SITUATION NOWHERE

"Situation Nowhere is a clever, dark, and often hilarious adventure through the most frustrating and endearing parts of humanity. In this fast-paced thrill of a book, you may not always know whether to scream at protagonist Lauren or with her, but there's no way you won't want to find out what happens to her next; and, possibly, question your own morals as you navigate a world of corporations, CEOs, and ethical dilemmas not all that far-fetched from our possible future. If the practice of laughing at your problems until they either go away or eat you alive took literary form, this is it."

—Alex Woodroe, Author of *Whisperwood*

"Situation Nowhere feels like a postmodern Truman Show made by Odenkirk and David Cross. What scared me most was how quickly the absurdity of it started to feel normal. Everyone go buy this book and read it before the world ends."

—Alex Dobrenko, Writer of *Both Are True*

"Bobby Miller's writing is beautiful, hilarious, and disturbing, the perfect combination if you ask me. I'm terrified of the world he has created in Situation Nowhere, and yet I can't look away. I also kind of want to get my hands on a case of this Energoo stuff he keeps talking about so I can suck it down during repeated readings of this excellent book."

—Dave Hill, Author of *The Awesome Game*

"This book tells your future through a funhouse mirror. It takes a blowtorch to your five-year plan while downing a toxic waste cocktail made of corporate America and robot circuitry. Read it while you still can because objects in the mirror are closer than they appear."

—Claire Hopple, Author of *Echo Chamber*

SITUATION NOWHERE

BOBBY MILLER

A MAUDLIN HOUSE BOOK

MAUDLIN HOUSE

maudlinhouse.net
twitter.com/maudlinhouse

Situation Nowhere
Copyright © 2025 by Bobby Miller
ISBN 978-1-7370222-8-2

May you live in interesting times.

One

What does it mean to be a badass boss bitch?

Most people agreed it meant you were fierce in the workplace, yet beloved. Just a hint of sass. You could be a badass boss bitch at any job, too, whether it be a teacher, custodian, or head of a large corporation. Yes, everyone wanted to be a badass boss bitch. Striving, worrying one might never attain such status. And it was this very worry that kept Barry Gray up at night.

The middle-aged man was alone in his penthouse apartment, dead-eyed, scrolling through work emails. He sipped a beer and stared out his floor-to-ceiling windows. Skyscrapers surrounded him, filled with rows of empty apartments. Luxury penthouses no one could afford. In the opposing unit, a robot maid dusted pristine new furniture, everything a shade of gray.

Barry fired up his ninety-inch television and settled in for his favorite reality TV show, House Pickers International. His job kept him city-bound, so House Pickers was the only way to see the world. But something about tonight made him restless, and he couldn't pay attention. He retreated to his phone, finger hovering over a name in his contacts: CAROL.

He closed his eyes. Willed himself not to call. Instead, he opened a dating app, changed his profile from private to public, and grabbed another beer.

BEEP! A woman named Gillian sent him a date request. He smiled: his rugged good looks were still viable in middle age. Either that or she was attracted to his elite star account. On her profile, she listed her job as "social media influencer" with over ten million followers. She was thirty-two, fifteen years his junior. He worried about speaking to her in public.

A robot maid appeared in the doorway, feminine energy purring through creaking gears. "Do you need help getting dressed for your big date?" it asked.

"Big date?" Barry laughed. "I haven't agreed to anything yet."

"A date would do you some good," the robot chirped. "I'm tired of hearing you talk about Carol."

"I don't talk about her that much, do I?"

"You do," the robot replied. "And according to my data, you really need to get laid."

Barry accepted the date and got dressed.

FOMO was the most exclusive cocktail lounge in the city, a place for millionaires, movie stars, and the ever-growing influencer crowd. Gillian, Barry's date, wanted to meet at the high-end establishment, but he preferred a pub. Barry was a man's man, a guy's guy, a real...*dude*.

Barry entered the pulsating lounge, a mix of young folks, heads on swivels, eyeing him.

"Do you have a reservation?" the maître d' scoffed. "We're quite booked tonight."

Barry flashed his corporate credit card, which bore the shiny green words: Atlas Wake.

The maître d's eyes widened. "I'm so sorry," he said. "Right this way, sir."

He showed Barry to a balcony seat perched above the crowd. Everyone below him stared. He enjoyed the spotlight.

"I'm assuming you'll want an Energoo cocktail to start." The maître d' smiled.

Barry nodded. "Yes, that would be fine."

He really wanted a beer.

A gooey neon-green cocktail appeared. The scent of artificial lime curled his nostrils. He gulped the cocktail down and used a spoon to break up a glob of green sludge stuck to the bottom of the glass.

"Gooey Green, oh Gooey Green, we love that, love that, Gooey Green," he hummed to himself.

Those were the lyrics to the first television jingle for Energoo™, the syrupy substance now sliding into Barry's digestive tract. He set the glass on his napkin and watched a slimy green ring form around it.

"Hey, Barry," said a woman's voice.

It was Gillian, beautiful, wearing a skin-tight black dress. She ascended the stairway, Energoo cocktail in hand. Barry was overcome with nervous excitement.

"Hi," he replied. "I'm Barry."

She smiled. "I know who you are. I just said your name."

Barry wasn't sure how to respond. "So, you have ten million followers. That's pretty impressive."

Gillian settled into the booth opposite him. "It's not that big of a fanbase," she said. "Not as many as Joey Paul, that's for sure."

Barry had no idea who Joey Paul was but pretended he did. It pained him to feel out of touch, and he wondered if he needed more young people in his life. Maybe this woman, this Gillian, was the key to his salvation.

"So, how did you become CEO of Atlas Wake?" she said, inching closer. "I always see your face on the news."

Barry was used to people pretending they didn't know he was a big-shot CEO. So, her directness made him nervous. He glanced at the patrons downstairs, some of them still staring.

"How did I get the job?" he said. He wanted to wow her, make her think he was a badass boss bitch for the ages, but the alcohol and the energy-packed Energoo made his brain wobble. "Well," he trailed off. "I'm very good...in the room."

"Are you now?" She twirled her cocktail straw. "How good *are* you in a room?"

Barry glanced at the crowd below and noticed they were no longer staring. They were already over him. Melancholy.

"Seriously," she said. "How *good* are you in a room?"

"I have to be good," he replied. "Because I'm not very smart. Just ask my ex-wife."

The comment hung in the air like a weak fart.

"She left me for a doctor," he continued. "Because I was too dumb for her."

Gillian licked her lips and played with her hair, struggling to flirt. Barry stared into the middle distance.

"Are you okay?" she asked.

He tried to smile and rescue the conversation but faltered. He explained that the divorce was fresh, and his wife took him for everything.

"Sure, I make a lot of money now that I'm CEO of Atlas Wake," he sobbed. "But it still stings."

Barry's wet eyes rose to meet hers, and he noticed she was bored. If he continued this outpouring of grief, he might end up masturbating to a ZipDee2Dah pornographic hologram tonight. His robot maid would be so disappointed.

"But, uh...I can't complain," he said. "I may not have been the sharpest tool in the shed, but I moved up the ladder like you wouldn't believe. Tech companies, private equity firms...Sure, they all eventually fired me. But Meryl saw something in me. And if I'm being honest...I'm grateful for the opportunity."

Gillian sighed with relief. "Thank God," she said. "You were losing me with that divorce talk. You sounded like a real fucking sad sack."

Barry locked eyes with her. Who was this angel, telling it like it is? Could she be his soulmate? He knew his employees at Atlas Wake didn't respect him, thought he was a dummy, but maybe Gillian would give him the confidence to become the badass boss bitch of his dreams.

"You're funny." He smirked.

Gillian smiled and pulled out her phone. "So, Mr. Barry Gray," she said, videoing him. "How does it feel to be head of the largest beverage corporation in the world? Maker of Energoo! Destroyer of the coffee industry!"

Barry shrank in his seat. "Oh, we don't need to livestream this."

"We're not livestreaming," Gillian replied. "I just think this would be fun content to post later. C'mon!"

Barry fidgeted. "Okay," he said, reluctant. "How's my hair?"

A loud explosion thundered through the lounge. Barry's ears rang, and his chest rumbled. He recoiled, huddling under the table for cover. Gillian joined him, eyes wide with fear. She searched his face, hoping for comfort, but his hands were shaking.

One of the walls collapsed, crushing the entire bar. A priceless chandelier crashed to the floor, shards of glass everywhere. Three military officers entered the flickering lounge, brandishing weapons. They searched the ground floor for a while until their gaze found the balcony.

"Are they looking at us?" whispered Gillian.

Barry said nothing. He had no idea what was going on. His hands kept shaking. The officers climbed the stairs. They were intimidating men, men who had seen some shit, clearly badass boss bitches. Barry hyperventilated.

"Are you Barry Gray?" one of them asked.

Barry stood to greet them, and the officer pulled the trigger on his weapon. A metal claw hurtled toward Barry, thwacking him in the neck and pinning him to the wooden table.

Gillian screamed.

An electronic tablet scanned Barry's eyes, and a loud beep ricocheted through the lounge. Every patron received an alert on their phone. They looked at each other, concerned, speaking in hushed whispers.

Gillian lifted her phone and started livestreaming, pissed that these "fascist officers" would have the audacity to ruin her night out. Barry overheard her say they were having a "nice time together," and his heart grew two sizes. He didn't know why he was pinned to the table, but he knew he would pursue Gillian once freed. Age difference be damned.

There was more noise among the crowd.

Gillian paused her livestream to read an alert on her phone.

"What does it say?" Barry asked.

Gillian's face fell.

The entire crowd stared in quiet disgust.

"What does it say!?!?"

"You've been X-ed," an officer said.

Barry was confused. This must have been a mistake. There was no way he was X-ed. But before he could offer a rebuttal, the officers removed him from the table, cuffed his wrists, and pushed him down the stairs. Barry looked to Gillian, his eyes welling with tears as they exited through the crumbling wall.

Gillian had never witnessed someone being apprehended for being X-ed. She didn't realize authorities would bomb out the side of a building just to get at someone quicker. But one thing she *did* know was that she needed to get the hell out of that private booth.

"How do you know Barry Gray?" an officer asked.

Gillian stared at her phone, unpaused her livestream, and greeted her fans.

"Hey, I'm talking to you," said the officer.

"I know," Gillian replied. "But I want to address my fans about this incident too." She looked into her phone. "Hey guys," she said, "just wanted to say that I don't know Barry Gray at all. So, please disregard my previous stream. However, I *do* know he deserves to be X-ed for whatever he did because Barry Gray is one giant piece of shit. I spoke to him for five minutes, and he's a real garbage person who should be prosecuted to the fullest extent of the law."

Her statement received thousands of likes on her livestream and, more importantly, satisfied the officer's inquiry. At first, Gillian felt terrible about lying, but the sentiment crumbled with every like and thumbs up from her fans. Nobody liked anyone who'd been X-ed; they were social pariahs, scum of the earth. And Gillian was glad to have distanced herself from the imploding mess called Barry Gray.

BARRY GRAY FIRED BY ATLAS WAKE AFTER LONG HISTORY OF PROBLEMATIC COMMENTS SPOTLIGHTED

Matthew Bustafson
Associated Press

CEO Barry Gray's tenure with beverage giant Atlas Wake is over after problematic comments were spotlighted on his Friendbook social media account some thirty years ago, leading to his subsequent X-ing out by authorities. Barry Gray (47) had only occupied the top spot for a few months before the comments came to light.

Gillian Davis, known to fans as GillzzyD, was seen canoodling with the disgraced CEO at FOMO minutes before his apprehension. Afterward, she denied knowing the man, stating to the television crew, "He tried to hit on me, but I shut him down like a badass boss bitch."

The problematic comments in question were quickly scrubbed from the internet, leaving many to speculate what was actually said.

Meryl Evans, longtime CFO and highest-ranking member of Atlas Wake's inner circle, told the press, "We have seen the offending comments on Friendbook and assure you: they are very problematic."

The disgraced CEO was transferred to a federal X Facility on Tuesday night, where he will remain until trial. If convicted, he will be formally declared X-ed and imprisoned for at least a decade.

Atlas Wake rose to fame for its green energy-packed syrup, Energoo, spinning off several products including a soda, coffee substitute, and cocktail mixer. Spokeswoman Geena Jackson believes the company's search for a new CEO won't impede the unveiling of its newest product, Energoo Formula Two, which is primed to become the best-selling beverage of all time.

Two

Inside the Atlas Wake building it was a day like any other. Employees hopped up on Energoo lattes, smiling, proud to be part of the corporation. Their morning meetings spread across the metallic building's thirty-plus floors. But deep in the bowels of the monolithic structure, it was a different story.

Two Atlas Wake executives paced the expansive basement floor. Surrounding them were large industrial vats of Energoo, the green sludge gurgling and churning between metal gears. Service robots with long hooked arms swayed above the vats, monitoring a massive Energoo production line. The grinding noise of the operation obliterated human speech, allowing the two executives to speak confidentially.

"What are we going to tell Meryl?" asked Dan. Dan Lowry, a slight thirty-something man with glasses, skin so white he verged on transparent. "We need a new face," he continued. "Someone low-key bulletproof. We can't afford another X-ing this close to product launch."

His colleague, Geena Jackson, a middle-aged corporate lifer, possessed much darker skin pigmentation. She stared at the bubbling green goo and remained calm. Her silence unnerved Dan, and he dry-gulped a Xanax.

"I'm bugging out, dawg," he said.

"I can see that," she replied. "C'mon, let's take a walk."

They strolled by several gurgling industrial vats.

"Did I ever tell you the intern story?" Geena asked.

Dan shook his head, still vibrating with nerves.

"I guess it's not much of a story," she continued. "This intern—Herbie, I think his name was—well, he decided one day that he really wanted a selfie with one of those Energoo tanks. Now, he shouldn't have taken any photos with the NDAs we have to sign. But, still, he got up one of those ladders, angled over ever so slightly, and WHAM! Fell right in. Got ground up by those metal gears. No one knew about it for days. He died a horrible death. Sad, really. I think his name was Herbie."

Dan popped another Xanax.

"I was scared to tell Meryl," Geena said. "But he completely handled the situation, and no one ever found out about it."

Dan looked unsure.

"My point is, you need to relax," she said. "We'll figure this out. Besides, I could always become CEO."

Dan agreed she was the heir apparent. Overqualified really. But, he argued, she was more valuable behind the scenes. "We need someone shiny as CEO," he said.

"I'm not shiny?" replied Geena, pretending to be offended.

She knew what Dan was getting at. Barry Gray was the corporation's gregarious front. His square jaw and kind eyes assured the public their growing addiction to green sludge was safe. Geena, for all her positives, was not a teddy bear.

"Do we know what Barry got X-ed for anyways?" asked Dan.

"Meryl wouldn't tell me," Geena replied. "But, if I had to guess, it was probably something homophobic."

"Really? He doesn't seem homophobic."

"Maybe it was something heterophobic?"

Dan scrunched up his face. "That doesn't track either. It was probably something misogynistic. Right? Er, no...maybe it was something *phobic*."

Geena shrugged. "Who knows? And honestly, who cares? What matters now is what we tell Meryl. Like you said, we need to figure out a SHINY CEO."

"Word is bond," replied Dan.

Geena winced just slightly.

They walked around the vats, looking for inspiration, but came up short. They needed a pick-me-up, a mental boost. They needed a fresh Energoo latte.

The Green Goddess was a chain of Energoo-branded cafes that sprouted like weeds across the United States. At first, they only existed in the city, but they eventually took over the suburbs. These cafes helped spread the gospel of Energoo, and Atlas Wake employees were treated like celebrities there.

Dan and Geena entered and flashed their corporate badges. The patrons, the staff, everyone smiled. At the far end of the cafe, a twenty-eight-year-old barista seemed nonplussed by their arrival. The tattooed woman went as far as an eye roll. Dan flashed a megawatt smile at her, but she offered nothing in return. He moved closer and read her name tag: Lo.

"Sup, Lo," said Dan. "You should smile more."

Lo parted her lips into a scary, exaggerated grin. Her dark eyes lit up with mischief.

"Uh, okay," said Dan, blinking a few times in annoyance. "I'd like an Energoo latte with extra foam, two shots, caramel, fudge, whipped cream. And a cherry."

Lo gagged, but Dan didn't notice. He'd already turned to Geena, looking desperate. "I hope this latte slays," he said. "We need to get our brains lit AF. Because in a few hours, it's...Meryl."

Lo made Dan's order.

Geena smiled at her, amused by her displeasure. "I'll have an Energoo espresso," she said, "with no cherry."

Lo leaned forward. "Does he order that shit all the time?"

"Like clockwork," Geena said, pulling out her Atlas Wake corporate card. It was thick and made of bronze. The reflection caught Lo's eye. Her demeanor melted.

"Holy shit," she said. "Where can I get a card like that?"

The question rubbed Geena the wrong way. Sure, she wanted to ingratiate herself with someone young and hip like Lo, but she also wanted respect. Obtaining that shiny bronze card took decades of hard work. One couldn't just "get a card like that."

"What a fucking loser," Lo said under her breath.

"Excuse me?" Geena replied.

Lo pointed to a gawky middle-aged man livestreaming his Energoo mochaccino. "I bet you he's a virgin."

Geena looked at Lo in disbelief. Openly mocking a customer was titillating blasphemy. She soaked it up, this rare treat. Lo smiled and handed her the espresso.

"Look at that turd over there," Lo said, pointing to a heavyset man with a tiny microphone. "He's on episode seventy-three of his latte podcast. What a fat dickhead."

Geena suffocated a laugh. "Why do you work here if you hate it so much?"

"I'm dead broke," Lo replied. "Why do you think?"

Geena's eyes drifted to Lo's arm, which featured a tattoo of a woman bound and gagged.

Dan grumbled impatiently, and Geena felt the need to end the conversation.

"You have an interesting…personality," she said, whipping out her phone. "How can I follow you?"

"Huh?" asked Lo.

"Y'know, on social media."

"Nah," Lo replied. "Social media is for losers. A bunch of people with no lives pretending they have one."

"Wait. You're not on *any* social media?"

"I mean, I am, anonymously," said Lo. "But I never post or anything. I just lurk."

Geena was speechless.

"Yeah, man," Lo continued, "I would *never* post anything online. Everyone's getting X-ed for dumb shit. Why would I put myself at risk?"

Geena reeled. She had never met anyone who didn't have a social media profile. What was the point of existing without one? It was everything—a way to build your brand, further your career, meet people. The idea that Lo opted out was an electric shot to Geena's broken corporate brain.

"Look at this," said Lo, spinning her smartphone around. "Five minutes ago, this woman got X-ed for saying The Revengers 219 sucked a fat dick. A bunch of Narvel superhero fanboy douches lost their shit. Honestly, I think those fanboys should be considered a terrorist organization."

Geena shushed her without thinking. She wanted to protect her, ensure she wasn't fired for running her mouth about Narvel, the comic book mega-corporation.

"Sorry," Lo said, sarcasm dripping from her young frame. "Didn't know you were such a fan."

Geena took a sip from her Energoo espresso, and a bolt of energy coursed through her. Green sludge rushed through her bloodstream, pummeled her brain, and overwhelmed her cortex. An idea was forming. She turned to Dan, who was in the middle of livestreaming his disgusting latte to his five "followers."

"I know what we should tell Meryl," she said. "I know who should be our CEO."

Three

It was scary to get X-ed, for authorities to barge into your life and rip it from you. After the initial apprehension, most Americans were transferred to a federal facility for final sentencing. They were sorted quickly by an AI-powered judge and jury. Most went to prison. Some did community service. Everyone received an X tattoo on their neck. The rich, of course, had a different process. There was no quickie AI judge and jury. Instead, they were offered a luxurious holding room while lawyers worked out their plea bargains.

Barry Gray was in such a room, confident his team would get him off. He had no idea what he said thirty years ago on FriendBook. But, he believed it was a mistake, a bureaucratic error, a glitch in a software program. These FriendBook comments must have been from *Jerry Kray*, some piece of shit loser who deserved to be X-ed. Not Barry Gray—a nice guy. He'd be free in moments, returning to his role at Atlas Wake and rekindling his romance with Gillian.

"What a first date, am I right?" he'd joke. Maybe they'd have a passionate one-night stand, or perhaps she was his soulmate, someone to erase the memory of his ex-wife who lorded over him.

A speaker crackled in the room, thrusting Barry into the present. A woman on the other end cleared her throat.

"I'm sorry to say, even the biggest corporate lawyers in the world couldn't turn this the other way for you, Mr. Gray. You've been officially X-ed. Final sentencing to be determined."

Barry was stunned.

He shot up and gestured toward the speaker as if the woman could see him.

"This must be some sort of mistake!" he cried.

The speaker switched off. Barry hovered by it, awaiting a response. He collapsed, sobbing on the cold marble floor. A military officer watched from the corner, embarrassed for him.

"Could I have my phone back?" Barry asked.

"Nope," the officer replied.

"How about a glass of water?"

The officer ignored his request, cracked his back, and circled Barry like a wolf.

"What's wrong?" the officer asked. "Did you cry all the water out of you?"

"No," Barry said. "I-"

"You little crybaby!"

Another officer appeared in the doorway. "How's it going?" the new guy asked.

Barry's officer shrugged. "This piece of shit wants water."

"Ah. Crybaby wants water?" the new officer replied, unveiling a large tattoo needle. "So, Mr. Crybaby Bitchtears, what did you do to get X-ed?"

Barry tried to flee but was shoved into a chair and held down.

"He said something shitty on Friendbook thirty years ago," replied Barry's officer.

"No!" Barry cried. "I'm pretty sure I didn't say anything! I've been...wrongly accused!"

The officers laughed. "I'm pretty sure I didn't say anything!" they mocked.

The new officer shoved the tattoo needle into Barry's neck.

"Agghh!" he shouted, hands gripping the chair. His officer motioned for a mouthpiece to ease his pain, but the new guy shot him down. He had a better idea. Wouldn't it be funny to give Barry his glass of water now? While he was unable to drink it?

"Hey Barry!" the new guy said. "How about some H2O?"

"Huh?" Barry whimpered.

The officer filled a glass from a water cooler, his heart pounding out of tune with excitement. He couldn't wait to dump water into Barry's open mouth as he struggled with the needle in his neck. Couldn't wait to see his eyes bulge out in horror. Couldn't wait until-

POW!

The new guy's stomach exploded open. Guts and blood ricocheted out of him and whacked Barry's officer in the mouth. Confused, he turned around, only to witness his own stomach explode too. The officers toppled over like rag dolls, knocking the cooler over and spilling water all over the floor.

Three men in gray hoodies, sweat pants, and ski masks emerged from a heating duct in the ceiling. An alarm sounded, and the three mumbled to each other. They promptly fell out of the ceiling and dusted themselves off. They were fidgety and nervous. The one with the gun seemed disgusted by the weapon and tossed it to the floor.

"Is this the guy?" the man asked. "I hope it's the guy because that didn't feel good."

"It's him," another replied. "Get 'em and let's get out of here."

Barry sat dumb and afraid as the trio moved closer. Despite the violence, the gray men appeared beaten down and hunched. Their gray sweatpants and ski masks were worn out and raggedy. If this were a Narvel movie, these men were neither superheroes nor supervillains. They seemed like homeless amateurs.

"We came to save you," the group leader said.

Barry screamed, and the leader covered his mouth as tears began to flow. The man rubbed Barry's back, calming him like a toddler. Another alarm rang out, and the leader offered his free hand.

"Barry," the man said. "There is no time for tears."

Four

Meryl Evans, the top dog at Atlas Wake, was 123 years old and not easy on the eyes. Wrinkled skin sagged over his brittle bones, and his posture was so bent he looked like a horseshoe. He always had a sourdough roll clutched in his bony hands, never spread with butter or used as a sandwich, but eaten bone dry.

"When you live to 123, you can tell me how to eat," he'd bark to new employees. "You get to my age; you can tell me how to LIVE!"

A speaker on Meryl's desk buzzed. It was Geena.

"Come in," said Meryl, wiping the bread crumbs off his chest. Geena entered the dim office, and Dan trailed behind. Meryl slid a crisp new cowboy hat atop his head. The elderly man fancied himself a cowboy, or in his words, "a corporate cowboy."

Geena greeted him warmly, but Dan only nodded. Meryl's office spooked him. There was never a light on. There were no computers or glowing devices; the only thing that lit the space was a single pumpkin spice candle, its sweet perfume no match for the office's decaying scent. Dan's stomach churned, his anxiety about to explode. He found a Xanax in his pocket and discreetly swallowed it.

"What is it?" Meryl grumbled, his frail hand dusting a bread morsel off his desk. Geena inched forward and occupied the pumpkin candle's glow.

"We have a solution to the Barry problem," she began.

"Ah. Did you hear Barry escaped?" Meryl said.

Geena was shocked. It was uncommon for people to escape an X facility.

"It seems an extremist group may have helped him," Meryl continued. "But, the press isn't certain."

"Well, if Barry's with an extremist group," Geena replied, "that's an easy press release. 'Barry's gone nuts and doesn't represent the values of Atlas Wake anymore.'"

Meryl agreed and twisted a sourdough roll in his mouth like a cigar. "Distancing ourselves from Barry is easy," he said. "But who will take his place?"

Dan stumbled forward.

"You can't be serious," Meryl laughed. "You think Dan should take the top spot?"

Dan mumbled an incoherent reply.

"No. Dan is just zonked on Xanax," Geena clarified. "We want to hire a CEO with no social media history."

Meryl was confused. How could anyone not have a social media history? At 123 years old, even *he* posted on social media—mostly business advice, pan fishing tips, and scented candle reviews.

"That someone does exist," said Geena. "And they work at the Green Goddess."

Meryl's sourdough roll shot out of his hands. "Are you telling me a barista is going to oversee one of the biggest corporations in the world?" he yelled. "They can barely get my drink order right! And I don't clack my teeth, goddammit!"

"The barista would just be a figurehead," Geena said. "Dan and I would be doing all the work behind the scenes. She'll say and do whatever we tell her. And because she has no social media history, she'll never get X-ed."

"Hmph," Meryl replied, opening a desk drawer. He found another roll and gnawed on it, unconvinced.

"Let's be honest," Geena said. "Barry was no great shakes in the intelligence department. We had to help him a lot. I don't see much of a change."

"Yes...Barry was dumb as hell," Meryl said. "But I liked the guy."

"She's waiting outside," said Geena.

"What?"

"Her name is Lo. I'd like you to meet her."

Meryl furrowed his brow. "You're making me feel sandbagged," he said. "You're not trying to sandbag me, are you?"

"No. No one is trying to sandbag you," said Geena.

"You sure? Because this feels like textbook sandbagging."

Dan mouthed, "Sandbag."

"It's not. You pull the strings, Meryl," Geena assured him. "You don't like her; we figure out a new plan."

Meryl nodded and adjusted his cowboy hat. "Show her in."

Lo could hear them whispering. Not actual words, just agitated murmurs. She'd spent her day at odds with Geena's proposition. Running a large corporation was antithetical to her entire being. She just wanted to fuck off, skirt by. And yet, there was something attractive about it all. The corporate position, the wealth. Loads of cash to be an empty figurehead. Would it be so bad if Lo had a taste? Or was she about to walk into some weird sex thing?

The door opened, and Geena waved her inside. Lo inched forward, her eyes adjusting to the darkness. She was warned that some found Meryl reptilian, but gazing upon his frail figure, Lo would have described him as a fucked-up elderly spider.

"Ack!" escaped from her lips.

"Hello, girl," said Meryl, his tone coarse as sandpaper. He knew she found him disgusting and made the air uncomfortable in retaliation. "Tell me, why do you think you're qualified to be CEO of Atlas Wake?"

Lo laughed. "I'm sorry, who said I thought I was qualified? These guys told me I just needed to pretend, and they would do all the work."

There was dead silence. This was not the answer Meryl wanted, and his eyes burned. He noticed the tattoos on her arms, the bound and gagged woman, a knife, swirls of chaotic lines.

"Those tattoos are a problem," he hissed.

"We could get them removed," offered Geena. "Would you mind, Lo?"

Lo got the tattoos when she turned eighteen, thinking they gave her an identity, a vibe. But, ten years later, her arms felt like relics. If lasering off these high school memories meant a serious payday, she was all for it.

"No problem," she said.

Geena smiled. But Meryl remained still. After careful inspection, she realized he was quietly choking on a sourdough roll. "Sir!" Geena screamed, rushing over. "Are you okay?"

Meryl just looked at her, eyes popping out. His cowboy hat tumbled to the floor. He gestured to his chest, desperate crumbs sputtering from his mouth. Geena spun him around and performed the Heimlich maneuver. Dan, unsure of what to do, took another Xanax.

A wet piece of sourdough socked Lo in the face. She recoiled. "What the fuck?!"

Meryl breathed heavily, crouched over his desk.

"Thank God," Geena said, slipping away from his back and placing the cowboy hat atop his head. "I told you, you need to put something on those rolls. They're too dry!"

"I know," he squeaked, "You're right. Maybe I can start spreading mayooo-naise on my rolls." He coughed a little and said, "And she didn't try to save me! I could have choked to death. Is that someone we want as CEO?"

Lo was speechless.

There was no way she would touch Meryl.

Not in a million years.

"Things happened so quickly," Geena said, searching for an excuse. "She didn't have enough time to process."

"Her generation doesn't care about anyone but themselves," Meryl replied, swiveling his chair around. "I won't entertain any more of this. You can go now."

"But, Meryl." Geena choked out.

"This is bigger than just the CEO of a company! This is our moment for world domination! To corner the market! To be the biggest thing in the galaxy! And you're going to hinge it all on a low-class barista?"

Lo wanted to explode, but Geena took her by the shoulder, and they exited, tails between their legs.

With every step to the door, "low-Class Barista" rattled around Lo's skull. How dare Meryl think she was a nobody. A piece of shit. The decrepit turd knew nothing about her. Knew nothing about her intellect.

Lo turned around, adrenaline coursing through her. This was her fucking moment. And she wouldn't let it pass.

"You're one hundred percent right about me, Meryl," she said.

He swiveled back to her, intrigued, tiny eyes glowing in the darkness.

"I don't care about this company. All I care about is you paying me. And that's why I'm the perfect candidate."

Meryl made a surprised, low-pitched sound that echoed through his office.

"You already know I have no social media history, so I can't get X-ed," she said, "You'll never have to worry about petty office politics or power grabs. Because I could give a fuck. So, yes, I'll laser these tattoos off my body. I'll become a blank slate for you and Atlas Wake. And your stocks will rise, and you will never have to worry about another public relations disaster. All I ask in return is lots of money."

Meryl was spellbound. Unable to comprehend that Lo could be *that* articulate. Lo smirked. Her monologue was reminiscent of the pretentious crap she'd written in high school English class a lifetime ago. It worked for her English teacher Mr. Butterfield, why not this old fuck?

Meryl studied her and smiled, revealing tiny shark-like teeth. "You got yourself a deal, Lo."

They shook hands.

Dan and Geena stood at the doorway, transfixed.

"I told you it would work," Geena whispered.

Dan simply mumbled, "Fo sheezly."

Five

Barry Gray sat blindfolded and gagged in the back of an unmarked van. His captors remained silent, traversing the city sprawl. They arrived in a sketchy area populated by rats, exploding sewer pipes, and trash. The van hit a bump and violently rattled, causing Barry to tense up. A guttural noise escaped from behind his gag.

"Relax," grumbled the leader of the group. A creature sprang in front of the van, and he slammed the brakes, causing the vehicle to fishtail across the street. "Shit. Sorry about that," he said in a thick Italian-American accent. "Almost missed the joint."

The van's sliding doors opened, and the three gray men found Barry rolled over on his side. "Madone, you need to chill," the leader sighed, still wearing his gray ski mask. "You're giving me agita."

His two gray cohorts chuckled, and the leader removed Barry's gag, hoping it would calm him. "What's going on?! Where are we?" shouted Barry, still blindfolded.

"Shhh!" the leader replied. "What are you thinking, yelling like that?!"

Barry pushed himself out of the van and blindly barreled toward the sidewalk, only to collide with a stop sign. The three gray men laughed.

"You done acting up?" the leader said. "Christ, we're all on the same team."

Barry licked his lips and tasted blood. The leader dabbed Barry's mouth with a handkerchief, and he flinched. "Can you take my blindfold off now?"

"Not now," the leader replied. "Where we reside is a bit of a well-kept secret."

"Why?"

"Jesus, Joseph, and Mary. I thought you were the type of guy who didn't ask questions."

"You kidnapped me!"

The leader sighed and turned to his men. "Fellas, can you pick 'em up? Let's get his ass inside before I blow my top."

The gray men grabbed Barry and carried him through the desolate streets. A three-legged dog with matted fur barked at them.

"Don't humor it," said the leader. "Shoulda ran that thing over when I had the chance."

The gray men moved closer to a boarded-up building and stopped to survey for prying eyes. Barry used the moment to lunge out of their hands, bumping into the front door and blindly scrambling into the darkened building. The leader followed him inside, turned on a light, and discovered a blindfolded Barry skirting dangerously close to the basement steps.

"Hey!" The leader called out. "Don't move, or you'll fall down the..."

But it was too late. Barry tumbled down the stairs with such energy that the three gray men couldn't help but watch in awe.

"This fucking guy," the leader said.

Barry was in knots at the bottom of the stairs. His arms were somehow over his head, and his blindfold had slid off. The basement was dark and cave-like, and a musty scent flooded his nostrils. He noticed several more figures in gray sweatpants and hoodies playing cards by a flickering work lamp.

"What the hell is this?" he asked.

"See Barry," the leader began. "If you would have trusted us, we could have gotten you down here all nice. But, now, look at you. You look like a Philadelphia soft pretzel."

The leader lifted Barry to his feet and removed his handcuffs. His three captors still wore ski masks, but the rest of the men (and one woman) wore nothing over their faces.

"Who are you people?" asked Barry.

"Oh, you probably heard of us," replied the leader, puffing out his chest. "We have a bit of a reputation."

"I have no idea who you are," said Barry.

"Seriously?" asked the leader. "We're The Brotherhood of the Resigned!"

Barry stared into the darkness. "Yeah, that doesn't ring a bell."

The leader paced around the dank basement, growing flustered. "What the hell, Little Ricky? I thought we had more social reach than this!"

The youngest man in the group, Little Ricky, removed his headphones. "What?"

"Steez, you said, or whatever. You said we had steez. This fuckin guy doesn't even know who we are!"

"Well, how old is he?" Little Ricky replied. "The college crowd knows who we are."

"That a fact?" asked the leader.

"I wouldn't lie to you, Papi John."

Barry burst into laughter.

"What's so funny?" asked the leader.

"Your name is...Papi John?"

The gray men fell silent and looked to their boss. Under his ski mask, a grimace formed. He tore off the mask, revealing a dark-featured man in his mid-40s, potentially the most Italian-looking guy Barry had ever seen. "They call me Papi John," he said. "It's a sentimental nickname, really."

"Okay, *Papi John*," Barry said. "What's the deal with these gray sweatpants? You look like you're homeless."

Papi spit. "Y'know what, Barry. I was gonna tell you how I got my nickname. But now I'm not. Outta spite."

"That's fine," Barry replied. "Can I go now, please?"

"And where ya gonna go, Barry? You're X-ed," said Papi. "The moment you get into the city, they're gonna get your ass. And good. You want a life behind bars, or do you wanna see what we're about?"

Barry stared at the silent gray figures surrounding him. "Okay, fine," he said. "What's your guys' deal?"

A gray woman in the back was offended. "Hey, we're not all guys here, y'know."

"It's okay, Meghan," Papi said, "he didn't mean no offense."

Meghan was small in stature but ripped with muscles. She lifted a dumbbell and replied, "I'll let it slide this time," before tossing it to the concrete floor with a thud.

Papi John circled him with newfound pep. "My friend," he said, "we are known as the Brotherhood of the Resigned."

"Brotherhood *and* sisterhood," Meghan interjected.

"Can we table that conversation?" replied Papi, doing the prayer motion and wagging his hands.

Meghan grumbled, and Papi continued. "Every last person in here has been X-ed. Some of us have even served jail time, and some of us, like you, are on the run. Exiles. But, we've banded together against this unkind world, living underground and forging a new life on the run."

"Well. I never asked to be on the run," said Barry.

"Christ! You're like a broken record!" snapped Papi. "Y'know, Barry, you'd have an X tattoo on your neck and be behind bars right now if it weren't for us!"

Barry went quiet.

"Yeah, you're not running your mouth now, are ya?" continued Papi. "When you're X-ed, you lose everything. Your job, your friends, your family. At least we saved your ass before they finished your mark."

"Yeah," boomed a large bald man from the back. "You don't want to be marked!" He rubbed his neck, revealing a large X tattoo. It appeared angry, as if the tattoo artist had a mental problem.

"Oh, Gerald. Poor bastard has to put on lady's makeup every day to hide his X," said Papi. "So he can buy a sack of suds at the grocery store without any aggravation."

"I don't mind it," the giant replied.

Papi laughed. "He doesn't mind it! Oh, goddamn it, Gerald. You're too much! But many of us do mind our Xs, don't we, friends?"

The others nodded. In the corner, a slim man reading a porno magazine piped up, "I mind my fucking X, you cunts!"

Barry did a double-take. "Wait a second," he said. "Aren't you Delbert Chapman, that movie producer who jerked off to women on the phone without them knowing?"

Delbert threw down his porno mag and glared at Barry. "I am! And I'll jerk off on your face when you're asleep, asshole!"

Barry was disgusted. Delbert was a creep and deserved to be X-ed. Barry wasn't like these basement dwellers at all! He didn't belong in this so-called group of the resigned!

"Barry," Papi said, "they may not have finished that tattoo, but you're one of us now, whether you like it or not. You're in the system."

Barry touched the scab on his neck. "But...but...I'm too import-ant to be X-ed," he sputtered.

A loud grunt echoed through the cavernous space, and an older man emerged from the shadows. He wore a gray sweatsuit just like everyone else but sported a clown nose and smeared on circus makeup. "You're too important to get X-ed?" he whispered. "I was the most popular kids' show host of all time, and look at me now! The X doesn't give a shit about your station in life, friend!"

It was Mr. Bompity Bomp, a children's show legend. He got X-ed after chatting up a young female production assistant. Some say he had a history of wayward flirtations; others say he was a harmless old man.

Barry took stock of the basement. There was: Mr. Bompity Bomp (the clown), Delbert (the creep), Papi John (the leader), Meghan (the only female), Gerald (the friendly giant), and Little Ricky (the kid). Two other figures remained speechless in the shadows. What was their deal? Were they creepier than Delbert? *Real* lunatics? Barry didn't want to find out.

"It was nice meeting all of you," Barry said. "But I'm going to take my chances above ground."

"We have electricity down here!" Papi said desperately. "I got us a shit ton of generators. And me and Little Ricky have burner phones. Completely untraceable. We even got a TV down here!"

"I'm good," Barry replied, walking past.

Papi jumped in front of him, then realized it was an aggressive gesture and backed away. "Uh, listen," he whispered nervously. "We need you, Barry."

"Why?"

"Because you...know something," replied Papi.

Barry had no idea what he was talking about, and Papi took a long breath. "We have reason to believe something fucked up is happening at Atlas Wake. And that maybe you could provide some insight."

Barry rebuffed the idea. Atlas Wake was no different than any other giant corporation. "They all have skeletons in their closets," he said.

"But Atlas Wake is different," said Papi. "We have our suspicions."

Barry looked into Papi's desperate eyes and realized he needed to be forceful at this moment, tell him to fuck off. Or else he might never leave this basement. He had to be a badass boss bitch, even if it wasn't in his DNA.

"Fuck you. I'm out of here," Barry said. "Why would I tell you creeps anything?"

"Fine!" Papi exploded. "Get the fuck outta here! We don't want you! And I hope the authorities have fun hunting you down like a goddamn animal!"

Barry left in a huff, and Papi hyperventilated.

Gerald put his arm around him. "Take a breath, Papi. You don't want your blood pressure to go up."

"Yeah, yeah," Papi replied, trying to settle his anger. But he couldn't. He shouted loud enough for Barry to hear, "He's an entitled rich prick and deserved to be in jail as far as I'm concerned!"

Barry spun around atop the stairs. "Brotherhood of the Resigned?" he mocked. "You deserve to be stuck in this basement! I'm not resigning to anything! I still have a life to lead!"

The door slammed shut, and he was gone.

Six

A glorious amount of Chinese food piled up on Atlas Wake executive Dan Lowry's desk. Every type of noodle, protein, and vegetable imaginable, all slathered in garlic, red pepper, and sesame oil. It was late for Dan and Geena to be at the Atlas Wake office, but they were waiting for Mitch the intern to finish vetting Lo's social media history.

Mitch had been hunched over his desk all night, eyes bugging out. He had three laptops running searches, and they all said she didn't exist. It surprised him, for he had several social media accounts before he could even hold a phone, services his parents set up in utero.

"Did you find anything?" asked Geena, grabbing another egg roll.

"Nope," Mitch replied. "I think she really doesn't have a social media history."

"That's so fetch," said Dan, half asleep at his desk.

Mitch hovered over the three laptops like a puppy dog, ready to do whatever the execs asked. Geena smirked at his ambition.

"Mitch, maybe we need another laptop going?" she said. "We need at least four. Maybe five."

Mitch panicked and searched the room. "Uh, I could probably find another laptop somewhere."

"I was joking," said Geena. "That was a joke."

"Ah."

"Geena's a real comedian," Dan said.

"Well," said Geena, dropping a clump of egg roll back onto the paper. "I'm heading home."

"I have a couple more searches I can do," said Mitch. "I don't mind babysitting the laptops overnight if you want. I can shower at the company gym."

"You're a real G," said Dan. "Appreciate you, homie."

"I don't think that's necessary," Geena said. "You can go home now."

"Well, uh, goodnight, Ms. Jackson," Mitch said.

"Goodnight," she replied.

Geena walked the perfect concrete street outside Atlas Wake, scrolling through her phone and waiting for a car service. A silver vehicle arrived, and a taxi bot leaned out the window. It was tall and stick-like, with barely any facial features, just two glowing eyes.

"Geena Jackson?" it inquired.

She nodded, and the car doors opened. She got one leg in and noticed a figure in the backseat.

"Excuse me," she said to the taxi bot, "I didn't ask for a shared vehicle."

"You must be mistaken, Miss," the taxi bot chirped. "You did select a shared vehicle." The car went translucent, and a hologram rendering of Geena's ride request floated on the exterior.

"Huh," she said, confused. "Maybe I did by accident. Can you cancel, please? I'll wait for another car."

The figure in the backseat inched toward her, and the shadows shifted, revealing Barry Gray. "Geena, we need to talk," he pleaded.

Geena recoiled in shock. "I can't be seen with you, Barry. Cancel ride."

The taxi bot shrugged and began to close the car door when Barry stuck his hand out.

"Please remove all limbs from the exit," the skinny robot barked.

"Please, Geena! I need your help!" Barry cried.

Geena was too well-versed in corporate politics to humor this and walked away, leaving his arm stuck in the car door.

Barry panicked and continued screaming at Geena to no avail. The taxi bot swiveled around, and a laser popped from its metal skull. It scanned Barry's eyes and beeped.

"You said you were Larry Bay," it droned. "But you are not. You are Barry Gray."

Barry's face went dumb. He had hailed the ride using a fake name and paid with cash.

"I must transport you back to an X facility," the taxi bot said, straining to close the car door. Barry pushed with all his weight and forced it open, falling to the curb. He noticed a figure boarding another car across the street.

"Geena!" he yelled. But no reply. His heart sank.

An engine roared, and Barry turned to find the robot taxi barreling toward him. "What the fuck?" he said as the car jumped the sidewalk, the taxi bot wailing, "Take you back! Take you back where you belong!"

Barry ran as fast as he could, but the robot taxi was gaining on him. He noticed an alleyway and darted toward it. The car followed, but the path was too narrow, and it got stuck. Barry limped, exhausted, down the alley, looking for a hiding place. He found a dumpster and climbed inside, then peered out to see the robot taxi static at the entry—a sinister metallic presence in the moonlight. There was a loud clang, and the slender robot lifted itself from the car and crept toward him. Its movements were slow and jerky, a cost-saving measure relegated to all gig econo-bots.

Barry's mind drifted. He thought about his date with Gillian and the hope of new romantic love. If he could escape this taxi bot, he could live in exile until his name was cleared. He had to be optimistic. There would be no jail time. No cleaning up junk on the highway. No pimply teens making fun of his orange jumpsuit!

"Hiya!" he yelled, leaping from the dumpster. He punched the taxi bot in the face and its jaw flew off, whipping towards a raccoon, who shrieked into the night.

"Ow," Barry said, clutching his swollen fingers.

"Barry Gray located," droned the weakened robot, sparks flying from its shattered face. "Authorities notified," it sputtered as Barry unleashed a weak kick to its stomach. "Authorities on their way," it cried as Barry ran off. "Apprehension imminent," it whispered, powering itself down in the vacant alley.

Seven

Lo couldn't sleep. Her future hinged on Dan, Geena, and Mitch's work, and they'd been radio silent. If they found no social media history, she would become the CEO of Atlas Wake. If they did, she'd return to the Green Goddess, serving lattes to influencer-wannabes and the morbidly obese. She wished she had parents to talk to in times like these. But she didn't know who they were.

She was raised in an orphanage and moved into low-income apartments for troubled youth at eighteen. She was haunted by not knowing her parents and struggled to find an identity. Often cycling through friend groups like a pair of pants.

Before she was "troubled," before she went by "Lo," she showed great promise. As "Lauren," she shined in high school, garnering the favor of her English teacher, Mr. Butterfield. He encouraged her to write the truth in her short stories. And she excelled at it. But, when she entered her senior year, a scandal broke out. Mr. Butterfield was unqualified to teach. He had bluffed all his credentials. He was nothing more than a con man.

She was devastated, her entire existence thrown into upheaval yet again. She tried to write about the experience, to stay "truthful," as he once told her. But her prose became so raw, so filled with venom and misplaced emotions, that she was assigned a psychiatrist. She eventually changed her name from Lauren to "Lo" and covered her body with tattoos. She would be reborn a perfect jaded butterfly, no longer wishing to find her parents, she told herself.

The sun rose across the city, and there was still no word from the Atlas Wake execs. Lo squinted through her one-foot-square window, a "luxury" amenity in the low-income government housing she was afforded. The streets were empty. Desolate. Years ago, they were packed with bustling office workers. But those jobs fell victim to AI automation. Few people worked anymore.

Lo poured herself some coffee, which a grocer gave her for free. "We can't get rid of this stuff," the cashier said. She was one of the few people who still drank coffee. Most had moved onto Energoo, but she loved coffee's taste - bitter, nutty, acidic. It mirrored how she felt inside.

Her gaze drifted to the sidewalk, where a homeless man bent over and defecated into a bucket. She had to laugh. Sometimes it was the only recourse in the face of total economic despair. Her phone vibrated and displayed: "Unknown caller."

"Hello?" Lo answered.

"Hey," replied Geena. "How soon can we get your tattoos removed?"

Lo's eyes turned to saucers. Holy shit. Was this really happening?

"You there?" asked Geena.

"Yeah, whenever you want," Lo replied, pretending to be aloof.

There was whispering on the other end. Geena spoke. "By the way, we want you to go by Lauren now. Is that okay? The name Lo tested poorly."

"Tested poorly to who?" Lo asked.

"It's complicated," replied Geena. "So, what do you say?"

Lo looked out her window and locked eyes with the straining homeless man.

"I'm fine with changing my name back to Lauren."

"Great," said Geena. "We'll have a car pick you up tomorrow morning."

Lo nodded to no one, felt her legs wobble, and decided to sit on her tiny bed. It was wedged against her dining room table, which doubled as a desk.

"And hey, congratulations," said Geena. "Ms. Lauren Caldwell. You're the new CEO of Atlas Wake."

Eight

Barry was running out of options. Geena had rejected him, and a collect call to his ex-wife, Carol, went unanswered. Shit. Did he have *any* friends left? If only he could slip into his old apartment, have a bite, a nap, and maybe a refreshing dump. He could regroup and figure out a way out of this mess. His stomach ached, and he dreamed of the frozen bean burrito in his fridge, fantasized about the excess cheese squirting from its sides.

He entered the lobby of his luxury apartment, the AW Estates, only to find the front desk flanked by guards. The apartment was under heightened security, probably due to his escape. There was no way he could gain entry now. A guard grabbed Barry by the shoulder, and he seized up in horror.

"Where are you supposed to be?" the guard asked, his voice metallic and edgy.

Another guard stumbled over and placed his hand on Barry's other shoulder.

"Where are you supposed to be?" the new guard asked, possessing the same voice as the other.

Barry was confused by these twins, then realized they were AI-powered synthetic humans. Their skin appeared soft and supple, but behind the facade was a mass of computer chips.

A red laser emerged from the first guard's eyes, and its fingers squeezed against Barry's neck. He struggled, trying not to let them scan his eyeballs for identification.

"Hey!" another guard said, sauntering over. "What are you clowns doing?"

The synthetics were offended and beeped at the guard, whose sweaty forehead made it clear he was human.

"Why are you harassing that man?" said the human guard.

The synthetics beeped wildly, spinning their laser appendages in protest.

"Fine," said the human guard. "Scan him already."

Barry noticed their grip loosened, and he darted away before they could scan him.

"Wait a second," the human guard said. "That's Barry Gray! Get him!"

Barry plodded out of the tiled lobby and through its thick double doors. Outside, an intercom blared.

"Escaped convict Barry Gray sighted," a voice declared. "Exercise caution; he is wanted dead or alive."

Barry's heart almost fell out of his chest. Authorities wanted him dead? For what? A dumb comment on social media? He was nearly one hundred percent sure he never wrote anything controversial! Also, he didn't escape! He was kidnapped! This was all a mistake! He was a nice guy!

A fleet of synthetic guards stomped toward him, and he ran into the streets, almost getting clipped by a car.

"Shit!" he cried.

He wandered the alleys for a while, eventually finding a bench in an abandoned parking lot. He collapsed into a pile, sobbing, afloat in the events of the last couple days, like someone else's memories. And what were the options? There were no options. He had absolutely no idea what to do.

The revving of an engine brought him back to reality.

An unmarked van slowly snaked into the vacant parking lot.

"Oh God," Barry whispered.

He stood up, trying to summon the energy to flee. A figure stepped out of the van. Barry began to jog away half-heartedly when the figure shouted at him.

"Barry Gray!"

Barry eyed his exit options. The parking lot had a large metal gate to prevent vagrants, and there was only one way out.

"Madone! Look at this mamaluke!" cried the figure. It was Papi John.

Barry stopped, dumbstruck.

"Have you been crying?" asked Papi.

"No," Barry replied. He dried his eyes, smiling.

"So. You wanna reconsider our invitation?"

Barry didn't speak.

"Good," said Papi, "But first, the boys are starving. I need some soppressata. Stat."

Nine

Lo sat in a large black limousine provided by Atlas Wake. It was early in the morning, and she felt anxious. She rifled through the limo's amenities, hoping for alcohol to calm her nerves. Instead, she found Energoo products—fizzy water, pre-made lattes, chocolates with an Energoo center. She sighed and stared out the tinted windows at the monolithic Atlas Wake building, approaching fast. It dwarfed everything. The rest of the city felt like a playset.

The limo skidded to a stop, and the passenger door popped open. "What it do, chica?" asked Dan, peering inside.

Dan Lowry was in a suit, sipping an Energoo latte, steam fogging up his delicate glasses.

"What's...up," she replied, slowly stepping out of the long, gleaming vehicle.

"Did you sign your contract, Lauren?" he asked.

Lo wasn't sure who Dan was addressing until she realized she was the Lauren in question.

"I did," she replied, handing over a large paper packet.

"Outta sight," he said. "We'll have an Atlas Wake technician take care of your arms now."

Lauren wasn't sure what he meant.

"We're going to laser off your tattoos," he clarified.

Lauren found it odd that an employee would handle this task, but Dan assured her it was the only way to keep things private. She was becoming a shiny new corporate product, and the public shouldn't know her tattooed origins.

Dan took her by the hand and led her into the magnificent Atlas Wake lobby. It felt like a ballroom, with floor-to-ceiling windows that let in every drop of light. Above her were Greek gods on painted clouds. She was certain this lobby rivaled the Sistine Chapel. But she wouldn't know.

In the elevator, Dan removed a heavy bronze access card from his wallet. Lauren's eyes were drawn to it. "Pretty lit, huh?" he asked. He slid the card into a reader, and the elevator plummeted several stories. Lauren grabbed Dan's shoulder, and he smiled at the touch.

The restricted area was screeching loud and chaotic, machinery churning green goo into large metallic vats. Dog-sized robots skittered around, checking the temperature of the vats with their artificial tongues. It felt like the kill floor of a slaughterhouse.

The size of Atlas Wake began to register with Lauren, and dread nagged at her insides. Could she really do this? Could she fake her way through being CEO of one of the world's largest corporations? Could she eat shit and sell out? The swirling green goo in those giant vats nauseated her.

"Y'know," Dan said, "that's Formula Two in there. Top secret shiyat."

Dan seemed to be sharing insider knowledge to score points with Lauren. But she couldn't get involved behind the scenes. She had promised Meryl that she wouldn't meddle, just collect a check. She remained quiet.

"I said, that's Formula Two in that vat. Pretty pimpin', right?" Dan said.

Lauren cringed. "Do you always talk in outdated slang?"

"Not sure what you mean, dawg." Dan replied, popping a Xanax.

Lauren rolled her eyes. "Uh. We gonna remove these tattoos or what?"

Dan nodded and retook her hand, an awkward gesture he seemed determined to continue. She looked back and watched the hundreds of machines churning their gears, sloshing and funneling Energoo through various tubes. This underground lair, this kill floor, was the size of a football field.

Many floors above them sat Geena Jackson in her tiny office. Considering her tenure at the corporation, she deserved a bigger space, perhaps a corner office with a view. But she never complained about it. Or, at least, never did publicly. Sometimes, though, she would scream into her pillow.

She was crafting Lauren's speech to send to the PR department. A speech that would assure the public that their new CEO had no problematic history. Geena knew about Lauren's upbringing and absent parents and wondered if she should utilize that trauma in her speech. She glanced at the time and realized she'd been working for three hours without a break.

She stood up, cracked her tired back, and surveyed the open floor office outside her door. Mitch typed away on his laptop, sipping an Energoo latte. She tapped him on the shoulder, and he jumped out of his seat.

"Oh, it's you," he said, bending down to clean up the latte he spilled.

"I've been thinking about your position at Atlas Wake," she said.

"Oh no," he replied, dropping the latte again. "You're firing me?"

"What? No," replied Geena. "I thought you could be Lauren's assistant."

"You mean Lo?" he asked.

"We're calling her Lauren now. Lo didn't test well," said Geena.

Mitch let the information wash over him. "So, I won't be an intern anymore?"

Geena shook her head. Mitch's eyes dimmed. He seemed underwater.

"What's wrong?" Geena asked.

"Oh, well, I don't want to sound ungrateful," he replied. "But the position. It's paid, right?"

"Yes," Geena said. "But not very well."

It was worse pay than working at the Green Goddess, but being an assistant at Atlas Wake brought the whiff of corporate advancement, and that was enough for Mitch. He was fiending to climb the ladder, prepared to slop feces in his mouth, smile, and ask for more.

"When do I start?" he asked, newfound confidence swirling through him.

Geena wasn't sure why, but she had the sudden urge to bat Mitch down, keep him in line. The Energoo latte he spilled dripped off his desk, and she feigned disgust.

"When can you start?" she said. "As soon as you clean up that mess."

Ten

Barry sat on the dusty basement floor beside a pile of gray clothing. Thirty minutes ago, he had agreed to join the Brotherhood of the Resigned. But he debated donning their official uniform—gray sweatpants and hoodie. It seemed lame, an announcement of one's failures. A resignation he wasn't comfortable with.

"Put it on, Barry. Christ. We ain't got all day," said Papi John. He was perched on an old wooden chair, looking annoyed.

"Are you shy about your body?" asked Delbert, the creep. "Are you shy about exposing your skin to us?"

"No," replied Barry.

"It's okay if you are," said Papi delicately, "I eat so many carbs, I got a little gut too. No one mentions it around here because everyone is so nice."

"Who am I to judge?" said someone in the back, and like a bubbling brook, the others repeated. "Who am I to judge?"

Barry didn't understand why they wore the gray uniform. Why not wear a nice suit like they did in the movie Reservoir Dawgs 39? "You guys look like depressed college freshmen," he said.

"It's not all guys here," replied Meghan.

"It was a figure of speech," Barry countered.

"Ugh!" interrupted Papi. "We all wear gray sweatpants and hoodies because that's what the Brotherhood of the Resigned is about! When we got X-ed, we could have caused trouble or tried to work our way back into society. But we didn't! Although some of us did try..."

"I tried to talk to my mommy," said Gerald, the giant. "I tried to talk to my mommy, and she said she can't talk to me anymore."

"See," said Papi. "Gerald can't talk to his mommy. And he's one of the most beautiful S.O.B.s I know."

"Dank you, Papi," replied Gerald.

Behind Gerald's big blocky features, Barry sensed a profound sadness. "No one wanted to talk to me either," Barry admitted. "I tried to collect call my ex-wife, but she didn't pick up."

Gerald shook his head knowingly. A brother in arms.

"Is your ex-wife hot?" asked Delbert.

Papi chose to ignore Delbert and put an arm around Barry. "I figured you had a woman on your mind," he said, turning to the group, "I found Barry crying in a parking lot like a big ol stugotz."

"I wasn't crying," replied Barry. "It was dusty. It was very dusty."

"Uh-huh," said Papi. "Listen, Barry. If society doesn't want us, fine! We ain't gotta cry about it! Let's throw on sweatpants and live underground! Let us hold hands with the great resignation! 'You can't fire us, world! Because we quit!'"

The members whipped their fingers across their chins and spat on the concrete floor. Barry was delighted by their synchronicity.

"We'll live underground and eat pizza like Teenage Mutant Ninjak Tortoises 47!" said Gerald, finding a withered slice of pizza from a takeout box.

"That's right. We pooled all our cash together for food," continued Papi. "Speaking of. Empty your wallet, Barry."

Barry complied, but his mind was elsewhere. "Wait a second," he said. "You guys-"

"—and women," interrupted Meghan.

"You *folks* are saying you're resigned," Barry continued. "But why did you shoot those officers? That's not very resigned of you."

Papi looked sheepish. "When you're right, you're right," he replied. "It was against our principles. And we took no pleasure in their deaths. But, we felt your case was particularly special."

"And why is that?" asked Barry, confused.

Papi grabbed two beers from a tiny fridge. He offered one to Barry, who politely declined. Papi kept motioning the beer to him as if he would change his mind, eventually shoving the beverage into his hand. He forced Barry to drink and "Salud." Seeing that went okay, he presented him with salty snacks, "aperitivos," which he had whipped up earlier.

"I'm not hungry anymore!" snapped Barry. "Why do you think my case is different?"

"You sure you don't want a little bit of bread or something? Couple of crackers?" Papi offered.

Barry shook his head, growing tired of Papi's Italian need to feed.

"Fine. More for me," replied Papi, throwing salted nuts into his mouth. "Truth is, Barry. I think you've been set up."

"You do?" said Barry, surprised.

"Yeah. I do," replied Papi, searching through jars of homemade bruschetta. "I don't believe you said those things on Friendbook thirty years ago. Whatever those things were."

The authorities never revealed what Barry actually said. Was it a lewd comment about women? A disparaging remark about the gays? Did he tell the president to eat shit? He had no idea. It was maddening.

Papi finished an olive and burped. "You were never on Friendbook," he said.

A lightning rod hit Barry's brain, and he downed the rest of his beer. "You're right...I was on FaceFriendz."

Papi ate roasted peppers straight from the jar. "The important question is. Why would anyone make this up?"

Barry shrugged. But Papi had a theory he savored telling, the same way he savored those roasted peppers. "I think you knew something about Atlas Wake," he said, licking his finger, "something no one wanted you to know."

"Like what?" replied Barry.

"Well," said Papi, rocking back on his old wooden chair, prepping himself for the big question. "What do you know about Energoo Formula Two?"

Before Barry could respond, Papi's chair cracked in half, sending him to the floor with a thud. The others quickly surrounded the defiled chair like magical elves and fixed it for their leader. Barry wandered over to the mini-fridge and grabbed another beer. Then, he took a handful of crackers and devoured them like an animal. Papi was pleased to see him finally enjoying the food he had thoughtfully prepared.

"Barry," Papi said. "Put on the suit. Join us for real. Let's figure out why you were really X-ed."

Barry glanced at the pile of gray clothes. "I don't get it," he said. "What does my X-ing have to do with all of yours? Why do you care so much?"

Papi nodded in silence and rose to meet him. "An honest question deserves an honest answer," he said. "We believe if we can crack your case, maybe some of ours can be cracked too. Maybe one day soon, we won't have to live underground."

Barry's eyes widened. This was bigger than him. If Atlas Wake made up stuff to get him X-ed, who knows how many people suffered the same fate? He finally agreed to don the uniform and slowly slid off his pants.

"Nice legs!" shouted Delbert. "Almost makes me wanna squeegee right now!"

Barry shuddered at the thought. He continued disrobing, eventually putting on the resigned's trademark gray sweatpants. He slid the gray hoodie over his head, but it got stuck. He tried unzipping to give his giant head more room, but the zipper wouldn't budge. He fumbled around, half-blind, and toppled to the floor. The zipper gave way, and his head burst through. He stood up and noticed the room of outcasts was teary-eyed.

"You look great," said Papi, an emotional dam about to burst.

"In solidarity," the others cheered, trying not to sob.

A warm feeling passed through Barry, and it surprised him. In college, he was in fraternities, and on the job, he had colleagues. But, if he were pressed to name an actual friend, he'd come up short. Could it be, after all these years, he had found his kin in this dirty, musty basement?

"I don't know much about Formula Two," Barry said, feeling the gray fabric between his fingers. "But I can tell you everything I know."

The others slowly crowded around him, eager, when a horn echoed through the room. They turned to find Mr. Bompity Bomp, the elderly clown, strolling in, squeezing his squeaky nose. A piece of toilet paper stuck to his giant red clown shoe.

"What did I miss?" the clown asked.

They all laughed. Papi pointed to his shoe, and Bompity sheepishly removed the toilet paper. Barry smiled and found himself appreciating these social pariahs, these underground trolls, these X-ed scum. He shrugged and joked, "Who am I to judge?"

The others replied in unison and broke into more laughter, tears of joy streaming down their faces. Eventually, the laughter died down, and Papi moved closer to Barry.

"Tell us, Barry," Papi whispered. "Tell us everything you know about Energoo Formula Two."

Eleven

Barry Gray was the CEO of Atlas Wake for only three months before he got X-ed. During his tenure, he learned Energoo Formula Two was secretly being tested at the Green Goddess cafe chain. An early version first appeared in their Macchiato Whipped Creme Nut Blast. Customers had no idea. At a test site in Newfield, New Jersey, one man was talked down from a telephone pole after consuming ten nut blasts. The jolt of power rushing through him proved too intense. He later told buddies over beers, "I didn't know where to put that nut blast energy."

But it wasn't just these early incarnations of Formula Two that got people climbing telephone poles. Despite being FDA-approved and widely available in America, Formula One also had its share of problems. A man in Park City, Utah, OD'd on the original formula. He was partying hard at the Sundance Narvel Entertainment Film Festival before the premiere of Metal Man 241. He somehow consumed a gallon of Energoo-enhanced vodka and was rushed to a hospital, where his stomach was pumped. Unfortunately, when the green goo left his body, he had a seizure and died. His last words reportedly were, "I will never know how Metal Man 241 ends."

A woman in San Diego, California, downed several bottles of Formula One before running a 15K charity run. She collapsed in a kid's park, careening onto a roundabout and upchucking green goo at children before finally perishing.

"But, you will never hear about these cases in the media," Barry said to the Brotherhood, his voice softening. "They were always swept under the rug. Families seemed happy to get compensated for their loss. Some even preferred a lifelong Energoo subscription over a cash settlement. They loved the product that much."

"Madone," said Papi.

"I looked the other way," said Barry. "But, eventually, I became concerned. Especially around the secrecy of Formula Two."

He even tried to confront Meryl about the ingredients of the new formula. But his timing was terrible. On that particular day, the old man had lined up a tasting menu of sourdough rolls, determined to find the best bakery in town.

"Why are you disturbing me?" the old man asked, carefully arranging the bread on his desk like a fine art gallery.

Barry tried to ask what was in Formula Two, and Meryl was shocked by the question. He figured Barry knew the rules of corporate culture. It was all about putting on blinders, staying in your lane, and collecting a paycheck. To question authority was subhuman, to "whistle blow" a dirty word. Meryl was pissed.

"I was X-ed a day after I spoke with Meryl," Barry concluded.

"Christ. They really are X-ing anyone who asks questions," the Italian leader replied. "Even their own CEO."

Papi believed Atlas Wake was out to destroy anyone who didn't publicly adore their products. Barry's story only corroborated this belief.

"I wish it weren't true," Papi whispered.

Formula One had created a nation of Energoo addicts, thirsty and fiending for more. But what would happen to America if this mysterious Formula Two proved the greatest fix of all? How could anyone compete with them? Or voice displeasure about their products? Who could stop Atlas Wake, the almighty corporation, from world domination?

Barry looked queasy.

"Hey," Papi said, taking him by the shoulder. "I can tell this is making your stomach upset. Let me show you something."

An ancient CB radio sat in the far corner of the basement. Papi grabbed the microphone, eyes glowing. He pressed a button and made clicking noises with his mouth.

Silence.

"Uh..." Barry said.

Papi shushed him. Static filled the room. Several click noises returned.

"There are other chapters of the Brotherhood out there," Papi said. "This organization is larger than you think."

Barry went quiet. "What are you guys saying to each other with those clicks?"

Papi smiled.

Twelve

Desean James was one of the most talented and underrated basketball players on the planet. But he didn't talk smack or flap his gums to the press. He believed in keeping his head down, doing a good job, and getting off the court to be with his family. Because of his low profile, he wasn't a sought-after player for endorsements. But then something changed, and it happened the first time he took a sip of Energoo.

Desean was so addicted to the stuff he had an Energoo soda fountain installed in his family room. At first, his two young boys, Derek and Dominik, thought it was "super cool." But, things took a turn when a koi pond was constructed in their backyard, complete with a giant animatronic fish spurting Energoo from its mouth. "It was bizarre," said the usually shy Dominik to his friends. "The pond smelled funny."

Desean married his high school sweetheart, Tanisha, and had no vices. He didn't drink or do drugs. He didn't even use the word "hell" amongst mixed company. So, it was a surprise when Energoo became his vice of choice. The addiction happened overnight, and the family questioned whether they should seek help. But Desean wasn't interested in intervention. He was interested in an endorsement deal.

His agent was shocked to hear from him. The two hadn't spoken since he extended his contract with the Philadelphia 76ers. Desean never wanted anything more than to play the game. But now, he was a different man. He spoke faster, every word dripping with desperation. He needed to be part of the Energoo story.

"I don't know what to tell you," his agent said. "But they like Travis right now and signed him to an exclusive endorsement deal."

"You know I'm a better player than fucking Travis," said Desean, testing out the F word for the first time.

"Yeah, everyone knows that, but what can I do?" the agent rebuffed.

"You can get me this endorsement or find someone else to represent," replied Desean.

There was a long pause on the other end. "I'll see what I can do," the agent said in a tiny voice.

"You better," said Desean, his temperature rising, "you know when I'm serious about something, I'm serious."

"I do," said the agent, worried, and hung up.

Desean was furious. He downed another can of Energoo, quickly crushed it into an aluminum pancake, and grabbed another. He noticed his two boys staring at him as if he were a stranger.

"What?" Desean asked. "You think Daddy's losing his damn mind?"

The two boys remained quiet. Derek stepped toward his father and nervously read a prepared statement.

"Dear Papa," he started.

Tanisha, his mother, had helped him with some of the more challenging words. But, Desean didn't hear an awkwardly worded sentence, for his attention was zeroed in on a large television mounted on the wall. There was a breaking news bulletin.

Atlas Wake had found a new CEO, and her name was Lauren Caldwell.

Thirteen

Lauren entered the Atlas Wake lobby wearing a pantsuit and heels for the first time in her life. She walked past a mirror and didn't recognize her reflection. Who was this dark-haired woman with no tattoos? Holding an Energoo latte.

Mitch, her new assistant, found her. "Ms. Caldwell?" he said, holding out a Green Goddess to-go cup. "Oh, darn, you already got one?"

"They made me take one in the limo," Lauren explained. "And please. You don't have to call me Ms. Caldwell. Lauren is fine."

"Ah," replied Mitch. "I thought I was making a grand gesture on my first day."

He tossed the cup into a trash can mounted on the wall. "This is not trash," barked the receptacle, one of many computerized items in the lobby. "This is not trash," the can warned, "Energoo lattes are for consumption."

Mitch awkwardly smiled at Lauren. "Uh, I'll handle this one," he said, pressing a few buttons. "Gotta be some sort of override switch, right?"

"This is not trash," growled the can. "Consume!" it shrieked, spitting the latte back at him. He screamed and clutched his face, the latte searing his skin.

"Holy shit!" cried Lauren, shoving him underneath a drinking fountain and rinsing his face. The cool water temporarily relieved him, but it was short-lived, for the fountain also took offense. "This drinking fountain is not for bathing!" it squealed.

A Security Guard approached the two. He thumped a baton in his hands and recalled his training for such situations. Vagrants often used their drinking fountains for bathing, and security needed to relocate them, keep them hidden. The corporation needed to project an aspirational image of upward mobility.

"Now, now," said the Guard. "Why don't I give you a coupon for one free can of Energoo and get you two on your way?"

Lauren and Mitch backed away from the fountain, and the Guard noticed their Atlas Wake badges. "Oh, I'm so sorry. I thought you were homeless," he said, embarrassed. "But if you do need to bathe, you really should use the gym facilities."

Lauren had been told what to do her entire life by schools, orphanages, and shitty jobs. For once, she had power and decided to wield it.

"I could have you fired," she said sharply.

The Guard was confused.

"Do you know who I am?" she continued.

"No," the guard replied, growing worried.

"Do you see my name on this badge?" she asked, stepping closer.

The guard squinted and noticed "CEO" under her name. "I'm so sorry," he whispered, lowering his head. "I would never tell someone of your stature to shower in the gym, Mrs. Caldwell."

"It's Miss," she corrected.

"Miss," he replied and hurried away. Mitch was impressed and a little scared of her. He pawed at his blistering face and moaned, but Lauren was oblivious. Pulling rank on that guard was the most fun she had in years. And she wanted to linger in the feeling.

Geena Jackson sat in the Atlas Wake press room, revising the speech Lauren would give in a few hours. She noticed Dan playing on his phone, dazed. His Xanax intake had increased recently, and he was becoming a non-entity.

"Hey Dan!" she said, testing to see how fucked up he was. He turned around slowly, eyes glazed over, mouth dry.

"W'sup?" he mumbled.

"Nothing," she replied.

Lauren and Mitch walked in, Mitch holding onto his peeling face.

Geena stood up in horror. "Oh my God," she said, "what happened to you?"

Before he could answer, Lauren interrupted, "Those trash cans in the lobby are psychotic!"

"I'm sorry?" replied Geena. "Those are top-of-the-line garbage bots."

Mitch locked eyes with Lauren. "It's no big deal," he shrugged. "I'll be okay."

Geena looked to the young CEO for an explanation. Lauren remembered she needed to stay calm and collected. Above the fray. If Mitch shrugged this off, so would she.

"By the way, I'm still not ready with your speech," Geena said. "Can I give it to you a little later?"

"That's fine," Lauren bluffed. She was nervous about speaking in front of a crowd. She hadn't done it since high school, her short story days.

"OK, boomers," mumbled Dan, staring at his phone. "Looks like social media is finding out about our new CEO. We're deadass trending right now!"

Everyone huddled around Dan's phone and watched Lauren's name ripple across his screen. "There's nothing on the internet about this woman," read one comment. "Who is this badass boss bitch?" read another.

Dan doubled over with laughter. "This is deadass going to work," he said, coasting on his Xanax high. "Lauren is deadass bulletproof."

Geena looked at Lauren for any sign of life, a signal she was processing the magnitude of the situation. But Lauren remained steadfast and cool.

The Brotherhood of the Resigned was also digesting the news. They crowded around Little Ricky's laptop while the young man read the press release. When he finished, Papi John asked Barry if he knew this "Lauren Caldwell broad."

"No," replied Barry.

"Seems like no one does," said Ricky.

Barry was bummed out. He thought he was pretty good at his job, a real team player. How could he be replaced so quickly? He stared at the press photo Atlas Wake released. Lauren looked like a girl-next-door badass boss bitch. Shiny and approachable.

"Those sneaky little fucks," said Papi. "I wouldn't be surprised if she was a clone or something. Or they grew her in a lab! They don't want anyone asking too many questions over there, do they, Barry?"

Barry went quiet. Was the Brotherhood a bunch of conspiracy theory nutbags?

"Oh shit," said Papi, "the press conference with this new broad is about to start!"

"Do you have to call her a broad?" asked Meghan. "It's demeaning."

"It is?" asked Papi in all sincerity. "Madone, I thought it was a term of endearment this whole time."

Meghan laughed.

"Well, I wonder what this *nice young woman* will say," said Papi, a mea culpa to Meghan, who returned his gesture with a smile.

"Hmm," said Delbert, studying Lauren on the screen. "She looks like a dyke to me."

Fourteen

For hours, Mitch assured other Atlas Wake employees that his injury was "nothing" and "not a big deal." But his face told a different story: red and leathery, like a grapefruit gone bad. He stood at the doorway of Lauren's new office, nursing his now-oozing jaw.

Lauren was oblivious to his plight, too taken by the real estate of her new office, which dwarfed her apartment. She was surrounded by state-of-the-art amenities, a massage chair, entertainment center, and small kitchen. A large window overlooked the city, and she squinted through the haze that hovered outside. A smile weaseled its way onto her face.

"Looks like we have some work to do," said Mitch, pointing to a stack of papers on her desk.

Lauren furrowed her brow. Work was the last thing on her mind. She figured she could kick back in her new massage chair, stare at the city below, and listen to music before the big speech.

"Uh, this is weird," Mitch said. "These papers all have Atlas Wake letterhead, but they're blank."

Lauren picked up her phone to call Geena, but the line was dead. No dial tone. Suddenly, it hit her. This was all theater, props for her to pretend to be CEO. She wanted to laugh, but she wasn't sure how much Mitch knew about her arrangement. So she shrugged and changed the subject.

"Did I show you the corporate card they gave me?" she asked. It was shiny, made of bronze, and sharp enough to cut a person.

"Whoa! Careful!" Mitch joked. "I don't want to get injured again!"

Mitch smiled through his mess of a face, and Lauren reciprocated. She wanted to treat him to lunch, make him happy, help him forget his oozing face. But mostly, she wanted a friend in this place, someone she could trust.

"Are you ready to slay all day?" a voice asked. Dan leaned in the doorway. "The press is waiting for you, playa."

Reporters from all over the country were huddled inside the pressroom, waiting for the arrival of the new CEO. Usually, the room was home to awkward silence, but this time it was alive with chatter. This new CEO, this woman with no history, titillated the press, and they craved more. Lauren arrived with Geena by her side. Everyone applauded.

Geena couldn't help getting caught up in the spectacle, the camera bulbs flashing, the smiling faces. She felt an invisible spotlight forming around her and took a bow. The room went quiet, and everyone looked at Geena, confused. They were here for Lauren, not her. Geena quickly straightened, pushing Lauren to meet her adoring public.

Lauren handled it like a pro, smiling and waving to the press as if nothing had happened. Geena excused herself to the far corner of the room where Dan and Mitch waited in the wings. Mitch had a giant ice pack on his face. Something Dan requested he do because his face looked "grody AF."

"Nice bow," Dan said with a shit-eating grin.

"That was bad, wasn't it?" Geena replied, embarrassed.

"Chillax. Ain't nothing but a thang."

Mitch mumbled under his ice pack, but Geena couldn't understand him and wasn't looking for his opinion anyway. The press settled in, and Lauren stared into the teleprompter. There it was. Her future. Blinking up there on the screen. She took a breath and read.

"Hello. My name is Lauren Caldwell, and I'm the new CEO of Atlas Wake," she said. "As you know, Barry Gray, our previous CEO, was X-ed out for terrible comments he posted on social media years ago. I know Barry was well-liked by some of you. But, his actions were reprehensible, and his recent flee from authorities unconscionable. Barry is not the person we thought he was, and Atlas Wake does not condone his behavior or life in general."

The journalists sat stiff, in quiet judgment.

Lauren fidgeted. "But enough about the past," she said. "Let's talk about the future of Energoo!"

The reporters leaned forward, eager for more.

"We're thrilled to announce we'll be debuting Energoo Formula Two at the Narvel Entertainment complex," she continued. "NBA superstar Desean James will welcome us for what should be quite a show!"

Lauren watched the hungry crowd lap up her words, and she decided to lean in. "The Energoo Formula Two debut event will be sponsored by the charity 'Dunk on Homelessness', an organization committed to eliminating homelessness in America. They urge you to, 'Hey, dunk on homelessness, America!'"

The press room was instantly bored by this homeless talk. They wanted to know more about the event. More about Formula Two. The room erupted, everyone shouting questions. But, one sailed through the air like an arrow.

"What's in Formula Two?" a chubby disheveled man shouted.

"Good question," Lauren replied. She scanned the next few sentences in her speech but found no details. Nervous sweat collected on her forehead, and she rocked on her heels. "Uh, if you want to know more about Formula Two," she ad-libbed, "you'll have to come to our event and find out!"

The press applauded, and Lauren smiled and paused to take a drink. She reviewed the last paragraph of her speech, and nausea overwhelmed her. She looked to Geena, the writer responsible, and found her steely-eyed, immovable.

"And lastly," she continued, "I want to thank Meryl and the team at Atlas Wake for trusting a young woman to be CEO. In the history of this company, it has never happened before. Yes, I stand before you, a young woman who has faced many hardships..." Her mouth went dry. Lips mouthing words she didn't want to say. She gripped the podium and drank more water.

"I may not have much of a social media history," she continued. "But I do have an emotional history. I stand before you, a young woman who grew up...in orphanages all her life...A young woman who..." Her gaze met the crowd, and she noticed everyone was riveted. "A young woman who never met her parents." A hush filled the audience. But the speech wasn't over. "I have survived my trauma," she cringed, "and now I'm the CEO of the biggest beverage company in the world...I look forward to getting to know all of you and understanding your truth."

The reporters gasped. Some sobbed. Lauren forced a smile for photos. She noticed Geena, in the back of the room, and the two locked eyes.

NBA superstar Desean James sat shell-shocked in front of his big screen TV. Did Lauren really just say his name? Did his agent secure him an Energoo endorsement deal after all? He quickly dialed the man.

"Desean!" the agent said proudly. "Did I kill that or what?"

"You killed it!" Desean yelped, excited. "I've never been this happy in all my life! God bless you!"

His wife Tanisha and two sons crowded around him, wondering how he could say this was his happiest moment.

"When do I get to taste Formula Two?" Desean asked.

"We'll figure that out soon. Don't you worry," assured his agent.

Fifteen

Lauren was in her executive office restroom having an executive emotional breakdown. She wiped tears from her eyes with toilet paper, devastated that Geena broadcasted her personal story. She never told a soul about not knowing her parents, let alone the entire world. How could Geena pick at her parental scab? She would have stormed out and quit if this were any other job.

"You okay in there?" said Mitch from outside.

"Yeah, I'm fine. Just taking a massive dump," she lied.

Mitch didn't know what to do with that information. So, he sat on her oversized black leather couch and played on his phone. Every so often, the phone's reflection would remind him of his melting face, and he would recoil as if seeing a ghost.

Lauren took a deep breath. She needed to make this work and roll with the punches if she wanted to be wealthy. She flushed the toilet for effect and exited to find Mitch sprawled on the couch. He immediately hid his phone, not wanting to appear like he was goofing off.

"You don't have to do that," she said. "You don't have to be on all the time."

"Are you sure?" he asked.

"Yeah, I want us to be friends," she replied.

"Oh, friends?" asked Mitch. "That's odd. Most assistants are treated like garbage."

"I know, and I think that's terrible."

"I dunno," replied Mitch. "If I ever attain a job of your stature. I'd treat my assistant like dog shit. Like a steaming pile of dog shit! Y'know, as payback for all the time I was stomped on."

"That's really old fashioned of you," smiled Lauren. "You better watch it. That talk might get you X-ed."

Mitch's eyes widened. He grabbed his phone and turned it off. "Don't joke about getting X-ed," he whispered. "You didn't record what I just said, right? The bit about me using my future job position to punish my underlings?"

"Why would I do that?" she replied. "Unless this office is bugged."

Mitch looked worried. He wandered to her giant desk, grabbed a blank sheet of paper, and wrote, "I wouldn't be surprised if they were listening in." He shoved the paper into a shredder, where it buzzed like a chainsaw to its demise.

"In other news," Mitch whispered, "You're trending on all the social media platforms—the orphanage stuff...The, uh, not knowing your parents stuff. People identify with that. Some even shared inspirational stories about their own family trauma."

"Really?" asked Lauren.

Mitch nodded and showed her his phone. It was a video of a woman saying she didn't know her parents. She described Lauren as a "badass orphan boss bitch". And was so thankful Lauren shared "her truth" with the world. BadAssOrphanBossBitch was trending.

"You're connecting with strangers," said Mitch.

"Yeah," replied Lauren. "I hate that."

Sixteen

Barry watched the Atlas Wake press conference with the rest of the Brotherhood. He felt woozy, not from the tequila shot Papi forced him to drink, but from Lauren's complete dismissal of his life. Was he *really* that replaceable?

The others raced to devise a plan, but Barry couldn't focus. His hands trembled, and a foul stench overwhelmed his nostrils. The Brotherhood rarely bathed, and their body odor was finally too much for Barry. He excused himself to take in some air outside.

The streets were desolate, the Brotherhood's secret headquarters far from society's reach. Barry took comfort in knowing he could stroll the streets unmolested. A shadow appeared on the sidewalk, and he recoiled. It belonged to a large rodent the size of a cat. It reminded him of a coypu, a large rat-like creature in Florence, Italy. It was the only trip his ex-wife seemed to enjoy with him, probably because she was drunk on Negronis the whole time.

He didn't want to believe the alcohol was the only reason for her smiles, though. She must have still enjoyed his company, right? Or was she already fucking that doctor? The rat skittered away, and a cold breeze made him shudder.

When he returned to the Brotherhood's lair, the stench of body odor blanketed him. He studied everyone's faces, trying to see if their noses flinched, but everyone seemed unaware, used to the smell. Barry couldn't take it anymore.

"Do any of you guys bathe?" he asked.

Meghan frowned. "Hey. There's a woman here, you know."

"Can we just let the record show that whenever I say 'guys,' I mean everyone," replied Barry. He looked to Papi as if to say, "Can you believe this broad?"

Papi shrugged. "Who am I to judge?" he said. "I like eating pizza with a sidecar of marinara sauce so I can dip the crust in afterward. Know what I mean?"

"What's that got to do with anything?" asked Barry.

"We're talking about personal preference," replied Papi, "it's a personal preference thing, capisce? Meghan would prefer you address her as a woman. Is that so hard? On a personal preference-type level?"

"I guess not," Barry said.

"A fanabla," replied Papi, "And to answer your question, no, Barry, we haven't showered in a long time. And if you have a problem with that, let me know."

Barry went quiet.

"I found some stuff for tomorrow," Little Ricky interrupted. He had been locked in on his laptop for the last half hour, reading about the Atlas Wake event. "They're going to debut the new can. But no one can purchase Formula Two until the day after tomorrow."

"We should go," said Barry. "Let's break into the convention center tomorrow and get a can of Formula Two before they release it. In twenty-four hours, we could figure out what's inside it."

"Look at you! I love it!" replied Papi. "But, who's going to analyze this can? Do you think we have some top-secret research lab that can magically analyze it within a night? We have factions nationwide, but not that type of scientific infrastructure."

"I know a guy," said Barry.

"You know a guy?" replied Papi.

"Well. Not a guy per se. But, I know someone who could test this new formula, break it down, see what's in it."

Papi couldn't help smiling. "See, my friends," he said, "I told you Barry would lead us to the promised land. Aren't we glad we rescued him? We're all gonna get un-X-ed!"

The Brotherhood nodded along, and Barry felt their warm embrace.

"Alright. Let's talk logistics," Papi said. "How are we getting into this joint?"

Two men emerged from the darkness. Barry had never heard them speak, for they always remained in the shadows. They wore matching gray construction helmets and appeared to be identical twins in their mid-forties. Rumor had it their parents, overwhelmed by having twins and the number of decisions that came with it, named them both Robert to save time. As adults, they went by Bob and Rob.

Bob surveyed the room and cracked his meaty fingers. His hands were caked in calluses, a side effect of years of manual labor. "Don't worry about getting into that place," he said.

"We know someone who can help," finished Rob.

Barry whooped and shot his fist up, triumphant. But everyone else remained quiet and in shock. He studied their faces, confused. "What's wrong?" he asked.

"Well," replied Papi, "I've known the twins for many moons, and I've never heard them talk. I don't think anyone has." He turned toward Bob and Rob and said sweetly, "You both have really nice voices."

Seventeen

The Narvel Entertainment Center, the largest sports complex in the city, had a line wrapping around its massive structure. Over forty thousand people were foaming at the mouth for their first look at Formula Two, the same people who crashed the Atlas Wake website within a nanosecond of ticket release. They knew they wouldn't taste the new formula, but it didn't matter. Being in the same building as the aluminum can was enough.

Reporters were on the scene and interviewed these folks, who stared crazy-eyed into their cameras. They regaled the TV-watching public about how Energoo changed their lives, some traveling thousands of miles to be there. They claimed the green goop solved all their problems even though many were barely hanging on, living in low-income housing, or on the streets.

Lauren watched the news coverage from the Atlas Wake Lobby and couldn't get over the fanaticism around a beverage she thought looked like alien cum. She glanced over at Mitch, whose face was like a melted candle. She wanted to reassure him about his appearance, but nothing escaped her lips.

"What up," asked Dan. "You stoked?"

Lauren nodded.

"So, uh, here's the thing. Mitch needs to hang back for this one," said Dan.

"Why?" asked Lauren.

Dan checked for eyes. "Well, I'll keep it a hunnit with you," he whispered. "The Atlas Wake shareholders saw a recent picture of him, and the corporation doesn't approve of his face."

"What the fuck are you talking about?" cried Lauren.

"Quit trippin'," Dan replied. "They just think having a guy with a melty face is a bad look for the company. They've recommended he have facial reconstructive surgery if he's to stay on as your assistant."

Lauren looked behind her. Mitch had heard everything, and his melty face sank. "This is bullshit," she said, trying to comfort him.

"Nah it's all good," replied Dan. "Unfortunately, Mitch has to stay home. But we do have another assistant for you tonight."

Lauren was speechless. She wanted to hug poor melting Mitch but felt it might not look appropriate.

"No need for the long face, bro-bro," said Dan, "Atlas will pay for the surgery."

The offer only upset Mitch, and Lauren feared his face might slide off.

"Maybe I don't want surgery," Mitch mumbled.

"You goofy," said Dan. "If you refuse the surgery, you're fired."

Mitch took that in the gut, and Lauren escorted him to the exit, apologizing the whole time. "I think you should get the surgery," she said at the gates.

Mitch twisted his hair between his fingertips and contemplated the offer. She was about to tell him how much she needed him. How much she needed a friend, but he vanished onto the street before she got the nerve.

A limo pulled up, and Lauren asked Dan who would be her assistant tonight. "Oh," he replied, pulling a miniature robot from the limo's trunk. "This lil' homeslice will take care of you."

The robot looked cheap, a step above a child's toy. Its eyes lit red, and Lauren noticed an Atlas Wake logo emblazoned on its chest. "Nice to meet you," it said. "Can I get you a bottled unit of water?"

The Brotherhood of the Resigned trudged down a dark sewer tunnel, their shoes growing thick with muck. Papi typically led such outings, but tonight, Bob and Rob, the quiet twins, had the honor. Eventually, they found a long metal ladder that ascended to street level. Bob and Rob nodded toward it, and Papi translated. "Okay," he said. "We'll exit through this sewer grate, then skedaddle to the overpass and into the staff parking garage of the Narvel Entertainment complex. Once there, Bob and Rob's connect will greet us."

The overpass would expose them to the outside world. They had to be quick or risk detection.

Barry whispered to Papi, "The twins. Why don't they like to talk?"

"Ah," said Papi, "they took a vow of silence after they got X-ed. They believed they *did* say something wrong and felt it wasn't their part to speak anymore. Sort of a monk thing, I guess."

"That's pretty serious," said Barry.

"Well, they're pretty serious guys," replied Papi. "They ain't a bunch of goofballs like the rest of us."

The Brotherhood entered the street and was overwhelmed by the mass of people in line. The Resigned had been disconnected for so long, living in self-imposed quarantine underground, that being this close to humanity hurt their hearts. Mr. Bompity Bomp was the most rattled, tears tumbling down so quickly they caused his clown nose to flip over.

"Aw, Bompity," said Papi. "Aw, Bompity boo my boy, it's okay. Let it out. But, at the same time, don't let it out because we need to get across the street now. There's no time for tears."

Barry saw this as a moment to connect with his new brotherhood and put his arm around Mr. Bompity. The Clown winced, and Barry was unsure if he had overstepped. He decided to double down and told Bompity about the last time he was at the Narvel Complex. "It was just me and my ex-wife," Barry said wistfully. "I wanted to see a wrestling match here, but she wasn't interested. But, when the orchestra came around, boy, was she into it. She loved it so much...I loved *her* so much, too."

Delbert rolled his eyes, annoyed by Barry's constant ex-wife talk. He seemed to have a story about her every half hour. Bompity, however, sniffled and smiled, won over by Barry's sudden vulnerability. The group moved through the overpass undetected, then entered the parking garage. They found a jolly heavyset woman holding the backdoor open for them, scanning for eyes.

"There you are," she said. "My favorite twins!" The twins beamed, and she gave them a bear hug. She apologized, knowing it wasn't politically correct to do so. "I can't help it. I missed you."

The twins, ever the consummate professionals, refused to get caught up in sentimentality. They slowly removed themselves from the big, gregarious woman's grip and ushered the Brotherhood inside. The woman asked the twins a hundred questions about their life. But the twins never replied, never uttered a word. The woman hadn't noticed their silence and filled the air with mindless chatter. They climbed what felt like a million stairs until, finally, the woman pointed to a two-foot hole in the ceiling.

"That's where you wanna be, boys," she said. Meghan was about to correct her when the woman continued, "*And* ladies."

Barry stared at the tiny hole and couldn't remain silent anymore. "Did we really come all this way to hang out in the rafters and watch everything from afar? We need to be downstairs where they're storing this stuff. We can't get a can from up here."

"Relax," replied Papi. "We have to trust the nice lady. She has a restricted access card and should be able to get us a can while we wait in the wings. We can't exactly hang out in the open, can we?"

Barry agreed to this plan earlier but hoped he could change the mission once they were inside. The problem was he didn't have a better plan.

"You think I love this idea?" said Papi. "I don't. I'm afraid of heights! Madone, I'm not looking forward to those rafters."

Barry wanted to continue arguing the plan's merits, but everyone looked annoyed. So, he climbed the rickety wooden ladder toward the hole in the ceiling, and the rest of the group followed suit. The twins were the last to go, and the woman stopped them before their ascent.

"I know you didn't mean what you said," she whispered. "You didn't deserve to be X-ed. You both have good hearts."

The twins stared at her for a long moment. "No, we don't," they said in unison.

Eighteen

Desean James and his family sat in an empty locker room one hundred and fifty feet below the Brotherhood. Desean paced like an addict, banging his fist against a locker, upset. The loud clattering sent shivers down his wife Tanisha's spine.

"How could they not give me a taste of Formula Two yet?" he cried, "I'm supposed to go out and endorse this stuff without ever tasting it?"

Tanisha closed her eyes and took a breath.

"I don't like how irritable you've become," she whispered.

"I'm only like this because they haven't given me that taste!" he yelped, flipping over a bench.

"Did you talk to your agent?" she asked.

"Nah, that fucking asshole is acting like an asshole!" he shouted.

Tanisha's face fell. Her youngest, Dominik, noticed and whispered, "Don't worry, Momma. We're used to Daddy talking like that."

Tanisha grabbed Desean's phone.

"What are you doing?" he asked.

"I'm calling the asshole myself," she said, finally getting through to the agent. "Hey motherfucker," she shouted, "My husband wants a can of Formula Two in his dressing room ASAP, or we're walking. You hear me?"

The agent was shocked. He stuttered, tried apologizing, but nothing made sense. Every word got chopped in half, flipped around, and swallowed under his tongue. The boys stared at Tanisha, as if she were a stranger. She felt terrible, but it worked, and the agent eventually agreed to make some calls.

But Desean didn't trust his agent. Didn't trust anyone anymore. He barreled into the hallway. "Where's my Formula Two?" he barked at Narvel staff. A frightened young man pointed Desean to a windowed room. Desean pressed his face against the glass. A security guard stood inside, babysitting a yellow cardboard box with the familiar green Atlas Wake logo. A small red label underneath read "Formula Two."

Desean's excited breathing fogged up the window. He knocked on the door, trying to suppress his frothing anticipation. The guard noticed him and grinned.

"Desean!" said the giant guard, opening the door. "Hey, I'm a big fan."

"Oh yeah?" DeSean said, sidling inside.

The guard lifted his uniform to reveal a Desean jersey. But Desean didn't notice, too fixated on the box.

"You think you could sign my jersey?" the guard asked.

Desean snapped out of it, "Sure," he said, signing the uniform. "Hey, uh, is it cool if I try one of those?"

The Guard instantly went from giddy fanboy to nervous company man. "Um, I'm sorry, Mr. James. I can't do that," he said. "My boss wants you to try it for the first time on camera."

"I just signed your jersey, and you're gonna deny me? C'mon, man. Don't be a punk-ass bitch."

The guard stared at the still-wet autograph, knowing he didn't want to be a punk-ass bitch. Not in the eyes of Desean. So he turned and dramatically looked the other way. Desean nodded, satisfied. He moved toward the sacred twelve-pack of Formula Two. His hands shook with expectation.

"Don't injure your hand on one of those cans, man!" joked the Guard. "You gotta sink some threes tonight!"

Desean could no longer hear him. He was lost to the crisp snap of the can opening. It echoed through him like a thousand tiny knives. He placed the cool aluminum to his stubbled mouth, took a gulp, then another.

"How is it?" asked the guard.

Desean closed his eyes. "God bless it," he said, giving the sign of the cross. "God bless it."

"Heh, that must be some good shit," said the guard with a weak smile.

"It is," replied Desean. "Fact, I'm going to need at least one more can."

Nineteen

The Brotherhood of the Resigned hung in the rafters like flies in a web. Below, an audience of forty thousand people, with only plywood holding back a fatal plummet. Sweat dripped off Papi's terrified face.

"I picked the wrong day to be afraid of heights," he said.

Meghan looked at him with sympathy and grabbed his hand.

Across from them, Delbert eyed the crowd. He could make out some details if he squinted. A busty woman in a neon green halter top. The words "Energoo" scrawled across her giant breasts. He smiled, unzipping his pants.

Mr. Bompity Bomp was beside him, oblivious, mid-nervous breakdown. The crowd of humanity was too much for the old clown. He cried so hard it shook the rafters, causing Papi to clutch the wood plank beneath him.

"Bompity!" he whispered. "Are you okay?"

Bompity was a wreck, makeup smeared with tears. "I'm okay," he sniffled.

"I know it's a lot," Papi said.

"I miss my family. I miss my friends."

"Hang in there, Bompity. Stay strong." Papi felt sorry for the elderly clown, but his face went astray when he noticed Delbert. "Ay, what the hell are you doing?!"

"Fuck off!" replied Delbert.

"I told you, he's a creep!" shouted Barry. "Why do you guys keep him around?"

"Fuck you, Barry!" yelled Delbert. "I'm gonna pretend that woman down there is your wife!"

"I don't have a wife, dumbass!"

"Whatever! No one wants to hear your ex-wife sob story anymore! Shut the fuck up so I can squeegee already," said Delbert, pumping his arm faster.

Gerald punched Delbert with such force that he flew backward into a row of steel columns. His body rag-dolled and hung precariously above the crowd. The Brotherhood stared in rapt silence. They slowly peered down at the crowd, terrified, to find everyone cheering. Something exciting was happening below, and no one gave a shit about the unconscious pervert in the rafters with his dick hanging out.

The crowd cheered as Lauren walked onto the court. Her tiny robot assistant trailed her, asking if she wanted bottled water. She passed Geena on the way to the podium and couldn't help whispering, "Did you write about the parents I never met again?"

"Hi, everyone. I'm Lauren Caldwell," she announced, "Are you ready for Formula Two?!"

The crowd went nuts as a suited man rolled a golden beverage cart to center court. Atop it were three sparkling cans of Energoo Formula Two.

Geena eyed the cans from the sidelines and turned to Dan. "There's supposed to be twelve cans on that cart," she said.

Lauren looked at the teleprompter and clenched her jaw. She took a deep breath. "As you all know, I don't know my parents. I never met them. And it haunts me every day." She waited for the crowd to finish a modest applause. "Anyways," she continued, "It's time to welcome one of the greatest NBA players of all time! Are you ready, everyone? Come out here, Desean James, and get ready to dunk on the homeless!"

Everyone cheered.

Lauren realized she'd read the last line wrong. It said, 'Dunk on homelessness.'

Music blared, and Desean barreled onto the court, bouncing two basketballs simultaneously. He sank one of them at half-court, ran up and dunked the other. Then he raced back and forth, pretending he was competing against a phantom basketball player. Lauren was supposed to greet him after a few minutes of play, but he was so laser-focused she let him do his thing.

After fifteen minutes, Desean showed no signs of stopping. Geena signaled for Lauren to step in. But, as she got closer to Desean, Lauren realized he was under the influence. The sweaty face, clicking jaw, bloodshot wild eyes. He kept mumbling, "God bless it."

Delbert lay limp over a creaking wooden beam with Papi moving slowly towards him. A drop of sweat fell from Papi's forehead as he gripped a wooden plank with both hands.

"Seriously, Papi," Meghan said, "let me handle this. You're shaking."

"No," Papi refused. "I got this."

He inched closer to Del. Del's eyes flickered open. Color returned to his face, and he began masturbating as if nothing had happened.

"You're going to fall! Grab my hand!" Papi said, wincing at the gesture.

"What? No! I'm trying to jerk off!" barked Delbert.

Desean sank another basket and lifted his hands to the heavens. "God bless Formula Two!" he shouted.

Lauren approached. "Hey," she said. "They wanna get you on camera drinking the first can of Formula Two. You ready?"

"Born ready," he replied, sinking another three. He laughed, scrambling to the golden beverage cart. "Formula Two, baby!" he said, picking up the can, giving it the sign of the cross. "This is the blood of the new and everlasting life!" he shrieked as he downed the can, then had another.

The crowd cheered. The glowing phones flickered through the stadium like torches. Excitement pressurized the building.

"I can feel your love!" shouted Desean, wishing he could crowd surf and become one with the pulsating mass of people. "Formula Two!" he screamed, running around the court at top speed. He high-fived Lauren, "C'mon girl!" he shouted. "Play with me!"

Lauren was taken aback. The way he said, "play with me," sounded so childlike. So innocent. A grown man wanted someone to play with him. It softened her heart until a ball hurtled toward her. She narrowly dodged it, and Desean laughed, urging her to catch the ball next time. He turned to the sidelines and shouted to no one in particular. "Anyone got another ball?" An official quickly tossed him one, and he dribbled toward her.

But, this time, his stride was off. His body began to vibrate. "Toss the rock up for me," he said, handing Lauren the ball. She was confused. "Throw the ball up, and I'll dunk it," he explained. He directed photographers to crowd around the basket.

"Come on, girl!" shouted Desean, barreling toward the basket. The crowd leaned forward. Lauren tossed the ball. Time seemed to slow down as Desean jumped. His hungry eyes zeroed in on the ball.

The crowd seemed to scream in silence as his hand gripped the ball. His eyes sunk back with pleasure, and his tongue let loose. Descending on the net, time returned to full speed, and Desean exploded the moment he dunked the ball.

Gallons of green goo flew out onto the crowd.

The entire arena went quiet.

You could hear the last few bounces of the ball he'd dunked.

The only recognizable thing left of Desean was his hand, which grasped the rim, dripping green goo.

Lauren fainted.

And before the crowd could fully process the horror, just seconds after Desean's implosion, a body fell from the rafters and splattered onto the court, hand still on dick.

A BRIEF INTERLUDE ON THE STATE OF THE NARVEL ENTERTAINMENT COMPLEX

It's important to note there are actually two Narvel Entertainment complexes. There's the physical building, where Narvel debuts their film and television series (and where Desean and Delbert met their unlikely demise.) But there's also the *Narvel Entertainment complex* that has slowly infiltrated society. This one isn't a physical space but something intangible that permeates all life. It's in the *content* people consume at home and what they buy.

Content used to be a word only business types used behind closed doors. It referred to television, internet videos, and feature films. It was a corporate term designed to make art feel disposable and interchangeable. "We need three more hours of content to fill our programming slate," the executives would say.

The word content flatlined the financial worth of art and helped devalue the artists themselves. Over time, artists became known as "content creators." And even introduced themselves as such at parties. Eventually, most content creators worked for the Narvel Corporation—a company determined to resuscitate every intellectual property they owned. One such property was Metal Man, starring Robert Dooney Jr.

One hundred years had passed since the original movie. But Robert's death wouldn't stop the Narvel corporation from making more sequels. On the night Desean exploded, Narvel was prepping the release of Metal Man 243. It was hot off its premiere at the Sundance Narvel film festival. And the corporation was particularly excited about its partnership with Atlas Wake. In the new film, Energoo Formula Two would be the official beverage of Metal Man.

When Dooney was alive, he famously killed his Metal Man persona to rid himself of the cinematic universe Narvel created. He wanted to return to more varied artistic output and contribute to culture in a way that wasn't just superhero movies. However, after a while, he realized pop culture didn't exist anymore. It was only Narvel culture, and he wanted back in.

Narvel welcomed him with open arms but under one condition - that he would agree to undergo a digital capture process called "CGI spirit-mation." It would allow Narvel to continue making Metal Man movies starring Robert Dooney Jr. even after he died. Thanks to AI, the CGI spirit-mation process yielded realistic results, and Narvel was able to crank out two Metal Man Movies a year after Robert's demise.

The Metal Man movies, post-death, were a huge hit. The audience loved to see Dooney crack wise from the great beyond. Creating him with AI was also cheaper than re-casting another Metal Man. Soon after, the Narvel corporation decided they didn't need film or television directors either. The digital wizards at Narvel created an AI app that allowed shareholders to text what they wanted the movie to be. Everything about its creation would be computer automated from shareholder texts. Even better, the app would sniff out past film critiques and ensure the criticisms were addressed in the follow-up sequels. What resulted was the perfect corporate product. Fan service plus artificial intelligence equaled endless predictive profit.

It was a flawless process, except when computers generated a weird bit of dialogue. For example, in an early draft of Metal Man 197, Metal Man proclaimed, "That's abouta it for you, boyz!" then farted on TarantulaBoi's head. Fortunately, Narvel engineers, called "The Narvel Dream Wizards" fixed these errors. The Wizards were poorly paid but thrilled and even honored to work for the mighty corporation.

The films generated by this process were so slickly produced that even the harshest critics loved them. They always earned 100% approval ratings on movie aggregate review sites. However, some of the positive reviews felt ambiguous at best. One critic wished "There'd be anything remotely interesting in these movies" while also applauding how well-made they were. If any critic dared to say the movie was mediocre, they would be shamed out of existence by "Narvel Fanboys." An extremist online group that grew more and more powerful as the years rolled on.

When Meryl Evans, founder of Atlas Wake, was a boy, he watched Star Force for the first time on VHS and fell in love. As an adult, he watched endless sequels and reboots of his boyhood love. But it felt different. He often had to excuse himself to the restroom, where he would quietly weep. He thought of the kids wearing Dinosaur World 203 t-shirts or playing with Star Force 387 toys and cried profound tears. He mourned a generation of kids with nothing original to hold onto, kids forced to eat the regurgitated leftovers of his pop culture past. It sickened him.

But, he never vocalized these feelings to a living soul. He learned early on that voicing opposition to corporate culture was a bad move for his career. He suppressed his feelings so much that he began sympathizing with shareholders, a sort of Stockholm syndrome. It was their money funding all of this *content*. He should respect and honor them.

As for his generation? Meryl eventually forgave them for making Dinosaur World 75 and Star Force 187. After all, his colleagues had seen their jobs sucked up by company mergers, AI automation, and environmental ruin. They lived through school shootings, terrorism, pandemics, financial and institutional collapse, and world wars. Who was he to judge if they needed a nostalgic pacifier to get through the night?

While most of his generation resigned themselves to nostalgic comforts, he privately strived for more. He wanted to be an American original, someone who left his mark on the world. And he was on the cusp of that and much more. But something terrible happened one night. His company's new product imploded one of the greatest basketball players to play the game.

Twenty

Lauren had blacked out. It could have been for two minutes or two hours. She had no idea. She awoke, groggy, to find a medic above her, holding smelling salts. She felt seasick, dazed by the madness swarming the Narvel Entertainment complex. The medic mumbled and swept her away on a stretcher. The stench was terrible. Her nostrils flared. She looked to the basketball court, the scene of the crime. Desean's severed hand still gripping the rim. Below it was a puddle of green goo, all two hundred and nineteen pounds of him.

Police pushed through the crowd of hysterical onlookers. The medics carried Lauren through a private corridor. People cried and screamed around them. "My Desean!" a woman wailed in the distance, her face slick with tears, kids hovering. Lauren realized they were Desean's family and pretended to sleep as her stretcher careened past them.

A mob of reporters was outside, closing in on the ambulance. One journalist shoved a microphone into Lauren's pretend-sleeping face and asked what she had to say for herself. She pretend-snored into his mic.

As the ambulance pulled away, Lauren's heart beat hard, and she couldn't bring herself to open her eyes. Thinking 'Fuck' over and over. Desean's disembodied hand on the rim. The crowd screaming after the silence. Pure horror. After a few blocks, she heard a familiar voice say, "Yo dawg, open your eyes. Presto."

She opened her eyes and saw Dan dressed like a medic, with two Atlas Wake security bots.

Twenty-One

Geena had escaped the Narvel Entertainment Complex earlier and had trouble settling her nerves. She tried meditating in her office but couldn't focus. Footsteps approached, and she straightened and formed an uneasy smile. Lauren appeared in the hallway, on the verge of tears. Geena instinctively hugged her. They were both surprised by the gesture.

"I know that was a lot," Geena said softly. "But there has to be a valid explanation for everything."

"Okay," Lauren replied, gathering her wits. "What am I supposed to do now?"

Dan strolled in. "Meryl thinks Lauren should have a spa day," he said.

"Really?" Geena replied. "You talked to him? I'm still waiting for a text back..."

Dan shrugged. "Dunno what to tell you, holmes."

Lauren's bronze corporate card slowly slid into an unmarked door. "You'll have the spa to yourself," Geena said, "and the sleeping quarters are quite nice. You should stay the night."

"I'd really like to go home," Lauren said. "I'm freaking out."

"This place will heal you," Geena replied. "Besides, Meryl insists you stay." Geena looked down at her phone. "Speak of the devil, he finally texted me back. Looks like Desean drank a 'bad batch' of Formula Two. Says he'll have more details tomorrow."

Lauren took a deep breath.

"Seriously, enjoy yourself," Geena said. "It's important you look rested and camera-ready tomorrow."

Lauren opened the door and noticed Geena looking wistful at the executive spa. Plants filled every inch of the darkened space, and a warm breeze blew by her. Her tense shoulders began to settle, relieved to press pause on the Atlas Wake nightmare. She walked through the vacant lobby and toward a temple filled with clay hot tubs.

She dangled her foot into one of the tubs and noticed other rooms dotting the perimeter. A tiny robot monkey chirped to life in the shadows and skittered up a fake tree. It wasn't shiny or metallic like her short-lived robot assistant but made of branches, leaves, and fur. An attempt by the robot's creator to make it seem approachable.

"Massage?" it asked.

"Not now," Lauren replied, "Maybe later."

"Namaste to you and yours," the creature said.

It hopped off its fake tree, landed on another, and continued hopping away into the darkness. Lauren was curious about what other amenities the spa offered and sauntered off, letting the warm jungle vibes consume her. She found a kitchen where fake woodland creatures cooked macrobiotic foods. She sampled a hot tea labeled "chill" from a small fox.

"Is it yummers?" the robot fox asked.

Lauren studied the furry thing and found seams in its design, the AI-powered robot poking through carefully stitched fur.

She disrobed by the hot tub and noticed her reflection in the water. Her skin seemed foreign to her without the tattoos, like looking at someone else. A small robot bear scurried by, picking up her clothes and arranging them neatly on an artificial beach. She got into the hot tub, and the water was warm and more buoyant than usual.

The robot bear explained the tub contained magnesium sulfate and was heated to match her body temperature. The intended effect was for her to feel weightless and disconnected from her body. She thought it was neat to hear this information but wished the bear were silent. It risked spoiling the meditative vibe.

She let her legs go limp and floated in the tub. But her mind kept turning over and over—Desean exploded. He exploded right in front of her. She could see the green goo every time she closed her eyes.

An artificial tree sprayed water into the tub, and she paddled to it. The pitter-patter allowed her to focus on something that wasn't her thoughts. She looked up at the darkened temple, and her mind finally cleared. Just pure. Nothingness. Her body felt like it was melting and turning into thick, viscous black goo. Somehow she was merging with the hot tub, becoming one with it. She imagined being stuck, fused to the tub, and it made her laugh like an idiot.

People may have viewed her as a carefree stoner. But these people were wrong. Her mind was always going a mile a minute, and she had trouble turning it off. Trouble sleeping. But now, for the first time, she felt free. Her nervous system seemed to detach from her body, floating above her, just a silly brain and spinal cord. She wanted to wave to it, say, "What's up?" but she no longer had control over her limbs. She was just a pile of goo stuck to a tub. Out of nowhere, she thought, "Fear is dumb," and it felt profound.

She imagined she was a baby re-entering her mother's vagina. "Fear is dumb," she wanted to stream. "Fear is dumb," she laughed, like a child. She remained in this state for an hour until the tub began to drain, an automated feature to ensure executives didn't hallucinate for too long.

She dried herself off with a towel and felt like a new person. Things seemed clearer to her, less muddled. Instead of contemplating her job, Desean's Death, or the parents who abandoned her. She thought about how she wanted to be rich for the rest of her life.

Twenty-Two

The Brotherhood of the Resigned was trudging through an abandoned subway tunnel. En route to home. Thanks to Bob and Rob's contact, they had escaped the Narvel Entertainment complex. But they stank with defeat.

"I made Delbert die," Gerald moaned. "I made him die with my fist." He sobbed. Papi shushed the crying giant. "No, you didn't. I should have grabbed his hand, but I was too afraid of heights."

"He was jerking off," shot Barry. "I mean, I wouldn't feel too sorry for that asshole. Especially with what he said about my ex-wife."

"You tend to talk about her a lot," Papi said. "Besides, you don't know Delbert as we did. We should all take a moment and say a few words about the man."

The Brotherhood stared at each other in the dimness. No one said a word. "Okay. I can go first," said Papi. "Delbert...Delbert...Well, what can you say? He was troubled for sure. A sex addict, yes. But was he a good guy? I'd like to think so at least." Papi paused, unsure of what else to say. "Actually," he continued, "I remember when he first joined the group. He bunked with Little Ricky. You remember that, Ricky?"

"Yeah," replied Ricky.

"Hah!" yelped Papi, eager to tell the story. "So, Ricky and Del had to share a bunk bed. And let me tell you, Delbert wanted that top bunk more than anything. But when Ricky said that's the bunk he preferred. Boom. Bam. It was so, and he let him have it."

Little Ricky cleared his throat to speak and then didn't.

"I mean, am I right. Or am I right?" asked Papi.

"You are," started Ricky, "but I also caught him jerking off to a magazine he taped to the bottom of my bunk."

Papi tried to remain upbeat despite this new information. "Well, he had a tremendous carnal spirit," he offered. "Anyone else have a story?"

The tunnel fell silent, and Bob and Rob, the quiet twins, spoke in unison. "I know he liked to jerk off every chance he got," said the twins. "But, he was always nice to us."

"Look at that. Will you look at that?" Papi strained. "Sure, the man, in his words, liked to 'squeegee' a lot, but he treated us with respect. For the most part. Right?"

"Nah," said Meghan, joining the conversation. "Barry is right. The man was a piece of shit and deserved to die with his hands on his dick."

Eventually, Papi found a platform with a ladder marked with red tape. Everyone followed him up and back onto the street near their boarded-up building. When they entered, they found the place had been ransacked. Every object, from chairs to shelves, was on its side. Papi raced to a tiny filing cabinet and found documents missing. He turned to see his CB radio bashed and gutted like a fish.

"Oh God," he said, crumbling to the floor.

The others scrambled in, horrified, noticing each one of their personal effects, reminders of their previous life, had been destroyed.

Little Ricky's laptop reminded him he was a budding genius coder, and Meghan's old notepad reminded her of being a well-liked teacher. Even Barry's wallet, with the photo of his ex-wife, reminded him he was capable of a romantic relationship. These little objects kept them sane. And now they were gone.

"We have to get out of here," said Papi. "Get your shit together, and let's move out."

"Who did this?" asked Barry, upset.

"It doesn't matter who," said Papi, trying desperately to find any document left.

In short order, the Brotherhood was back on the streets, eyeing shadows on the sidewalks as if the bogie man was waiting to leap out.

"What are we going to do?" asked Gerald.

Everyone looked to Papi, waiting for a plan, but Papi's mouth went dry. They walked some more, and a light bulb went off in the leader's brain. "I know of a place," he said.

The place was yet another nondescript, crumbling building in a weed-covered parking lot. Papi rushed ahead of everyone, opening the front door, which detached and thudded to the floor. But the Italian leader didn't seem to care about the busted door. He was too busy taking in the details of the old place.

Booths covered in dust.

Tablecloths tattered and worn.

Mouse turds.

So many mouse turds.

He was blind to it all, acting like a realtor showing off a new property to a prospective buyer. He didn't see cobwebs and dust but beautiful large windows with rays of sunshine that could fill a space and warm him.

"By the way," Papi said with a twinkle in his eye. "It's got a basement."

Lumpy bags of flour littered the place while precarious stacks of tomato sauce threatened to tumble over. Gerald carefully plucked a tomato can and wiped off a thick blanket of dust, revealing a past-due expiration date. "What is this place, Papi?" the gentle giant asked.

Papi tried not to get emotional. "This, my friends, was my pizza parlor." He stared at the ceiling full of cobwebs. "Ain' it a beaut?"

They smiled weakly.

"It was Atlas Wake, wasn't it?" asked Barry. "They ransacked the place, didn't they?"

Papi's smile faded. He nodded. "Yes, I believe so...I think Delbert's death clued them in on our whereabouts."

"But...how could they have found our place so quickly?" said Mr. Bompity.

"I'm sure it doesn't help we're parading around with their ex-CEO," Meghan said.

"Yeah," Barry replied. "I guess not. I hope I'm not responsible for what happened to your place."

"Nah," said Papi. "It's like the serenity prayer says. Y'know?"

"Serenity Prayer?" asked Barry.

"Eh, we don't have to get into it," replied Papi. "Everyone, get some rest. I'm sure we can't stay here too long, considering they're probably on our scent now."

Little Ricky's pants vibrated. He was about to look at his phone when Papi stopped him.

"Oh no, Ricky," said Papi. "Let's not read any more news."

Little Ricky examined his phone anyway. "It's not a news alert. Joey Paul put up a new video."

Barry looked confused.

"I'm a silver subscriber to The Joey Paul Truth-Telling Experience," Ricky said proudly.

The other members, all fans of the social media influencer, crowded around Little Ricky to watch Joey Paul's latest 6-second video loop. All of them except Mr. Bompity and Papi, who retired to their sleeping quarters.

Barry watched Papi prep his little area: the ratty sleeping bag, a jar of olives. He watched him pull a shred of paper from his back pocket, the only document he could save from his filing cabinet. The others laughed so hard at the Joey Paul video that it made Papi's despair seem sadder. Barry couldn't take it anymore.

"Hey," he said. "Are you okay?"

Papi nodded.

"What was in the filing cabinet?" Barry asked. "Was it important, Brotherhood of the Resigned documents?"

Papi laughed. "What do you think, we're the CIA?" he said. "That we keep important documents around? What would those documents even be, Barry?"

Barry shrugged. He was trying to be nice.

"Nah, Barry. They weren't fancy secret documents," Papi said as he rolled to his side. He noticed a bag of flour had spilled over, and some insects were using it as a playground. "They were my nonna's recipes."

Barry watched Papi's eyes shift to someplace far away. A memory perhaps of a simpler time when he didn't have to camp in dusty basements. A time when he was probably the proud owner of a pizza parlor people adored. Maybe he had a wife and a small child. Maybe they enjoyed watching him spread dough on the counter and toss it into the air. Maybe one day, Barry would feel comfortable asking about this previous life. He put his hand on Papi's forehead.

"I'm so sorry, Papi," he said. The two had never been this intimate before, and realizing this, Barry removed his hand and stared off.

Little Ricky motioned for Barry and Papi to join them, informing them the new Joey Paul video was hilarious and "so true." But Barry waved them off, wanting alone time with their depressed leader. He wanted to say something hopeful, perhaps a rousing speech, but the words wouldn't come.

"Maybe we're all miserable wretches and are finally paying for our sins?" Papi said.

Barry nodded, but the sentiment didn't sit well with him.

"This isn't the end," Barry countered. "We need a new plan."

"No," Papi replied, his voice deflating to a whisper. "This is a situation nowhere."

"A what?" asked Barry, confused.

Barry kneeled by the leader's side, contemplating their current predicament. Yes, they had failed. But there must have been a way to get a can of Formula Two before it went on sale tomorrow. He thought long and hard, and then it hit him. He would go rogue and find Lauren himself. Convince her to work with the Brotherhood. Be their woman on the inside. A whistleblower. Perhaps then, and only then, would Barry transform into a badass boss bitch, and the hero of this story.

Twenty-Three

Lauren dragged her feet down the hall to Meryl's office. She'd spent the night at the luxurious executive spa, per Meryl's orders. Returning to his office felt like homework.

"There she is," said the old man. "Grab a chair."

There were several pumpkin spice candles flickering on his desk. Underneath their glow was a curious spread of sourdough rolls cut into tiny bite-size pieces. He was hunched over, studying them like a scientist. Lauren joined an already seated Geena and Dan. They were sleep-deprived and dead-eyed. Meryl pinched one of the sourdough cubes and then dusted off his hands and folded them in his lap.

He reclined in his seat. "Okay, let's get to the nut of this," he said. "As you know, and as our company memo will state, Desean drank a...bad batch of Formula Two last night. Very unfortunate all around. And he drank a lot of it. He also had a rare heart disease that he hid from teammates. Those two facts alone are enough to declare last night a freak accident. But we'd still like to do something as a brand. So, we'll be placing a warning label on every package of Formula Two, instructing consumers not to drink more than three cans in thirty minutes."

Lauren was confused. "Why do we still need a warning label?" she asked. "Wasn't that just a bad batch? The regular batches shouldn't be...dangerous, right?"

Meryl sputtered. Geena stepped in to explain.

"Lauren, all you need to know is that the real Formula Two, which will be on store shelves today, is completely harmless," she said. "That bad batch from New Jersey has been recalled and is in the process of getting destroyed."

"So why the warning label?"

"It's to cover our asses," Geena blurted out. "Besides, everything we eat and drink has some kind of warning label on it these days."

Lauren realized she was right. The frozen dinners she usually ate every night had some sort of label on them. The Salisbury steak even warned of hair loss.

"So, what's the plan for me today?" Lauren asked.

"Your main thing will be the press conference at eleven a.m.," replied Geena. "We're hoping everyone will watch it and feel good about purchasing the new product, which will be available at noon today."

"Okay," replied Lauren. "Does that mean I could hang out in the executive spa for a while? It's open 24-7, right?"

"Actually, we have a limo waiting for you outside," said Geena. "Desean's family wants to speak to you. They're obviously very upset. We've prepared a financial compensation plan for them."

"Oh." Lauren deflated.

"We need to nip this in the bud before the press conference," said Geena. "Don't want them causing a scene."

Lauren couldn't hide her nausea.

"We'll have security escort you out there," Geena said, trying to comfort her, "You'll be in and out. We'll make it as painless as possible."

"Are you up to the task?" Meryl interrupted, his eyes glowing.

Lauren faked a smile. "Yep, not a problem."
She wished she was in a hot tub.

Twenty-Four

Reporters crowded outside Atlas Wake, waiting in anticipation for the corporation to address the public. They were surrounded by Atlas Wake superfans holding signs.

"We want Formula Two!" a man screamed.

"Desean is still alive! That explosion was fake!" a woman shouted.

Lauren watched from her office window, growing queasy. A security guard entered and placed a wrapped present in her hands. A token for the bereaved. He guided her to a secret exit and rushed to a limousine.

"Hey, Lauren."

A stunningly handsome man stood by the limo.

"I decided to take Atlas Wake up on their offer," he said.

"I'm sorry?" she replied.

"About my face."

She studied him for a long moment.

"I got the face surgery," he said.

"Mitch?"

"In the flesh," he smiled.

Lauren couldn't help but touch his new face. Her finger bounced off his skin like it was rubber. "Wow, they really did a number on you," she said. "In a good way."

Mitch beamed. "It's okay. You can say it. I'm hot now."

Lauren didn't want to admit it.

"It was crazy," Mitch continued. "They let me pick out any face I wanted."

Outside Desean's house there was another crowd of reporters. Lauren's limo snaked toward the gates, and her appointed security guard urged her to stay low. The last thing they needed was this clandestine visit leaking to the press. The gates opened and Lauren nervously crouched below the passenger window. She looked to Mitch for a reaction, but because of his plastic surgery, couldn't tell if he was nervous too.

Inside the compound, dozens of Desean's closest friends and family mourned him on the opulent front lawn. Some took to each other's arms for comfort, while others remained distant, gesturing to the sky and shouting at God. Some sniffled into tissues, while others swirled bottles of brown alcohol and smoked cigarettes down to stubs. Desean had touched so many lives that the place felt like a community center rather than a man's home.

The limo passed a few intoxicated mourners, who raised their heads, whispered, and stared bullets through the vehicle's tinted windows. Lauren felt their ammunition and crouched lower. The car stopped, and the security guard asked for her to step outside. She did, nervously clutching her wrapped gift.

Inside the house, every curtain had been drawn. There were candles scattered around and the smell of frankincense in the air. An elderly man stumbled out of a room, where faint sobbing trickled out. A cigar hung from his lips, and he steadied himself on a coffee table.

"You Lauren?" the man asked.

She nodded.

"You can see my daughter now," he said, pointing a crooked finger at the door.

Lauren asked Mitch to wait outside. There was no need for him to go through this too. But Mitch's face was so rigid that she couldn't register if he was bummed or relieved by this request. She wanted to tell the Guard to wait too, but he was already inside the room.

Tanisha, Desean's wife, was sobbing when Lauren walked in. The new widow sat on a chair, surrounded by her family, the dark green walls covered with photos of Desean, a smiling dad, and a caring husband. When Tanisha noticed Lauren, she stopped crying.

"Is that for me?" she said, noticing the gift under Lauren's arm.

"Yes," Lauren said, almost inaudible. The whole scene was already too much. Tanisha asked what it was, and Lauren was surprised by the question. She also didn't know how to answer.

"Well?" asked Tanisha.

"I'm not sure what's inside," said Lauren awkwardly. "But it's only part of a financial package Atlas Wake would like to offer you as compensation."

"Hold up," replied Tanisha. "You're bringing me a gift, and you're not sure what's in it?"

Lauren shook her head, embarrassed. And Tanisha stood up, her legs finding strength. "I asked to see you today because you're the CEO, are you not?"

"I am," Lauren said weakly.

"I asked to see you because I wanted to put a face to this," Tanisha said. "I wanted someone to own up and be responsible for my husband's death."

"I know. That's why I'm here," replied Lauren.

"Is it? And you don't FUCKING know what gift you're giving me?" Tanisha said, growing animated by grief. "My husband was a great person before he started drinking that Energoo crap! You turned him into an addict and killed him in front of everyone!"

"I'm so sorry for your loss," Lauren offered, trying not to feel personally attacked.

"You fucking killed him," Tanisha replied. "My boys have no father because of you. Do you understand?"

Her sons looked up at Lauren. Eyes encased in tears. Lauren couldn't meet their gaze. Too chickenshit. She wanted to bolt.

"You motherfuckers are all alike!" shouted Tanisha. "You don't give a fuck! You don't give a fuck about people like me!"

Lauren felt cornered. Her only tact was to speak carefully, like a public official or a man apologizing after getting X-ed. "Our team informed me that Desean had a medical condition," she said. "Which led to his reaction on the court."

"His reaction? He fucking exploded!" Tanisha screamed. "You killed him! Desean had no goddamn 'medical condition'!"

The security guard tensed, unsure what to do, and Lauren shifted her eyes to the floor, apologizing for their loss. Tanisha mocked her. "I'm so sorry for your loss," she said in a whiny voice.

Lauren glanced at the Guard, whose eyes urged her to walk away. But Lauren denied him, knowing she had business to finish. "Like I mentioned, Atlas Wake has prepared a rather generous compensation plan for your loss," she said. "I'm happy to talk about the details if you like. Essentially, in exchange for your silence during the rollout of Formula Two-"

"Fuck you!" shouted Tanisha. "Fuck you and your money!" Tears rolled down from her eyes. "You think I give a damn about YOUR money," she continued. "Desean was one of the greatest basketball players who ever lived! We're fine with money! I want someone to take RESPONSIBILITY for destroying his life!"

Lauren moistened her lips for another round of bargaining, but all she could taste was bile. Her guard strained by the doorway, waiting for her signal. But she refused.

"Could you leave us a moment?" Lauren asked.

"Are you sure, ma'am?" the guard replied.

Lauren nodded, and the guard reluctantly left. She turned to Tanisha, who no longer appeared human. She was a frayed nerve, a spewing bag of sadness. "It's quite a lot of money," Lauren said, knowing this was the only card she could play. "It's enough to make sure everyone in your family is well off. You could start a school in Desean's name."

"Oh, fuck you and your school," said Tanisha. "Fuck you and your school. You silver spoon-fed bitch."

"I'm not a rich kid," Lauren said, going cold. "I've only been CEO for a few days. I'm not even qualified. I'm just a mouthpiece."

"That supposed to make me feel better?"

"I came to your house to be nice," replied Lauren. "But, I feel no personal responsibility for the death of your husband. I got this job after struggling my entire life, and I'm just trying to get a piece of the pie now. You can be rich beyond your wildest dreams, your family's wildest dreams, and I suggest you take it."

Tanisha was speechless, and the room felt thick with tension.

"Are you asking me to sell out?" the widow asked quietly.

"Is that a problem?"

Tanisha shook her head. "You child," she said, "my husband could have played for the Lakers and made ten times as much money as he did. But he wanted to stay in his hometown. He wanted to lift his community onto his shoulders. He cared more about that than the all-mighty dollar. You look at that lawn out front and see the people mourning him. You stand here, thinking I'm going to feel sorry for you because you had it rough growing up? So did I. So did Desean. So, did fucking everyone! The difference is Desean chose the way of the light. He was a good man before he got hooked on that shit you peddle! And you? You don't take responsibility; you don't ask for forgiveness. You pay us off and continue selling sugar water to future addicts! Addicts that you create! How dare you say you had it rough.

You had it rough. All you care about is profits and your own miserable existence!"

Lauren was rattled.

"Momma, can I open this?" Derek asked, pointing to Lauren's gift.

"Don't touch that," Tanisha replied, catching her breath.

"Please Momma."

His mother eventually obliged, and he ripped the box open with his brother. They were both disappointed by the cotton balls inside. Derek fished around to find a small object buried underneath. He slid the thing onto his finger and displayed it proudly.

"Look, Ma," he said. "It's Dad's championship ring."

Twenty-Five

Lauren couldn't feel a thing as she walked out of that sad little room. She floated to her limo like a haunted specter. *Sell out.* The words bounced around her skull. Why did the phrase suddenly feel so ominous coming from Tanisha? Lauren's entire generation was obsessed with selling out. It was the ideal, the American dream.

She recalled the speech she made to Meryl, the one that got her the CEO job. She told him she would do anything for the corporation as long as the check cleared, but she knew this was a pose she couldn't support. She always had trouble keeping her mouth shut, towing the company line. She was a ticking time bomb.

A TV in the limo blinked on and jolted Lauren out of her existential daze. Geena was on the screen.

"How did it go?" she said. "Did they accept the compensation plan?"

Lauren sank into her leather seat. "No, they took the ring, but not the money."

Geena froze up as if she were a computer program malfunctioning. "Did you explain how much it was?" she asked.

Lauren looked out the window as the limo passed a crowd of mourners.

"I did," she mumbled.

"She turned down that much money?" asked Geena. "I've never heard of such a thing."

"I guess money isn't everything," Lauren said to her reflection, which danced on the window pane. Uttering that phrase would have caused her to cringe a week ago, but somehow, at this moment, she meant it. Geena gave her a look, but Lauren was oblivious. Her mind was a million miles away.

"We'll have our legal department speak with Desean's lawyers privately," Geena said, growing flustered. "I'm sure we can make a deal. Besides, we need to discuss your press conference in a few hours."

Lauren turned back to the TV and locked eyes with Geena. Her hands trembled. She sat on them, trying to hide what her body told her.

"We're going to lead with the details of Desean's medical history," continued Geena.

Lauren wanted to burst. But Geena kept talking, outlining the important aspects of the press conference, how essential it was to assure the American people that Formula Two was okay to drink.

"And we're one hundred percent he had a medical history, right?" interrupted Lauren.

Geena was bewildered. "Of course," she replied. "Why would you ask that?"

Lauren removed her hands from underneath her seat and breathed out slowly. "No reason," she said. "Sorry."

The Limo exited the gates and made its way toward the city. Lauren tried to breathe slow and steady, calm herself, but it was useless. She was on the verge of a panic attack.

"You okay, Lauren?" said Geena, noticing her weakening demeanor. "Seriously, I'm sure that was a lot to handle. And we can hire a therapist for you to discuss it after the press conference. But I really need you to focus. We have to get this message out ASAP. Formula Two will be on shelves in a couple of hours."

Lauren stared at the clouds through her window and felt trapped. She stared at her phone; people were arguing over Energoo on social media. It's safety. It's promise. Insanity. In her past life, when she went by the name Lo, she would have bailed on any situation that made her uncomfortable. Bailing was always there. The eternal option. She blinked, saw an image of her old self in her mind. Lo. She waited for the limo to approach a red light, opened the passenger door, and leapt out.

Twenty-Six

Barry was pissed. He believed finding Lauren was the key to the Brotherhood's salvation, but Papi was too depressed to do anything. So Barry decided to find her alone. He wore the Brotherhood's trademark uniform: gray sweatpants and hoodie. But this time, he felt the need for a proper disguise. He swiped his finger across Papi's old pizza oven and used the soot to pencil in a fake mustache. He looked ridiculous.

He emerged onto the streets, hiding behind walls, hoping to make his way to Atlas Wake headquarters and catch Lauren out on her way to lunch. He heard a thump and saw a woman bouncing off the pavement. She got up, and Barry realized his search had already concluded.

It was Lauren Caldwell, dusting herself off and running toward the subway.

Barry couldn't help but smile. He had never seen an actual human being leap from a moving vehicle. He had only witnessed them in movies like Metal Man 203, when Tommy Stark skipped off the pavement, shouting, "I'm Metal Man, baby! You better belieeeeve it!"

Lauren descended the stairs, and Barry ran after her, quickly joining her on a subway car. She was scared and breathless, her dark hair matted to the side from sweat. She was pretty cute, he thought, more attractive in person.

A teenage girl watched a video on her phone, and a loud explosion emanated from her headphones. Barry craned his neck to view her screen. It was a video of Desean exploding in slow motion. A banner at the top read, "Joey Paul: The Truth Sayer," and a teenage boy (Joey Paul) commented from the screen's corner. "Whoa! Let's see that again!" he exclaimed.

Barry noticed Lauren was also watching the video, and the two locked eyes. It seemed like the start of a romantic comedy, a meet-cute. Barry, the ex-CEO sporting a dumb soot mustache, and Lauren, the current CEO, who had just lept from a moving vehicle.

The girl with the phone noticed Lauren and raised an eyebrow. "Do I know you from somewhere?" she asked.

"No," Lauren replied.

The girl wasn't buying it and looked at her phone. She rewinded the Joey Paul video. Then, paused it on an image of Lauren.

"That's you!" the girl said.

Lauren's eyes widened, anxious, and she quickly exited the subway car. Barry followed along as a business crowd emptied into the underground corridor.

She entered a souvenir shop and perused the cheap tchotchkes. She found a large floppy bucket hat that read, "Make mine Narvel," and a pair of goofy purple sunglasses. It was a half-assed disguise but nowhere near as ludicrous as Barry's soot mustache.

Barry moved closer, trying to figure out what to say.

Lauren reached into her pocket to pay for her impromptu disguise and froze. She had no cash, and Barry realized she didn't want to pay with a card.

"What's a matter, pretty lady?" asked the stand's proprietor, a smiling old man.

Lauren rolled her eyes.

"Lotta people are scared to say when a stranger is pretty," the man said.

"I hear ya," replied Lauren.

"Glad you hearin' me," he smiled. "You single?"

She stared at the man for a long moment, her gears turning. Her eyes went dull. Switched off. "I don't believe that's an appropriate question," she said.

The man wilted. "My apologies if I offended you."

Lauren appeared uncomfortable, her words unnatural and foreign. "Well...you, uh, did offend me," she stuttered. "To be honest... And I'm, uh...not here for your sick amusement, sir."

"I'm so sorry, miss. I'm so sorry. Please. Please don't be offended," he cried.

"I appreciate the apology," Lauren replied, pleasure bubbling up. "But you *should* be careful. You could get X-ed for saying that sort of thing."

"Take them," he said, pointing to the hat and sunglasses. "For the trouble. Here, you like beef jerky? How about some turkey jerky as well? It's less fat."

Lauren struggled not to smile. She clearly never pulled that card before and sort of enjoyed it. She walked away, only to turn back and yell, "Words Matter!"

The elderly proprietor almost fainted, and Barry was impressed. He followed her up the stairs and onto the streets. His heart raced. Now was the time to stand up and be a badass boss bitch. Now was the time to become the romantic lead of this film.

"Lauren Caldwell?" he blurted out.

She turned around, frightened.

"Barry Gray?" she asked.

He smiled. She knew who he was. What a feather in his cap. "Nice disguise," he replied. "Who are *you* hiding from?"

She checked the streets for eyes.

"Uh, you can trust me, y'know," he continued. "I've been on the run longer than you."

Lauren leaned up against a wall, wheels turning.

"What's that shit on your face?" she asked.

Barry looked at his reflection in a nearby window. The soot mustache had smeared, causing his entire face to turn brown. It was problematic, to say the least.

"Jesus!" he said, trying to wipe it off.

Lauren laughed. A police car roared its sirens, and the hair on the back of their necks stood up. They ducked behind a parked car, and Barry took in her scent. She noticed and narrowed her eyes.

"So, uh, why did you jump out of a car?" he asked.

She peered at the ground. "I need a break from Atlas right now... Just a moment to think about things."

He nodded and noticed a sewer grate across from them.

"I know a place that is off-the-grid, very private..." he said. "In fact, there are some people I'd like you to meet."

Lauren grew uncomfortable. "What people?" she asked.

"The Brotherhood of the Resigned."

"Oh, I don't know about that," she replied.

"You've heard of them?"

"Yeah," she said. "I know a little bit."

"Oh, that's good. Papi will be glad to hear," he replied. "That reminds me, I promised I'd pick up some snacks while I was out. Do you mind waiting here while I pop into that bodega?"

She nodded. What other choice did she have? Barry smiled, quickly returning with a baguette and wine bottle teetering from a grocery bag. He walked toward the sewer and tried lifting the grate, but it was too heavy. "Little help?" he asked.

Lauren looked at him oddly. He contemplated her standoffish posture, and it dawned on him he needed to say something heroic for her to spring into action. He wasn't the most creative person, though, and repeated a trademark phrase a man once told him.

"No time for tears," he said.

Lauren was confused by the statement.

"Uh," Barry mumbled, "It was a figure of speech."

Lauren stared into Barry's kind, dumb eyes and softened. She helped him slide the sewer grate off.

"Are you claustrophobic?" Barry asked.

She shook her head, and he climbed down into the sewer. "Good," his voice echoed, hand reaching back to her. "Come on down."

Lauren didn't budge. Another police car roared by, and she recoiled, startled.

"Someone will pick you up if you stay on the streets any longer," he said. "If you really need a moment to get your head straight, I suggest you take my hand."

Twenty-Seven

The sewer tunnel was slick and dark, with human waste matted to its walls. Barry and Lauren clomped through murky water while a sliver of light flickered above, a faint reminder of the world they'd left behind. A small creature brushed by Barry, and he looked back at Lauren. In his eyes, he didn't see a stranger unnerved by this sludge-filled tunnel but the continuing adventures of a romantic comedy film.

"This is pretty fucking gross," said Lauren. "You don't live down here, do you?"

"Oh no," said Barry, "We all live above ground."

"Oh...so you...all live together," she replied flatly.

Barry realized this was a buzz kill, the equivalent of admitting he lived with his parents, and led the rest of the way in silence. They eventually waded through the weeds outside the pizza place, and Barry sped up, swelling with pride. He couldn't wait to present Lauren on a silver plate to Papi, who doubted his sleuthing skills.

Barry opened the door to the pizza parlor and led her down the creaking basement steps.

"Ta-da!" he said, pointing to Lauren, who slowly entered the musty basement.

Papi's eyes widened. "What the fuck, Barry?"

The Brotherhood instantly tightened up around the two, and Barry was confused by their reaction.

"What are you all getting excited about?"

"She could be loaded with tracking devices and shit!" Papi explained. "Did you check her out first?"

Barry's face fell with disappointment. This was supposed to be the next chapter in their romantic comedy. The part where his buddies, The Brotherhood, high-fived him and told him, "Good job." He did it. He located their "inside man." The one who would lead them to salvation and freedom.

"Listen," Lauren said, "The last thing I want is for Atlas to know my whereabouts. I'm wearing a disguise, for Christ's sake." She pointed to her large goofy glasses and "Make Mine Narvel" bucket hat.

"You call that a disguise?" barked Meghan, doing push-ups in the corner.

"Papi," Barry interrupted, "she's on the run from Atlas Wake. She could help us."

Lauren was annoyed. None of this was discussed with her. "Help you how exactly?" she asked.

Barry was about to explain, but Papi shushed him. "Let's search her before we say anything. Meghan, can you do it?"

"Why me?" she replied.

"Cause you're a broad," said Papi, "and I'm trying to be sensitive to the situation."

"I don't feel like it," Meghan replied. "Besides, she might be a big lesbo and like it."

"Fanabla," snapped Papi. "I can't win! I'm just trying to be decent to everyone. Is that so wrong?"

"I can do it," Barry offered, turning to Lauren, "if you don't mind."

"I don't give a shit," she replied. "Let's just get it over with."

Barry couldn't believe his luck. A patdown like this would totally happen in a romantic comedy. He took a breath and slid his hand across her soft shoulders and down the length of her arms. He lightly patted the sides of her stomach and bent over to slide his hands down her legs. He eyed her the whole time as if asking permission. But Lauren seemed bored, as if she were in line at the DMV. He finally slid his hands toward her ass and lightly stroked.

Barry stood to greet her eyes. He'd given so many massages to women in the past, one-night stands that ended in sex, that he met her eyes with a sense of expectancy. But, she remained elsewhere. The last uncharted spot was her chest. Barry usually relished this moment, but this time felt awkward and ashamed. He hovered by the holy grail, stuck.

"Just put your hands on my tits already," Lauren barked.

Barry recoiled, and the Brotherhood laughed. Even Meghan paused her push-ups to admire the new woman's brazen attitude. "I like this bitch," she said in the shadows.

Lauren's demanding tone initially put off Barry. But then he realized it was *so* romantic comedy of her. Very boss bitch. He put his hands on her waist and slowly slid them toward the tits in question. He awkwardly rubbed the sides of her breasts for a few seconds while the Brotherhood watched silently.

"We good here?" said Lauren.

Papi nodded, no longer wanting to suffer through any more.

"Hey guys, a press conference is about to start," said Little Ricky.

"Press conference?" asked Barry.

"According to social media, Atlas Wake is about to speak about the Desean explosion," Little Ricky replied.

The crew crowded around Little Ricky's phone to watch.

"Where's the snacks?" asked Papi.

Barry quickly produced the grocery bag, pulling out a baguette and a jar of roasted red peppers.

"Aw, man. No soppressata?" whined Papi.

On the live video feed, photographers clicked away at an empty podium. Lauren wondered who would stroll out and talk to reporters. It had to be Geena, not weird Dan or ancient Meryl. She knew the corporate lifer probably would relish this opportunity to be in the spotlight. Good for her, Lauren thought. But it wasn't Geena. It was another woman dressed in a black power suit. She approached the podium confidently. It was Lauren.

"What the fuck?" she said to her reflection.

On Ricky's phone, the other Lauren spoke, "Hello, everyone. We wanted to address last night's tragic incident before you pop over to your local grocer and buy Formula Two for yourself at noon today!"

"I never said any of this," said Lauren, aghast.

"Shh," said Gerald, the giant, "I'm trying to listen to you."

Barry pointed to the corner of Ricky's screen. "I don't understand," he said. "This says it's live right now."

Papi laughed, "They could say anything was live these days! It's all smoke and mirrors!"

"First of all," said the other Lauren, "Desean has a medical history that he hid from teammates. This, coupled with the 'bad batch' reported, was a recipe for disaster. So, while we know last night was hard to process for many of you, please know it was an isolated incident. The Formula Two you will buy in stores today has no relation to what Desean drank. So, thank you, and happy Formula Two day!"

The program cut to a Newscaster, who was all smiles, "That Lauren Caldwell, she's such a natural on camera, isn't she, folks? And she had no parents either."

Lauren was nauseous. "How did they do that?" she asked.

"Narvel Dream Wizards," replied Little Ricky, "It's their spirit-mation process. AI-powered."

"May you live in interesting times," Barry offered.

"I hate that phrase," said Lauren.

"Yeah," Barry replied, "Uh, me too."

"It's actually a pretty easy thing to do nowadays with consumer software," Little Ricky said. "I could probably make a video duplicate of Papi if I still had my laptop."

"Madone," said Papi, devouring some nuts, "Don't do that! There's only one Papi!"

"Fuck this," Lauren said. "They created a fake me just because I'm AWOL for a little bit? I'm gonna march back in that building and resign."

"No, no, no," interrupted Barry. "You can't quit. We need you on the inside."

"Barry's right," replied Papi.

Barry beamed. He was glad Papi recognized how valuable Lauren could be. He was happy to be useful to the cause.

"We believe Formula Two is the start of something big," said Papi. "Something very bad. You must return to Atlas Wake and get back into their good graces."

"Who knows what they could do to you," said Barry gravely. "I don't think you want to piss them off. Look what happened to me."

Lauren nodded. "Okay," she said. "I'll...uh...apologize for ditching them and...fix this."

Papi beamed with excitement. He turned to his crew, energized. "Let's buy a can of Formula Two today and get it tested. If there's something bad in it, we can use Lauren as our whistleblower. No one trusts journalists or newscasters anymore. But if the CEO of Atlas Wake speaks up, maybe we have a shot. Maybe the public will listen, and we'll save lives."

The Brotherhood cheered, and Barry smiled weakly. He had tried to sell Papi on this plan earlier, but the leader wouldn't listen. Oh well, he thought. He would have his badass boss bitch moment one day. For now, he was glad to see Papi smiling again. The Italian man exchanged numbers with Lauren for future communication.

Barry wished he was the one exchanging numbers, but he had no phone. He watched Lauren leave like a clingy teenage boy, his heart filling up. He believed they were entering the second act of their romantic comedy, the one where they banded together to take down an evil corporate empire, an action that would free him and the Brotherhood of their shackles.

"May you live in interesting times," he said to himself.

Twenty-Eight

The city vibrated with energy as the minutes clicked down to the release of Formula Two. Every grocer, health store, and bodega had a line out the door with people waiting in fevered anticipation. And it wasn't just cities. The suburbs had crowds too. In small-town Newfield, New Jersey, where the bad batch of Formula Two originated, elderly folks waited outside a WaWa.

"Well, that Desean fella was all fucked up, health-wise," said an old man, clutching his oxygen tank. "He should have told people he was fucked up, and he wouldn't have exploded!"

"Yeah," a chain-smoking lady agreed, "these players think their shit don't stink. They need to shut up and dribble."

Lauren emerged from an underground tunnel and hid inside an abandoned bus stop. She peered onto the sidewalk and saw a line of cheery people waiting for Formula Two. She was surprised there was no public backlash to the Desean incident. No riots in the street. Was everybody numb?

She knew she had to call Geena back, but her mind drifted to the subway car earlier. Desean's implosion had become a meme, a remixable piece of "content." It was sick, and she felt insane. Part of her wished she had never met that dork Barry and the Brotherhood of the Resigned. Why did she jump out of that limo?

She turned on her phone and took a deep breath. She had thirty-two missed calls from Geena and was not looking forward to returning them. She had to apologize, let go of her ego, and not ask questions. She had to be the person she sold them on, an empty vessel.

"What the fuck, Lauren?" said Geena instantly.

"I'm so sorry," Lauren began, "I just needed some time to think. Desean's widow rattled me."

"Everyone is pissed," replied Geena, "you could have phoned earlier."

Lauren wanted to tell her to fuck off. She was only gone a couple of hours. It wasn't the end of the world.

"I'm so sorry," Lauren said.

There was a deep sigh on the other end. Geena was livid and tried to compose herself.

"You still want me back, right?" asked Lauren.

"Of course, we want you back!" Geena blurted. "You think we want to hire Narvel's Dream Wizards every time you decide to go AWOL? We had our security team scouring the city all morning for your dumbass!"

Lauren's face lit up with anger. Geena was always the consummate professional, and here she was, calling Lauren a "dumbass."

"Where are you?" asked Geena, flustered.

Lauren gave her the cross streets.

"A limo will be there shortly," Geena said, hanging up the phone.

Lauren did it. She managed not to burn bridges, and Geena seemed anxious to bring her back into the fold. If all went well, she could be the "inside man" the Brotherhood desperately needed.

She stared at the clouds, relief washing over her. A huge billboard towered above featuring an ad for Formula Two. It sported a giant countdown clock to the beverage's release—there were ten minutes left to go.

Twenty-Nine

"We did it! Formula Two is killing it!" said Meryl, squeaking his wheelchair into Geena's office. "The shareholders will be thrilled! They were really chomping my ass the last twenty-four hours."

Geena tried to smile.

"What's wrong?" asked Meryl. "This success is all your doing! The idea to make a Lauren Spiritmation. Having Desean's doctor appear on morning shows. The warning label. It was all your genius!"

"I know," replied Geena.

"Then, what is it?" Meryl asked.

Geena bit her lip.

"Well...you know how qualified I am," she said. "And I'm proud of the company. But, and I feel lousy saying this, I want the credit. I know that sounds petty, but you *did* pass me over for Barry. And while I know Lauren was my idea..."

"I get it," interrupted Meryl. "You should be the face of this place. But you have to understand you're more bulletproof behind the scenes. You're so vital that it wouldn't make sense to put you out front, where you could get knocked down or X-ed."

Geena laughed. "There's no way I'd get X-ed."

"Many people who've been X-ed thought that," replied Meryl. "But, listen, if you need a different title and some more money, we can do that. What do we call you now?"

"Senior Executive Manager," she replied.

"How'd you like to be COO? It's close to CEO. It's off by just a letter!" he laughed. "And we'll make sure to give you a healthy raise."

It would have been a life-changing promotion to anyone in the world. But Geena wanted that CEO title. She wanted to lead press conferences, go on television, and get invited to fancy parties. Be the center of attention. It killed her to admit it.

"That would be great, Meryl," she winced, "Thank you."

"Good," Meryl replied, spinning away in his wheelchair, "Today we celebrate!"

Dan strolled in, oblivious, looking like a wet bag of shit. He asked what he missed, and Geena refused to fill him in. He was growing increasingly weird with her, and she didn't want to argue about why she was COO, and he wasn't. Besides, he looked sickly; his skin stretched taut across his bones. When he passed her, he made weird gurgle sounds.

Here is the result of a lifetime of drugs, she thought. She secretly applauded herself for resisting such things. She knew Xanax would be the perfect match for her anxiety and stress, but she chose the healthier path—exercise, meditation, and herbal tonics. She watched him bobble in his seat as if possessed by dark spirits and thought about how much better she was than him.

Thirty

The Brotherhood was back on the streets, ready for their date with destiny—a very long grocery store line. They all wore silly disguises except Mr. Bompity Bomp, who had no desire to hide. He wore a weathered ball cap with the name of his show, "Mr. Bompity's Hour," blazoned on the front. His eyes were red. Had he been crying again?

"Y'know," Barry said quietly, "I used to love your show. My mom and I watched it every Saturday morning."

"Ain't that something else," said Bompity. "Was your mommy pretty?"

Barry went quiet. Was Mr. Bompity a pervert? Was his sob story all an act?

"Was your mommy a pretty baby?" he said.

Barry felt foolish for believing the old man.

"I'm just messing with you," snort-laughed the clown.

"Hah," Barry replied, uneasy.

"You should have seen your face," the old man said to no one.

Papi noticed a gathering of people drinking Formula Two on the corner. They were a motley crew. Some young, some old—all culturally diverse, as if they were starring in a television commercial. A young boy in the group began drinking a can, and Papi's eyes widened in fear. He expected the boy to explode. But the boy finished his drink and smiled.

"Look at that!" The little boy yelped. "I didn't even explode neither!" The others laughed, and the boy puffed up, "You'd have to be a real PUSSY to explode from one of these, right?"

Everyone fell over with laughter, and Papi couldn't help feeling perplexed. "I really thought that little guy was going to explode," he muttered.

They walked to the grocery store and witnessed smiling people leaving, one after another. Underneath their arms were cases of Formula Two. They all seemed serene, as if they had just left church.

Barry was sure he'd never see peace on earth in his lifetime, but here on the street, the notion seemed close. "What if we're wrong?" he asked. "I mean, it doesn't make sense for Atlas Wake to kill off its consumer base. Maybe what Desean drank really was a bad batch."

"Nah, man," said Little Ricky, "I was X-ed because I said I didn't like the taste of Energoo on Social Media. And Barry, your X was completely fabricated!"

"Fanabla!" cried Papi, spitting on the ground. "We're not a bunch of conspiracy theory nutbags, Barry! How dare you!"

"That's not what I meant," replied Barry.

"What *did* you mean?" asked Papi.

The Brotherhood stared through Barry, and he shrunk with embarrassment. Luckily for him, the grocery store line inched forward and deflated the situation. The crowd pulsated with excitement, and it proved contagious. A beach ball floated over to the Brotherhood, and Gerald couldn't help punching it into the air. Musicians played nearby with tip jars that playfully read, "Formula Two fund." Bompity seemed unaffected by the good vibes, distant. He slowly removed his trademark red nose.

They entered the grocery store. Every inch of the place was filled with the new product. Papi quickly grabbed a can and studied its silver exterior. A striking green logo read, "Energoo Formula Two." He rotated it and found a small, sloppily affixed warning label, an afterthought.

"Woohoo!" yelled a man at the front of the line. He proudly paid for a case of Formula Two and wore a ball cap that read, "Metal Man is my Savior." He proceeded to chug a can in front of the cashier.

"We did it!" he screamed as if he had won the Superbowl. "Formula Two gets you lifted, baby!" He said, downing a second can.

The Brotherhood watched, spellbound. Meghan whispered, "He's making this stuff sound good. Maybe it doesn't taste like ass. Like Formula One did."

"Shush," said Papi. "Madone, I could shit!"

The Metal Man fan guzzled another can and danced on the counter. His eyes danced around in shock as if to say, "Can you believe I'm doing this?" He finished his third can and let out a triumphant belch, which caused the crowd of onlookers to cheer. He savored this new spotlight, cracked open another can, and jumped off the counter. He danced with the crowd, and everyone was game, the friendliest mosh pit in the world.

"Woohoo!" yelled the man as he sloppily guzzled some more. "This shit is awesome!" he shouted, high-fiving a stranger. "This shit is the bomb!" he said and exploded into green mist.

The grocery store went quiet as folks near the explosion reacted in stunned horror. The man's green, gooey insides dripped from the onlooker's shoulders and faces. Everyone froze in shock until they realized the green goo was acidic. They wiped the stinging goo from their faces. Panic rippled through the crowd.

Papi turned to the others, clutching his solitary can, "Let's get the fuck out of here."

Before they could exit, Bompity made a bee-line for a display shelf. He grabbed a can and began drinking. Papi rushed over, but by the time he reached him, the clown had already guzzled one can and was onto number two. Papi batted it from his hands, and the two fell to the floor. They wrestled for a bit, Bompity struggling, desperate to get more Formula Two into his bloodstream.

"What are you thinking?" screamed Papi. "You can't do this!"

Mr. Bompity summoned all the strength in his withered frame and pushed Papi off. He picked up the second can and drank from it.

Gerald tackled him. "No, Bompity," he said. "Don't do it. We love you."

But Bompity was a man possessed. He somehow wiggled from the giant's grasp and ran across the store like a feral cat, bouncing around, dodging the Brotherhood. It led him straight into the middle of the panicked crowd, where Metal Man Guy's insides began to dissolve the tiled floor. Bompity saw a woman scared, holding a case of Formula Two, and swiped them from her.

The crowd was spiraling out of control, and Papi tried breaking through the barrier of humans separating him from Bompity. Papi lost sight of the clown and grew desperate, loose fists and limbs swinging wild.

But Bompity was no longer in the center of the crowd. He had found a safe perch, a ladder used for re-stocking, where he watched the crazed melee of people. He downed another can and another. Papi ran toward him, desperate to get his hands on the clown.

Mr. Bompity's face drained of color. "I didn't do nothing wrong," he said. Then he exploded.

Thirty-One

Papi exited the grocery store, shell-shocked, his mind reeling. Strangers bumped into him as the chaos swirled. Gerald held up the weary leader, escorting him through the crowd, a contrast of frightened shoppers and oblivious onlookers. The rest of the crew were also in poor shape, slumped over, defeated, and unable to process Bompity's sudden departure from the world. They willed themselves forward, eventually getting underground.

They lumbered through the sewer system, speechless. Papi was usually good about rallying the troops, but this time he couldn't. He noticed an old advertisement matted to the sewer walls. It was for a pizza place—*his* pizza place. He mourned his past, and tears formed. But he refused to let them fall.

"No time for tears," Papi said.

"No time for tears," the others repeated soberly.

There were no smiles, not even for Papi's trademark phrase.

"Enough!" cried Meghan, barreling to the head of the line. "Bompity's dead. But that doesn't change our plans. Does it?"

Papi shook his head. He noticed his hands were still gripping a can of Formula Two. He must have walked out without paying.

"We have the can," Papi said in a shocked whisper.

"Exactly! So, let's get it tested," said Meghan. "Barry. When can we get this to your contact?"

Barry nodded enthusiastically but didn't offer an answer. He looked nauseous.

"So...when can we get it to them, Barry?" asked Meghan.

"Yeah, Barry," added Gerald. "We have to stick to the plan."

Barry stared at the sewer walls. "Uh...I could try and text her now if you guys want?"

"Yes," said Papi, handing over his phone. "Of course."

Barry scratched his chin, scrunched his eyes, and gestured to the phone like a mime.

"What the fuck are you doing?" asked Papi, getting closer.

"Uh, there's no signal down here," he replied.

Papi spied his phone and noticed he had reception. "You got two fucking bars!" he shouted.

"I do? Oh, wow," said Barry, mock surprised.

"Stop dicking around!" Papi screamed. "Bompity just fucking died! We gotta figure out what's in this can before anyone else dies!"

Barry gulped, and the others swarmed around him, urging him to call. "I know it's important," Barry squeaked. "I know."

"Then why are you pretending you can't get service, Barry?" Papi shouted.

Barry was sheepish.

"C'mon, Barry," said Gerald. "What's the drama?"

"Here's the thing," the ex-CEO sputtered.

"Yes?!" cried the Brotherhood in perfect synchronicity.

"The contact...the scientist who can analyze that can of Formula Two...Well, she's my ex-wife."

Papi looked at him thoughtfully, then cracked up. "Madone!" he shouted, smiling. "Madone!" he shouted, doubling over with laughter. The laughs grew intense, and Barry wished for them to stop. But Papi was out of control, free, the laughter inflating him with new life. The others eventually joined in, and the guffawing proved cathartic. They laughed at Barry, laughed at Bompity's death, laughed at the absurdity of living underground.

Barry grimaced, trying to find the comedy in all of this. He eventually offered a few fake chuckles, which caused the others to dissipate. Papi dried his eyes and went stone-faced. "Call your ex-wife, Barry," he said steely. "Do it fucking now."

Barry picked up Papi's phone, and the Brotherhood crowded around him. He waved his hand, preferring privacy, and walked away. They watched as Barry's posture sank, then bounced up as he shored up his nerves. He waited patiently for someone to pick up. Then, returned to the group.

"She didn't answer," he said.

"Well, call that bitch again!" said Meghan.

"She's not a bitch," replied Barry faintly.

Papi sighed. "You're working on my last nerve, Barry. Did you at least leave a message?"

Barry shook his head, and the entire Brotherhood made an annoyed Tsk sound.

"I don't think you realize how serious this is," said Bob and Rob.

Papi was shocked to hear them speak.

"Time is ticking," they continued. "We need that can tested and for Lauren to broadcast our findings ASAP."

"Okay," Barry replied. "Just, uh, give me space."

Barry walked away, let the phone ring, and left a message. He tried not to sound desperate or weak on the phone, but in trying, did precisely that. He hung up and looked at the others, hoping to see proud faces. But they were annoyed. Barry wished they viewed him as he wanted to be, a badass boss bitch, but surveying their faces, he knew in his heart that they considered him just a plain old bitch.

"You're on speaking terms, right?" asked Papi. "She will return your phone call, right Barry?"

"She will," replied Barry nervously. "C'mon, no use mulling around here any longer."

He walked away, and the Brotherhood was distraught.

"Fucking hell," Meghan said.

Papi agreed with the sentiment but knew they had to remain optimistic. "Barry may not be the brightest bulb," he whispered. "But, he *is* helping us. We have to remember that…it's like I always say—"

"—you get what you get, and you don't get upset," chimed the others.

Papi swelled with pride, glad they remembered another one of his goofy sayings. The group eventually rejoined Barry, and Papi put his arm around him in solidarity. Barry grinned, but Papi couldn't help feeling insecure. If Barry's ex-wife refused to call back, they were up shit's creek. They needed concrete proof that Atlas Wake was poisoning people. This was their last shot. They needed Barry's ex-wife to put aside their differences and help save humanity.

Thirty-Two

Lauren sat in the back of a limo en route to Atlas Wake, reading the latest news on her phone. Several press outlets proclaimed Formula Two a runaway success. But how could it be selling so well? She searched social media for "Formula Two Explosions" and found dozens of videos. People were exploding on the street, in their houses, at the office. Underneath were comments that said, "FAKE."

She stared out the limousine window and wondered how she could return to Atlas Wake. How could she pretend everything was fine? Even if it was a temporary arrangement, a bluff to bide the Brotherhood time, it was still difficult to swallow. She fingered the passenger door and found security had enabled child locks. She was trapped.

She entered the secret back entrance of Atlas Wake with a pit in her stomach. A young Security Guard led her to an elevator, and everyone in the building eyed her as if she were a celebrity or someone on death row. She tried to chat up the guard in the elevator and quiet her nerves. "So, how are things going today?"

The man smiled and replied, "Just another day in paradise."

Lauren didn't expect such a sarcastic reply and fumbled the conversation out of existence. The elevator doors parted, and a robot cat greeted Lauren, slowly leading her down a labyrinth of hallways.

The last time she felt this grinding in her guts was in high school, in the painful moments leading up to sharing her first short story with classmates. Ever since then, she rarely felt such nerves.

The robot cat pointed its tail to Meryl's office. Lauren entered the darkened space and noticed a mannequin in the corner. It startled her, and she let out a gasp. The figure nodded casually, and she realized it was Mitch, his perfect plastic face expressionless in the shadows.

"Hey," she whispered to him, "make sure I don't say anything stupid."

Mitch wondered what she meant.

"What do you think of this one?" called Meryl from the far end of the room. He was sitting across from Geena and Dan and wearing a cowboy hat. "Does this hat make me look strong and virile?"

Lauren was about to reply when Geena and Dan answered affirmatively. She realized Meryl wasn't speaking to her. He didn't know she was in the room.

"Well, look what the robot cat dragged in," Meryl said, finally noticing her. "Sit down."

Meryl's eyes turned into pieces of burning coal. "You know who runs away?" he said. "Children run away. Are you a child, Lauren?"

She shook her head.

"Then why did you act like one?" Meryl asked. "Why did our new CEO run away like a baby on our most important day?"

Lauren was about to squeak out a reply when he cut her off.

"Hmm?" He asked. "You gave me a whole song and dance about how you were comfortable 'selling out,' doing anything we asked, and then you fled at the first sign of difficulty. Now, I must ask, are you a child or an adult?"

"I'm an adult, sir," Lauren whispered.

"Speak into my good ear," said Meryl.

Lauren was confused but moved forward.

"Just kidding," Meryl said. "I have no good ears left!" He cackled long and hard and sunk into his chair, eyes no longer glowing with anger. Lauren tried to settle, too, hoping the hard part was over.

"There's a lot of fake news going on right now," said Meryl, reclining his chair so far back that it threatened to become a bed. "I'm sure you've seen some of these explosion videos."

She wanted to stand up and shout, "WHAT THE FUCK. WHAT THE FUCK IS GOING ON?!" But she didn't.

"Most people know the product is safe in moderation," offered Geena.

"Some even think the explosions are bunko," said Dan. "They think it was all done with computers. The press calls them 'explosion deniers.'"

Lauren laughed.

"Don't laugh. This shit is legit, cuz," said Dan. "Besides. Explosion deniers are our friends right now."

A strange noise escaped from Lauren's lips. A cross between the word "Huh?" and a vomit sound.

"Are you okay?" Geena asked.

"Yeah," Lauren weakly replied.

"There's a small segment of the population we're concerned about," said Dan. "A group of people who believe we're to blame for people exploding. Total chode-skis."

"Do you believe that?" said Meryl from his chair-bed. He closed his eyes. "It's like these people can't read a warning label or something."

"If this vibe grows, the idea that we're responsible could complicate our distribution plans," said Dan.

Another weird sound erupted from deep within Lauren. Geena offered her a glass of water, and she took it. If she could just focus on the cool, clear liquid and pretend she was elsewhere, maybe she could get through this conversation in one piece.

"Besides, it's only killing some people," Dan said. "Goofies. Addicts who can't read a warning label."

Every cell in Lauren's body screamed at her to speak up. She had plenty of addict friends in her previous life. She put a piece of ice in her mouth and cracked it with her teeth. She placed her fingers on the ice, trying to focus on the icy coolness, focus on anything that wasn't the bile streaming out of Dan's mouth. He noticed her fidgeting and let loose a shit-eating grin.

"Do you not agree with my assessment?" he asked. "Does it not sound dope and fresh to you?"

The room went quiet. All eyes were on Lauren. She dug her nails into her palms, trying to hold on, not say how she really felt. She knew if the Brotherhood found criminal ingredients inside Formula Two, a sitting CEO whistleblowing would be a powerful statement. But Dan's pale, smug face set her off.

"What's in Formula Two?" she asked.

"Excuse me?" said Meryl, shifting in his chair-bed. "What did you just say?"

Lauren eyed her colleagues. They seemed scared for her, hoping she would stand down.

"I don't even know what's in it," said Geena, hoping to reassure her.

"Me either, you jive-ass turkey," said Dan.

"The shareholders know," replied Meryl. "And that's all that matters." He reclined back into bed mode and considered the matter handled.

Lauren put down her glass of water and took a deep breath. "I'd like to speak to the shareholders," she said.

Geena stared daggers at her. "I've never even met the shareholders," she said. "You need to slow down."

Meryl's eyes grew fiery from his chair-bed. "I'm the only one who can talk to them," he said. "They're a...prickly group."

"So what? Let me talk to them," Lauren replied.

"They'd eat you alive!" Meryl shouted.

Meryl was furious, hyperventilating.

"If I may say something," said Mitch from the dark corner of the room. "I think Lauren needs an Energoo Latte." He tried to wink at her but couldn't due to his surgery. "I think if she had a latte break in her office," he continued, "she might feel a lot better about everything."

Lauren was speechless. She knew he was following her instructions and getting her out of a jam, but everyone's contempt made her want to burn it all down.

"Your assistant has a real brain on him," said Meryl, catching his breath. "What was your name again, son? Dicky?"

"Mitch," he replied eagerly.

"Ah, right. You're the one with the new face," said Meryl. "Looks good on you," he lied. "Real...natural."

"Fantastic idea, Mitch," Geena said. "Why don't the two of you go decompress."

Lauren calmed down and exited with Mitch. Meryl watched her every step, a menacing darkness sliding over his face. He lowered his cowboy hat till it almost blocked his steely eyes.

"What are we going to do about *that*?" he asked.

Dan and Geena weren't sure, and Meryl waved them away. He reclined back into his chair-bed and stared at the ceiling. In his mind, he pictured the cosmos, planets spinning precariously, stars shining—the vastness of space. And in this cosmic solitude, he formulated a plan.

ATLAS WAKE LOSES ANOTHER CEO

Kyle Bilamowski
Associated Press

CEO Lauren Caldwell's brief tenure with beverage giant Atlas Wake is over, mere days after previous chief Barry Gray was fired.

Lauren (28) was a relative unknown in the business world, leading many leaders to question her hiring. She was X-ed on Tuesday for problematic views shared on social media several years ago. Screengrabs were provided to media outlets, many choosing not to publish—this outlet among them.

Rumors are swirling about who could replace her in what would be an unprecedented third CEO in merely ten days.

"Lauren proved to be a disingenuous individual," said Meryl Evans, Atlas's longtime CFO. "She told us on day one that she possessed not a problematic bone in her body, but it turns out her bones were loaded with...problematic bone stuff."

The company is optimistic its new product, Energoo Formula Two, is still on track to become the biggest beverage of all time. Some analysts remain skeptical, considering it caused the alleged explosion of an NBA star.

Thirty-Three

Geena stared at the press release in shock. "Is this real?" she asked Meryl.

The two were alone in his office.

"It's real," he replied. "Some of the writer's commentary I don't agree with."

Geena was a mix of emotions. She had so many questions but wasn't sure which to ask first. Meryl interpreted her silence as acceptance and casually moved about the room.

"Did I show you this yet?" he said, wheeling to a shelf. "Just got this in the mail." He unfurled a leather bullwhip and draped it across his desk. "Kangaroo hide. Top of the line. Look how it balances in the hand."

He offered her the whip to examine, but she declined.

"Who found these posts?" she asked.

"What posts?" replied Meryl, confused.

"We vetted Lauren thoroughly," Geena said. "Where did you find these problematic posts?"

"Oh," Meryl said, lightly slapping the whip in his palm. "Our AI software was able to find it."

Geena wasn't buying it. Mitch had searched all over for Lauren's social media and came up empty. How could AI find it?

"I don't know how the tech works, to be honest. Not sure anyone does!" laughed Meryl. "But it found it. She's apparently a horrible person."

Geena studied Meryl's eyes for signs of bullshit, but he seemed to be telling the truth.

"I'm sorry we drafted a statement without you," he said, "but there's something more pressing I want to talk to you about."

"Okay," she replied.

"I want you to be CEO," said Meryl.

Geena wasn't sure she heard him correctly and asked him to repeat it. He did, and she almost cried. She drew in her breath and held it, hoping she could regulate herself. But her eyes couldn't help filling with liquid, and when she met Meryl's gaze, she blinked, spilling tears down her cheek. They embraced, and she sobbed into his chest.

"You deserve this," he said.

She absorbed the compliment, and it caused her whole body to shake. Her concerns for Lauren vanished. She daydreamed about the press conferences she would hold court in, the spa she would have access to, and the frivolous things she would buy with reckless abandon.

Lauren sat in her giant leather executive chair. She had cooled down since the Meryl meeting and was relieved to be back in her office. Without Mitch's interjection, she probably would have blown everything up. Gratitude swirled in her chest.

An alert buzzed on her phone, and that gratitude morphed into full-tilt panic.

"What?" Mitch asked, his phone vibrating too.

He checked his alert and promptly vomited.

"What the fuck?" he said. "Oh, God. This can't be happening. I checked everything. I never found any problematic posts!"

Lauren's life flashed before her eyes. She never remembered posting on a social media platform. This was fake, bullshit, but why? She wanted to scream bloody murder.

"This can't be happening," cried Mitch, awkwardly cleaning up his vomit with paper towels. "I worked so hard to get a job here!"

Lauren's horror quickly shifted into annoyance. How could Mitch be so upset when *she* was the one getting X-ed? He stood up to toss vomit-covered towels into the trash can, and she slapped him. His artificial face quickly reddened like a newborn's bottom.

"Get ahold of yourself," she said.

He rubbed his fake face, offended that she would strike him. Lauren said nothing more. She was terrified. She had no friends, no parents, no one to rely on in her time of need. She stared out the window and saw a homeless man streaking across the street. It hit her like a lightning bulb. She dialed a number.

"Hello?" answered Barry Gray.

"Barry?" Lauren replied. "I'm trying to get ahold of Papi."

"You can talk to me," said Barry. "You can *always* talk to me."

Lauren sighed and explained what had happened. But Barry already knew. He had read the alert on Papi's phone.

"I don't know what to do," she said nervously, eyeing Mitch, who sat on the couch, stroking his face.

There was some whispering on the other end, and she could hear Papi chastising Barry for stealing his phone. She walked over to Mitch and put her hand delicately on his shoulder. He recoiled like an abused dog.

"I'm sorry," she mouthed to him.

"Hey," said Barry, returning to the conversation. "I talked it over with Papi. As you can imagine, we're all bummed to find out you've been X-ed. That really puts a crimp in our plans."

"I know. I'm sorry," she replied. She heard the elevator outside her office ding and tightened up, worried about who was stepping off it.

"I'll make it up to you, I swear," she said. "But I gotta get out of here. Can I meet you somewhere?"

There was more hushed whispering on the phone, and Lauren grew anxious. She grabbed Mitch by the collar and stood him up.

"We have to get outta here," she said.

Mitch contemplated her request as footsteps grew closer.

"You don't have to leave the building with me," said Lauren. "But just help me get outta here, okay? Run interference or something."

The footsteps stopped, and Lauren went for broke.

"Barry, can I meet you or not?" she blurted out. "I remember where the pizza place was. Can I just meet you there?"

"No," exclaimed Barry. "Papi wants to meet somewhere neutral, just in case someone is tracking you. There's an abandoned overpass that cops never patrol. He wants to meet there. He'll text you the address."

"Thank you!" she said, hanging up and turning to Mitch.

The footsteps resumed; the clock was ticking down to her apprehension. Mitch finally came out of his stupor. "I know a back door," he said.

They escaped the hallway and slipped into the underground parking garage undetected.

"Thank you," Lauren said, hugging Mitch and exiting through the back door.

He lingered in the shadows of the parking garage and contemplated this new development. What did this mean for his career? His gaze drifted to a parking mirror, where he noticed his reflection. It appeared his cheek was slowly detaching from his new face.

Thirty-Four

It was dusk, and Lauren had been walking for a long time. The overpass she was to meet the Brotherhood loomed in the distance, and she could feel a blister forming on the inside of her big toe. Her CEO look, a fitted pantsuit and stocky heels, was no match for this journey. She entered a foggy area and passed a tent where two human shadows danced. She stopped to watch as if it were a puppet show.

There was a gurgling noise, and the smaller shadow exploded, eliciting a loud thud. A homeless man emerged from the tent covered in green goo.

"She exploded," the man said wearily. "My wife just exploded."

The goo on his face began searing his flesh, but he was too shocked to notice. There was murmuring in the distance, and Lauren realized she was in the middle of a homeless encampment.

"Fuck you, she didn't explode," said a man's voice. "Don't spread lies like that."

A homeless couple sauntered in, sipping Energoo cans.

"We've been drinking this shit all day," said the man, "And it doesn't make you explode. You bunch of pussies."

Lauren stole a look at their beverage. They were drinking Formula One.

"What are you looking at, bitch?" said the can-drinking woman.

Lauren glanced at the overpass. She was eighty yards away and needed to shut up and move on. But the woman's shit-eating grin pissed her off, and she had bottled frustration that needed uncorking.

"What am I looking at?" Lauren replied. "I'm looking at someone who thinks they're drinking Formula Two but is actually drinking Formula One. That's why you're not exploding. There's nothing wrong with Formula One."

"Bullshit," the woman said, sipping her can.

"You trying to tell us what we can and can't drink now?" her man butted in with a menacing look.

"If anyone is exploding," explained the woman, "it's because they ain't healthy inside. Nothing wrong with this draaaank."

Lauren realized she had spoken too much. "You're right," she lied, sprinting away. "You're absolutely right. People only explode if they're not healthy. If you're healthy, you have nothing to worry about!"

The Brotherhood trudged up a grass hill opposite the homeless encampment. It was night, and more fog rolled in, causing their vision to blur. They rarely allowed themselves to be in the open like this, but Barry convinced everyone they should take a field trip.

"This is giving me agita," Papi said nervously. "When is your ex-wife going to call back?"

Barry didn't want to think about his ex-wife, especially now, when he was moments away from rekindling his relationship with Lauren.

"What are we going to do once we get the can tested?" said Meghan, "Lauren got herself X-ed. We no longer have a megaphone."

"Christ, I think my colitis is acting up," said Papi. "Let's not talk about this anymore. Forget I brought it up. I'm gonna shit myself with nerves."

Lauren spotted them in the fog, and Barry darted to meet her, leaving the rest of the crew behind. She smiled and he hugged her tight. She seemed confused by the gesture.

"Do you know why I got X-ed?" she asked, pushing past the informal embrace.

Barry got shy. The Brotherhood caught up, and Barry deflected the question to Papi.

"Oh," replied Papi, forlorn. "It's very bad. I rather not repeat it. If you don't mind."

"I never even posted on social media," replied Lauren. "It's all bullshit!"

"Has anyone followed you?" asked Papi. "Should we check you for tracking devices?"

"I don't mind checking you again," Barry said, smiling. "As long as you don't mind."

Lauren rolled her eyes. "Dude, you're reallllly pushing it."

Two red dots formed on Bob and Rob's foreheads. And before anyone could say a word, their heads exploded.

"Oh, God!" Papi cried.

Large silhouetted figures emerged from the homeless encampment, fog obscuring their features.

"Get down!" screamed Papi, pulling them into the tall grass.

Barry couldn't look away from Bob and Rob's exploded heads. Why did he ask the Brotherhood to join him on this "field trip"? He could have gone by himself, and they'd both be alive. He knew the answer and didn't want to admit it. He was scared to go out alone in the dark.

"You are fugitives of the law," blared a robot voice in the distance. "Termination on sight."

The Brotherhood gasped in the grass. They had all fled their X sentences, and they knew what the punishment was. But hearing it out loud was alarming.

"Fuck this," said Meghan, pulling a small pistol from her boot.

"Whoa," said Barry, shocked to find her armed.

"No!" cried Papi, pulling her down. "Let's get out of here, get back underground."

"I'm tired of hiding underground," Meghan replied. "If I'm going out, it's on my two feet. Out in the open for a change."

Six giant ex-military bots emerged from the haze. They were fifteen feet tall and solid, with no "eyes" to speak of, just slick slabs of gunmetal, clanking horror shows. Meghan fired her pistol and landed two immediate headshots. The giants fell.

"Suck my dick motherfuckers," she laughed.

Papi breathed a sigh of relief. He hoped these military bots were just giant idiots, old decommissioned models that Meghan could dispose of quickly. She toppled two more, and Papi smiled. He was going to say "thatta girl!" but wasn't sure if it was considered offensive.

The rest of the Brotherhood had no weapons and watched in stunned silence as Meghan stood on the robot's metal carcass and whooped in celebration.

"I'm going to piss on their faces!" she said, unzipping her pants.

Two giant military bots appeared above her, weapons drawn. Papi quickly sprung into action, jumping on one's leg and causing it to spin around. Meghan smiled and aimed her pistol at the bot's head.

"See you in hell," she said.

But, when she pulled the trigger, all that emitted was a click. The giant robot fired at her, piercing her stomach and sending her tumbling into the grass.

Papi screamed in horror and grabbed a discarded robot arm. He swung it wildly like a baseball bat, knocking the two military bots backward. Gerald connected his fist to the back of one's head, and it exploded like a firecracker.

The final military bot pressed its foot onto Papi's neck and searched for its weapon, ready to end the man's life. But, the fog was proving difficult even for its advanced nighttime vision. It finally located the firearm, and Gerald rushed the metal being with all his might. The bot spun around to finish Papi, but the bullet meant for the Italian leader never reached him, instead striking Gerald clean between the eyes and killing him instantly.

"Noooo!" screamed Papi, rushing over to cradle the man.

Barry, Lauren, and Little Ricky were so grief-stricken they just stared at their leader, slack-jawed.

"What are you guys doing?" screamed Meghan, bleeding in the grass.

A rush of nervous adrenaline filled Barry's body. He had to be a hero—a badass boss bitch. He searched the grass, locating one of the fallen robot's guns. He tried to lift it, but it was so heavy his back seized. Lauren helped shoulder the weight, and they aimed the gun together and pulled the trigger.

The shot connected with the military bot's massive barrel chest and fell with a terrible thud. Papi clutched Gerald's body harder, shrieking into the night. He hoped his embrace would awaken the gentle giant, but it would not. Meghan gurgled in the distance, and the remaining Brotherhood found their way to her.

She was gulping blood, and Papi fell to his knees, removed his trademark gray hoodie, and held it to her stomach. She was fading fast, but his presence allowed her a weak smile.

"I was the worst one," she said between labored breaths.

"What?" asked Papi, confused.

"Out of all of you...I was the worst," she explained.

"No, you weren't," Papi whispered.

"I was," she cried, tears forming in her eyes.

"Please, Meghan, try to relax," Papi said.

She did for a moment, but turmoil roiled behind her eyes.

"I need to tell you something," she said.

Papi shushed her.

"No," she continued, "I...I really did fuck that kid."

Papi was speechless.

"Matty Boyle," she said. "I was his substitute teacher, and he hit on me...and I was all fucked about my marriage...I was drinking a lot back then. Getting stoned."

Papi couldn't believe what he was hearing. Meghan had always denied allegations that she had sex with a teenager.

"I told you that Atlas Wake was responsible," she said. "That they made it all up because I refused to serve Energoo at our school. But, it was all lies. I did it. I fucked that kid."

She closed her eyes. "I regret nothing."

Papi wanted to offer comforting words, but her revelation knocked him off kilter.

"Who am I to judge?" offered Barry shakily.

Papi didn't have the heart to repeat his mantra. But Meghan seemed to hear Barry just fine.

"Who am I to judge?" she said, fading away.

There was another rumble in the homeless encampment, and Lauren squinted, trying to find the source of the commotion. The disheveled widower, whose wife had exploded, was pointing at them.

"I know this is fucked up," Lauren said. "But we need to leave. We're about to have some more company."

The others nodded and stood up, ready to dart away, but Papi remained crouched in the grass. They watched as he clutched Meghan close to his chest and whispered a prayer into her ear.

Thirty-Five

In the doorway of Lauren's abandoned office stood Geena Jackson. She was proud of herself for confusing the authorities earlier, buying Lauren a few moments to escape. She felt a motherly connection to her for reasons she didn't understand. Still, she decided to get comfortable and reclaim the young woman's office as her own. She sat in her plush new executive chair and stared at the city. The streets were covered in trash and homeless people, a real buzz kill. She quickly drew the blinds, determined to enjoy this. It was a long and bumpy ride to the top of Atlas Wake, but she knew it would be worth it. It had to be. She sampled the luxury espresso machine and the VR meditation station, then meandered to the private bathroom and decided to shower just because she could.

The water was hot, and she savored the steam rising through the mirrored room. There were several shower heads to choose from, and she opted for the massage option, letting it linger on her lower region longer than necessary. The water gurgled and buzzed, and she thought about the women in business trophies lining her bookshelves at home. She hated being called a lady boss. Even the trendy title of badass boss bitch seemed beneath her. She wanted to be a great boss with no asterisk.

There was a knock on her door, and she jumped.

"Who is it?" she asked, annoyed.

"Uh, it's Mitch," he replied.

She quickly got dressed and joined him in the office.

"You scared the shit out of me."

Mitch apologized, clutching his sliding cheek. "Is there anything I can do for you?" he asked.

She daydreamed about seducing him for the hell of it. Let him finish where the showerhead left off. But she knew exploiting her new position of power would get her X-ed, and she stuffed down the impulse.

"Y'know. I wish you had found Lauren's social media posts," she said. "That would have saved us a lot of grief."

"I'm sorry," Mitch replied. "Can I make it up to you? Run an errand or something?"

Geena was annoyed. Her quiet moment in the shower was cut short, and now that she was dressed, playtime was over.

"I just figured I could be your assistant since Lauren doesn't work here anymore," said Mitch.

"I'm good," replied Geena, opening up her laptop.

"Here's the thing," he said. "I don't know what I'm supposed to do if you don't want me. I mean, I haven't been fired, right?"

"Not that I know of," said Geena, eyes focused on her screen.

"So, if you don't want me. What do I do?" Mitch asked. "Should I try and become someone else's assistant? Does Meryl need someone to catalog his whips?"

"I doubt it," said Geena, barely paying attention. "Anyways, I have a lot of stuff on my plate. So, you'll have to have this existential crisis somewhere else."

E

Mitch was devastated. He descended the long elevator and drifted through the empty Atlas Wake lobby. Was he still getting paid for this phantom job? Or was he off the payroll? Should he go home and try to find another assistant job?

Assisting was one of the few career options left. A surprise, considering AI replaced most jobs. Apparently, CEOS preferred humans for the position. They enjoyed bossing a *real* person around.

Sure, Mitch could find another assistant job, but he didn't want to leave the company. He believed in Atlas Wake's agenda—their quest for world domination—and needed to be part of it.

Mitch walked by a security booth and peered through the glass. A burly human guard eyed him suspiciously.

"Do you have any job openings?" Mitch asked.

"Nah," the guard replied. "Hasn't been for years. I mostly manage these clowns."

He pointed to three synthetic security guards. They saluted him dutifully.

"I like when they salute me, though," the guard admitted.

Mitch backed away from the glass, and his cheek detached and hit the floor. Splat! He scooped it in a panic and desperately held it to his face. After thirty seconds, the cheek appeared successfully reattached.

Mitch wandered toward the cafeteria. It was empty, and the company's glowing vending machines called to him. He purchased a can of Formula Two out of boredom. The warning label read: DO NOT CONSUME MORE THAN THREE CANS IN ONE-HALF HOUR.

He took a sip and drank from it. Damn. It was good. He recognized how some people might have trouble stopping at three. Not him, though. He had a brain on him. A brain he believed would run Atlas Wake one day. Green goo dribbled from his chin and splattered onto the floor.

A small, squatty Janitor emerged from a closet to clean up the mess. Mitch went silent, embarrassed a grown man was cleaning up after him. Suddenly, a light bulb went off in Mitch's head. He swiped the mop and cleaned the splattered beverage.

"What the heck are you doing?" asked the Janitor.

"I want to assist you," replied Mitch. "Can I be your assistant?"

"What are you some kind of asshole?" the janitor said, grabbing the mop back.

"But, couldn't you use an assistant?" Mitch floundered.

"Get the fuck out of here, you freaky piece of shit."

There was nowhere for Mitch to go, so he sat in the lobby and stared at one of the giant LCD monitors on the wall. A news broadcast featured eyewitness accounts of people exploding. A synthetic guard noticed the coverage and quickly changed the channel to another program. A handsome broadcaster downplayed the explosions, instead highlighting how good Formula Two tasted.

"Did you know it's on pace to become the fastest-selling beverage in American history?" he said.

Mitch was depressed. How could he find a way to stay in this glorious corporation? He scrunched his eyebrows, causing his cheek to loosen and plop to the floor.

"Fuck," he said.

The Security Guard gave him a dirty look, and Mitch skittered off, eventually finding sanctuary in a janitor's closet. He fumbled in the dark, trying to find a tool to fix his face, eventually locating an expired tube of crazy glue. He squeezed the remaining glue onto his detached cheek and held it to his face.

He sat on an upside-down mop bucket, contemplating his life. In the darkness, he decided not to feel sorry for himself anymore. If no one wanted him, he didn't care. He'd be happy to float around the building, glad to become a ghost in the Atlas Wake machine.

"I'm never going home again," he whispered to the void.

Thirty-Six

The abandoned pizza parlor basement never felt so sad. Meghan was dead. Gerald was dead. Bob and Rob were dead. Little Ricky broke down in tears. Papi tried to comfort the young man, only to blubber and sob into his neck. Eventually, the Italian leader couldn't take it anymore and moved toward the shadows to mourn privately.

Ricky searched Barry for comfort, a father figure, and Barry played the part. He hugged the boy firmly and motioned for Lauren to join in. She did, and they all cried. When the hug was over, Little Ricky recoiled in fear. He was covered in blood.

"Oh, fuck," Lauren said, pointing to her blood-stained shirt. "I'm sorry."

Little Ricky looked down at his dripping fingers, realizing the blood likely came from one of their fallen comrades. Barry grabbed a fresh gray sweatsuit from a shelf.

"Here," he said, handing it to Lauren, "you can wear this."

She gave him a dirty look.

"It doesn't mean you're one of us," he clarified. "Just means you'll have a clean shirt."

Lauren nodded and headed to the bathroom to change. Despite the harrowing situation, Barry was still head over heels for her. He turned to Little Ricky, a twinkle in his eyes.

"Ain't she something?" he whispered.

"What?" Ricky replied confused, horrified by the blood on his fingers.

Papi crouched by a makeshift sleeping bag that Gerald would no longer fill. He reached for a large bottle of bourbon, took several gulps, and sank to the floor.

"You okay?" Barry asked.

"They're all gone," Papi said quietly. "Just like that. They're all gone."

Barry's gaze drifted to the bathroom light. Lauren was visible through the cracked door, removing her blood-stained shirt and exposing a worn-out tan bra. Barry was taken aback, not at the tantalizing exposed skin, but that Lauren's bra was normal-looking. Average. He thought she would be wearing a black one. Something *edgy* to match her attitude.

Little Ricky desperately tried to wash the blood off his skin. But he was a mess, frequently pausing to sob in the doorway. He tried changing into clean clothes when his phone vibrated with a news alert. SEVERAL MEMBERS OF THE BROTHERHOOD WERE DEAD. The press seemed excited by this development.

Ricky's hands trembled. He stormed over to Papi and Barry, who sat quietly in the dark. "We can't just sit around here and be sad," Ricky said. "We need to do something!"

Papi took another sip of his brown liquor. "It's okay to be sad sometimes."

"But, you're the one who said 'no time for tears'!" yelped Ricky.

"I know," replied Papi, "and I'm starting to regret that catch-phrase. It keeps getting thrown in my goddamn face."

"We can still get that can tested," Ricky said. "What are we waiting for?"

Papi made a noise. He wasn't in the mood to discuss this and moved to another corner of the basement to sulk. Lauren found Barry and asked what was wrong.

"It'll be fine," he said.

She wore her brand-new gray uniform, and Barry smiled like a schoolboy. With Papi and Ricky gone, now was the time to reset the mood. It was time for romance.

Lauren was pensive. "I feel like I'm responsible for what happened," she admitted.

Barry shushed her. He wouldn't have any of that talk. Not now.

"I feel grateful you're still here," Barry said, grabbing her hand and peering into her eyes as if they were star-crossed lovers.

Lauren's face dropped. "Dude," she said. "Can we not?"

"Huh?" he replied.

"There's been a vibe," she explained.

"Yeah," he agreed. "A good vibe, right?"

Lauren sighed.

"Listen," Barry said. "I really like you."

"I'm gay," she replied.

Barry was floored. Speechless. He didn't expect this hiccup in their burgeoning romantic comedy. He stuttered like a broken record. "Wh-wh-why didn't you tell me this before?"

"What am I supposed to do?" she asked. "Hi. I'm Lauren Caldwell. Nice to meet you. I'm gay."

"A lot of people say that nowadays!" Barry whined. "They get it right there out in the open! Some even put it on all their social media accounts!"

"Well, I guess I'm not like everyone else," she said.

Goddamn it. Barry couldn't get over how cool she was. She *wasn't* like everyone else. That's what drove him crazy. "You could have warned me earlier," he said half-heartedly.

"I've only seen you a handful of times in my life!" she replied. "When was I supposed to do that?"

Barry wasn't sure.

"You're acting like a teenager," she said. "How old are you?"

"That's not important," he replied. "Although, I have worried about our age difference."

"You've worried about our age difference?" she said. "That's how far down this fake relationship rabbit hole you've gotten?"

Barry was embarrassed, his masculinity unfurling like a flag in the breeze. He appeared on the edge of tears. Lauren wanted to flee. The last thing she needed was more messy emotions. Luckily, Papi began wailing in the distance and broke up the awkward scene.

"It's all hopeless," the leader cried. "I shouldn't have stayed in this city. I should have left for Ceto Isles when I had the chance."

Barry hadn't heard the name Ceto Isles in years. "That used to be a vacation spot," he said. "But, then, I think it got overrun by rats, right?"

"Yeah, it used to be full of rats," Papi replied. "Some of the Brotherhood left the city to hide out there. I could have gone too, but I didn't want to leave my friends behind."

Little Ricky locked eyes with Papi, glad the man had stayed in the city all these years. Papi's phone buzzed.

"I don't recognize this number," he said.

Barry glanced at the number and froze. "That's my ex," Barry replied.

"Well, answer it, you idiot!" screamed Papi, life returning to his veins.

Barry got shy and walked away from the group. Lauren watched him. He looked like a puppy dog, nodding his head, eager to please his ex-wife. His eyes eventually drifted to Lauren's, and he gave her a defeated smile.

"Okay, here's the deal," Barry said. "My ex will analyze that can, but it has to be tonight, and she doesn't want a crowd. Just one of us can go."

Lauren volunteered. Considering how responsible she felt about their predicament, it was the least she could do. She also secretly wanted to see who could marry a guy like Barry.

"No way," said Barry. "You have the biggest target on your back right now. Besides, as much as I don't want to see her again, she is my ex-wife. I should go."

"Who cares who goes?" said Little Ricky, taking the liquor bottle away from Papi's hand and swigging it. He recoiled at the taste and spat it out immediately. "What's the real plan here?" he continued. "Say we discover there's something wrong with Formula Two. What's our next step?"

Everyone fell silent.

"This is why the other chapters of the Brotherhood don't talk to us!" Ricky said.

"Really?" asked Barry. "The other chapters don't talk to you guys? Papi, I thought you spoke to them on that CB radio."

"He was pretending!" said Little Ricky. "He was talking to himself the whole time! Just to make himself feel better!"

"That's not true," said Papi, taking his liquor back.

"It *is* true!" snapped Little Ricky. "I'm our 'communications guy,' and I'm telling you! No one talks to us because they don't take us seriously. We do everything half-cocked. We never have a plan. We're the laughing stock of the Brotherhood of the Resigned!"

Papi slapped the boy across the face.

"Watch your tongue," he said, upset. He wished he was on that rat island, away from all this drama. The other factions of the Brotherhood probably figured out how to make alcohol by now. Papi could have been sipping a tropical drink, fishing off the shore, living the life. Not arguing in a musty basement.

"Everything keeps changing," said Papi. "A day ago, we had access to a CEO willing to take Atlas Wake down from the inside. An old-fashioned whistleblower."

"You did," said Lauren.

"But now she's X-ed. And just as useless as we are," Papi continued. "No one will listen to what an X-ed person has to say."

"We should still get the can tested," Lauren said. "And if something bad is inside, we need a new mouthpiece. That's all."

"Couldn't we take this to a newspaper or something?" asked Barry.

Little Ricky laughed. "Yeah, maybe a million years ago. No one believes journalists anymore."

"Then who?" asked Papi. "Who could possibly get this potential information out there?"

"What about Joey?" asked Little Ricky.

"Who?" replied Papi.

"Joey Paul, the truth sayer," said Barry, proud to remember the influencer's name.

"Joey Paul?" asked Lauren. "That kid who does those six-second lip-sync videos?"

"He has a billion followers," said Little Ricky. "I think he's our only shot." The boy stood up, confident, the idea fortifying him.

"Okay," Papi said, witnessing the boy's transformation. "We'll take our findings to Joey Paul."

"It won't be easy getting to him," said Ricky, "But I am a paying subscriber to his feed. So, we have a leg up over most people."

"I can't believe we're hinging our plan on a teenager who makes lip-sync videos," said Lauren.

"He does more than that," replied Little Ricky, annoyed. "He's very creative. Although, if I'm being honest, I think I'm just as talented as he is."

The plan was set, and Barry walked away en route to his ex-wife. But something nagged at him. He didn't want to do this alone, not when Lauren existed in the world. He still wanted to spend time with her. Gay or straight, it didn't matter. Wow. Was this an evolution for him? Could he be friends with a pretty woman when sex was off the table? She agreed to join him, and they left, gliding up the staircase.

"Hey!" Papi yelled, slurring his words from below. "You forgot the can of Formula Two, you dumb mamaluke!"

Thirty-Seven

It was the dead of night, and the industrial part of the city emitted a low droning noise. Barry and Lauren were alone on the street, shadows creeping along their faces, when they heard an explosion. They crouched behind a barbed-wire fence and wondered if the sound was firecrackers or people exploding from too much Formula Two.

They looked at their hands gripping the earth and realized they were kneeling in chicken shit. A sign plastered on a crumbling building read, "Art & Vinnie's Poultry Mart."

"Ughhhh," said Lauren.

Barry found an old water spigot on the side of the building and turned it on, desperate to wash his hands. Lauren stood by, waiting for a turn, but only brown liquid choked out. Barry rubbed his hands in the dirt, hoping it would mask the scent.

"I can't smell like shit," he said desperately, "I can't smell like shit in front of my ex."

A loud explosion sent him on his ass. He sat up and locked eyes with Lauren, spooked. This explosion was closer to them than the others. They crept along the property line, trying to get a peek at the street.

"Oh my God," said Barry, freezing by the fence.

The smell was pungent, even at a distance, and they held their noses. Green goo bubbled and hissed on the asphalt road. It seemed alive for a brief moment, flittered, and died.

"Was that a person?" asked Barry.

Lauren shook her head. "Probably homeless. I saw one explode earlier."

"Christ," said Barry, slipping under the fence for a closer look.

Headlights flooded his face, and he quickly retreated, hiding behind the fence with Lauren. An ominous white van barreled down the dark road and skidded to a stop. Figures in hazmat suits slid open the van doors, boots thudding the pavement. Barry and Lauren tensed up.

A massive metal device was wheeled off the van. It was covered in switches and exhaust pipes. One of the figures removed a hose from it and began sucking up the green goo on the street.

"What the hell is this about?" Barry whispered.

The figures stopped vacuuming to peer into the darkness. Barry and Lauren ducked down as the three figures plodded toward them. They all held a beeping device. Barry watched in horror, his life flashing before his eyes. The figures seemed soulless, mechanical, unyielding. He searched for a getaway plan and dived into the pile of chicken shit.

"What are you doing?" whispered Lauren.

There was no time for an explanation. He grabbed her and pushed her under the shit.

The figures were inches away, gliding their handheld instruments above them. The beeping stopped, and the figures were confused. They waved their devices around the chicken shit some more, then moved them about the fence. Not a beep.

It didn't take long for Lauren to understand the game Barry was playing. And they laid together, buried in shit, holding their breath, trying not to move a muscle or make a sound. Another figure exited the van and joined them. The gait of his walk was looser.

"Did you find anything?" the new person asked.

The three others replied in sync, "Negative, sir."

Their voices were vaguely artificial, a bright hint of electronic noise to their breath. The new man was frustrated, breathing louder in his suit. He grabbed one of their devices and pointed it around the chicken shit. Barry and Lauren were about to come up for air, but they held on, eyes wanting to bulge out of their heads.

The device didn't beep, and the new man deflated.

"We told you, sir," the others said simultaneously.

The man grumbled, gave them back their device, and plodded back to the van. The others eventually joined, and they skidded away, leaving a faint outline of green goo sizzling on the street.

Barry and Lauren quickly pulled themselves out of the shit and gasped desperately, sucking in the air.

They walked for several hours in the dark, chicken shit slowly drying and flaking off. Barry noticed a warehouse emerging from the darkness. He stopped walking and clutched his stomach.

"You okay?" asked Lauren.

"I think so," he whispered. "I guess I'm just nervous about seeing her. Plus, I still smell like shit."

Lauren got closer. "I don't smell anything. I think you're good."

"Really?" asked Barry.

"Yeah," she replied. "Either that or I'm just numb to it."

Barry smiled weakly, and they walked some more.

"There she is," he said, pointing to a woman silhouetted by a lamppost. She was tall and slender and smoking a cigarette.

Barry's hand trembled. He tried to steady it, force himself to act.

"Hey!" he yelled from across the parking lot, hoping to get the awkwardness over with. "It's good to see you!" he croaked out.

His ex-wife only stared. Her features were angular, like stone, and when she spoke, she exuded a confident, icy air that drove Barry wild.

"Hello," she said. "Please don't shout."

She stared at Lauren, annoyed. "I thought you were coming alone."

"She's just a friend," said Barry. "She's cool."

"Uh-huh," his ex replied, slowly taking a drag from her cigarette. "Does she have a name?"

Lauren introduced herself, and they shook hands.

"I'm Carol," she said, exhaling more smoke. "But I'm sure you already knew that." She wrinkled her nose. "What is that unpleasant smell?"

No one answered.

The warehouse's exterior was shabby and in disrepair, but its inside was slick and modern. Carol led them down a long and winding white corridor. Barry was speechless, staring at his shoes the whole time. Wishing he could think of small talk. Any talk. Carol scanned her ID card and whisked them inside a lab. An older pudgy gentleman with glasses was working on a computer, and Carol's eyes widened. She grabbed Barry's collar in a panic.

"I wasn't aware Jenkins would be here tonight," she whispered. "Can you two hide in this closet while I facilitate his exit?"

Before Barry could answer, Carol pushed him into a tiny closet. Barry and Lauren were now inches apart. It was *so* romantic comedy of them, but he knew he couldn't think like that anymore.

"She seems cooler than you," whispered Lauren.

"Yeah," Barry said. "She's smarter, too."

"Well, duh, of course," Lauren replied.

It was dark in the closet, and Lauren searched for his eyes, only finding a faint glint. Barry couldn't discern any part of her either, and they became two disembodied voices talking in the abstract.

"I've always been dumb," said Barry.

Lauren let the comment linger.

"I guess I try to hide it," Barry continued, the darkness allowing him to be vulnerable. "I guess I've made a career hiding it. But Carol knew my secret. She knew how truly dumb I was."

"Dude, I was only joking," Lauren butted in.

"I thought I was getting a trophy wife when I married her," Barry continued. "But, I think I was *her* trophy wife."

"What's the harm in that?" Lauren replied. "It just means you guys were hot for each other, right?"

"I guess," Barry drifted, "But it also made it feel like we were cardboard cutouts in each other's story, a placeholder for a real relationship."

Barry sniffled, and Lauren braced herself for crying. She figured she would inch away from him, stare at the ceiling, and wait for the tears to end. But, once he started shaking uncontrollably, sobbing like a little boy, she was surprised to find herself hugging him.

"I'm sure you're struggling too," Barry said, sniffling. "Not knowing your parents, that's gotta be a weight on you."

Lauren forgot the entire world knew her backstory. She wished they didn't. She didn't want anyone's sympathy.

"You can't let your past define you," she said, resolute. "You are you."

"You are you?" asked Barry with a whimper.

"You're not a collection of your trauma," said Lauren. "That's bullshit, defeatist nonsense. You are you."

"You are you," Barry whispered to the dark.

Carol opened the closet door, and light spilled onto their awkward embrace. "Jenkins is gone," she said, rolling her eyes at them. "I'm not sure how long, so let's hurry."

Carol's laboratory was clean and organized. She wore a lab coat and eye goggles over her smooth tight skin and carefully removed the pull tab from Barry's Formula Two can. She poured its contents into a glass beaker, never spilling a drop. Every move she made was controlled and precise.

Barry watched her glide around like some sort of genius dolphin, picking up instruments and eyeing things on a computer. Guilt slowly overwhelmed him. He never visited her at work before.

"So, why are you doing this, Barry?" Carol said, eyeing the beaker. "I don't believe we'll find anything nefarious inside this beverage, but what is your endgame if we do? You're not one to rock the boat."

"I know. But now that I'm X-ed—" he started.

"Shush" she butted in. "I don't want to remember that you're X-ed. If someone caught you in here with me..."

"We don't want to be here any longer than you do," interrupted Lauren.

Carol laughed to herself and placed a metal probe into the beaker containing Formula Two. The probe was attached to a giant machine. It slowly sucked up the beverage, and a buzzing sound filled the room.

"It's thinking," said Carol giddily, her inner science geek spilling out of her prim and proper frame. Barry was spellbound. He had never seen Carol so joyous before. She waved them over to a monitor.

"It's detailing the contents now," she said. "High fructose corn syrup, citric acid...these are all standard fizzy water ingredients."

A few more words appeared on her screen.

"Yes. Ginseng," she said. "The 'energy' part of the drink, as it were." More words danced on the screen. "These are just color dyes."

Barry grew concerned. What if there was nothing terrible in this beverage? What if it was just another energy drink that some people's constitutions couldn't handle?

The machine buzzed and slurped while more words appeared on the monitor, Carol casually dismissing them. The probe made a grinding noise as if it were stuck.

"Is that normal?" asked Barry.

Carol didn't answer. She approached the probe, tapped her fingers to her lips, and stepped back to observe. The probe stopped grinding, and a word appeared on the screen: Unidentified element.

"Holy shit," said Barry. "Unidentified element?!"

"Yes," Carol replied.

"Well, what does that mean? Does that mean there's poison in there?" Barry yelped.

"No, Barry. It doesn't mean 'there's poison in there.' It just means it's unidentified. Not in our database. It can happen."

"Well, shit," said Barry, grabbing the can. "Isn't it illegal or something not to publish all the ingredients on the label? This is enough for Joey Paul to run with, isn't it?" he asked Lauren.

"I'm not sure," Lauren replied. "I mean, I would hope that a mystery ingredient that causes people to explode would be newsworthy."

"Oh dear," Carol said, "It only exploded people who can't control themselves. Your typical addicts and low-grade bums. People who would have shot themselves up with drugs and OD'd anyways."

"Excuse me?" Lauren said.

"Relax," Carol replied, "I've had a glass of Formula Two over ice with a shot of vodka and felt fine. I read the warning label. I showed restraint. One must have some personal responsibility after all."

"You had a can already?" asked Lauren. "Why did we come all this way?"

"I don't know," Carol replied, smirking. "I figured Barry just wanted to see me again."

Barry was annoyed by the accusation. "I didn't trust you'd do it," he said to Carol, his eyes narrowing. "You usually don't take me seriously. I wanted to make sure you tested it with my own eyes."

Footsteps echoed down the hall. Carol quickly removed the probe from the beaker.

"Time's up," she said.

"Wait!" Barry said. "I think we need something more than this... There's gotta be something more!"

The door opened, and the plump man named Jenkins entered. Barry and Lauren quickly hid under the counter.

"Hey," Jenkins called from the doorway, "I'm going to head out."

Carol nodded and smiled. "Me too. See you tomorrow."

The man left, and Barry stood up, grazing his arm on a large microscope. Blood pooled on his forearm.

Carol sighed. "I'll get you a bandage."

She walked away as Lauren stared at the blood dripping from his arm.

"Wait a second," she said, loud enough for Carol to hear, "What happens when we mix this unidentified element with blood?"

Carol turned around, intrigued.

"What happens to it," Lauren continued, "on a scientific level?"

Lauren leaned into the words "scientific level," hoping she had found Carol's weakness. She had. Enthusiasm bubbled through Carol, and she quickly grabbed Barry's arm, moved him to another empty beaker, and squeezed his skin.

"Hey!" he yelped.

His blood dripped into the second beaker, and Carol moved on to the first one with Formula Two.

"I'm distilling the Formula Two into its unidentifiable element," Carol said excitedly. "Next, I'll mix Barry's blood with it...and we shall see what happens."

She tapped some more buttons on her computer and readied a mechanical arm.

"Stand behind this, please," she said, pointing to a large protective shield.

"We're like ten feet away from those beakers. Isn't it a little overkill?" asked Barry.

"No. It's not," said Carol, handing them both a pair of eye goggles. She instructed the mechanical arm to pick up the beaker filled with Barry's blood.

"Please pour one milliliter of beaker one into beaker two," she said.

They hid behind the protective shield as the arm creaked and complied with her instruction. The blood mixed with the distilled unidentifiable ingredient, a swirling contrast of dark red and green. But, there was no chemical reaction.

"One more milliliter, please," she said.

The mechanical arm did as it was told. The two liquids mixed and yielded nothing.

"The hell with this!" Barry yelled. "Pour the whole goddamn beaker one into beaker two, please!"

"I don't think that's the right tack" Carol replied.

It was too late. The arm had heard Barry's command and dumped the entire beaker of blood into the distilled Formula Two. The glass instantly exploded into fiery shards, and they recoiled in shock, falling to the floor. The flames grew, threatening to catch the surrounding table on fire. Carol was shocked into silence, eyes wide with fear, suddenly out of snide remarks. Barry surveyed the situation, got to his feet, and ran away.

"Barry?!" Carol cried. "Where are you going?"

He returned with a fire extinguisher and quickly snuffed out the growing flames.

"I may be dumb," he said, "But I know how to put out a fire."

Thirty-Eight

Geena Jackson sat in her apartment, eyeing a screengrab sent to her by Atlas Wakes' legal department. It contained a homophobic text message Lauren had sent a friend. Geena wanted proof, and now that she had it, felt unsatiated. Something felt wrong. It didn't seem like something Lauren would say.

She guzzled an entire glass of wine, determined to move past it. She was CEO now, a role she had desired for decades. She poured some more wine and turned on the television. A news program breathlessly covered the Formula Two explosions, and it made her queasy. She hoped Lauren's exit as CEO would occupy the headlines, but people were already over it. She headed to the kitchen to find a more substantial drink.

She grabbed a glass and fixed herself a gin and tonic. She tried to remember the last time she made a drink for another person in this kitchen. It was at least a decade ago, back when she would date. She remembered when a man stood by the stove in tears, begging her to be more available, more "open." She sipped her gin and tonic and walked away from the memory.

A dozen "Women in Business" trophies were on her wall, each featuring a businesswoman with a briefcase. Their existence suddenly annoyed her, and she smacked the largest one. It fell to the floor with a crunch, and she bent down to pick it up. Small plastic balls had popped off.

They were tiny breasts. The businesswoman atop the trophy was just a man with glued-on tits. Rage overwhelmed her, and she grabbed the other awards and stacked them on the kitchen counter. She grabbed a knife and methodically chiseled their chests. She was heartbroken every time she discovered the boobs were pasted on. She dumped the trophies into the trash and made herself another cocktail. A pair of plastic boobs had settled on the counter, and she decided to keep them as a fucked-up keepsake.

Geena entered the luxurious Atlas Wake executive spa and tried to settle her nerves. She floated face up in the warm pool, staring at the cosmos. She was fine, she thought. Everything was fine. Her fingers slipped down her thighs, and she began to masturbate. She thought of Mitch and his perfect face, and the universe disappeared. She was about to climax when a robot frog hopped toward her.

"I have an important message," the frog chirped.

"Yes?" Geena sighed.

"The shareholders would like to see you now."

Geena's eyes widened.

She waited for an elevator to take her to the thirty-seventh floor, a floor she never knew existed. It was after hours, and the place was vacant and eerie. A chill rose up her spine. The elevator dinged, and the doors opened to reveal Dan.

"Hey, Geena," he said coolly.

"You seem relaxed," she replied, "considering the shareholders are summoning us for the first time."

Dan smiled. "I think it's totally dank that you're CEO," he said. "It makes sense it was you."

Geena studied his face and wasn't sure if he meant it. He led her down the thirty-seventh-floor hallway as if he had been there before. Geena's nostrils flared, and she stopped in her tracks.

"Whew," she said. "Do the custodians ever get up to this floor? It reeks."

Dan shrugged, and they moved closer to the meeting room. Whispers grew from inside, and Geena tensed up.

"Damn, Geena. Relax," Dan said. "These people have never been an issue. They just want to meet the new CEO, that's all. You should be turnt up." He knocked on the door and asked if the team was ready.

"We're ready for lift off!" replied Meryl from behind the door.

They entered, and the old man rolled toward them in his wheelchair, excited.

"There she is, everyone!" he yelped. "Our new CEO!"

The entire room erupted in applause. There were twelve shareholders, men in their early forties. They were all brown-haired and blue-eyed and possessed an all-American ruggedness. They seemed lifted from the Sears catalog of Meryl's youth.

"Thank you," said Geena, overwhelmed by the gesture.

The shareholders smiled at her like she was a shiny object they had adored for years.

"Please, have a seat," said Meryl. "We have serious matters to discuss."

Geena was the only woman in the room, and although she'd been in this situation countless times, it felt different. Anxiety-inducing. She was the CEO now and under the microscope. She sat at the head of the long conference room table, and a foul odor overwhelmed her. The same one she smelt in the hall. She tried breathing out of her mouth, which helped. But she could almost taste the rotting stench.

"I'm sure you've seen the news that several of the Brotherhood of the Resigned have been killed," said Meryl, looking to Geena for a reply.

"Well," she said. "That's good news for us. Isn't it? They're not exactly fans of our company."

Meryl smiled, hoping she was on the same page. "Yep. These Resigned folks are a bunch of extremist nut jobs. They see conspiracy theories everywhere!"

"There's still quite a few left," interjected one of the shareholders. Geena never got their names. And it was just as well. They looked so similar it would have been tough to sort anyway.

"Speaking on behalf of the others," the shareholder continued, "eliminating all factions of the Resigned would greatly benefit us."

Geena felt like she was in a war room, not a corporate shareholder meeting. Meryl noticed her confusion and patted her on the back reassuringly.

"Unfortunately, our recent ex-CEO has joined the Brotherhood," he said.

"Barry?" asked Geena.

"No, Lauren, I'm afraid," said the old man.

Geena was shocked.

"I know," said Meryl. "I didn't think she'd link up with them either." He turned to the shareholders. "We liked Lauren a lot. Until we found out she was a racist homophobe, of course."

The shareholders nodded agreeably.

"The Brotherhood has proven to be a thorn in our side," Meryl continued. "We need every faction, every chapter of that organization, to be brought to justice."

Geena glanced at Dan to gauge a reaction. He muttered under his breath and scratched his neck.

"The press coverage over these explosions has been unfortunate," said one of the shareholders. "We'd love to change the conversation."

Meryl agreed and turned to Geena for an idea. She didn't realize she'd be put on the spot, and her mind raced.

"What if we flooded social media with AI bots?" she offered. "We have the budget for it. All the bots could be explosion deniers."

Meryl smiled. "Did I tell you this gal was the tits or what?"

The entire men's Sears catalog laughed in unison. They stood up to offer their hands. "It was so nice to meet you," they told Geena as they filed out.

Dan scratched his cheek. He seemed uncomfortable and itchy, like he was fighting an allergic reaction. He eventually left, leaving Geena alone with Meryl.

She tried to smile at the old man but had trouble faking it. The meeting unnerved her. Was it the shareholders, their eyes gleaming, teeth so white, so eager to crush the Brotherhood? Or was it the weird stench that seemed to permeate through the room?

"Are you okay?" Meryl asked.

Geena mulled it over. "I need to ask you a question," she said. "The stuff about Lauren, the things in that press release. We didn't make that all up, right? She really did say all of that terrible stuff?"

"Of course," Meryl blurted. "Why would we make it up?"

"It's just...we really vetted her," she replied.

"That intern kid fucked up!" Meryl said. "He missed it! It's nothing to get hung up about. Besides, this is all ancient history. Lauren was the past, and you're our future! I know it sucks to say it, but the sooner we can get her and the Brotherhood behind bars, the sooner we can continue our world domination!"

Meryl smiled, urging Geena to join in. She did, but the meeting ate at her. She realized the plastic boobs were in her pocket and fingered them quietly as Meryl spun around in his wheelchair like a teenager doing tricks on a skateboard. The air conditioner kicked on and wafted a smell toward Geena, whose eyes watered.

"What is that terrible odor?" she asked.

"Oh," Meryl replied, slowing down his wheelchair. "You get used to it."

Thirty-Nine

Barry and Lauren were back in the basement, waiting for Papi to speak. In the Italian leader's hands was a vial containing the mystery ingredient in Formula Two. He rotated it, letting the viscous green goo slowly slide up and down. He moved it closer to his eyes, studying, trying to form words.

"I'll be honest," he said. "I secretly hoped you'd come back and say nothing was wrong...I didn't want to believe in a world where a corporation would purposely harm its customers."

"Well, let's not cry about it," Little Ricky interrupted. "Let's get this to Joey Paul!"

Papi nodded solemnly as if this were a funeral. He knew it wasn't, but he couldn't help feeling that something had died. Little Ricky grabbed his phone and logged into "The Joey Paul Truth-Telling Experience," a premium subscription service for the biggest and most well-heeled Joey Paul fans.

"Ugh," Little Ricky said, "I think my dad changed my login password."

Barry was confused.

"Yeah," replied Little Ricky, growing embarrassed. "He still pays for some of my stuff."

Ricky tried to guess the password for several minutes, but nothing worked. He couldn't get in. Despair spread across the empty basement.

"I think you know what to do," Papi said.

"Do I gotta?" Ricky asked. "Give me another couple minutes. Maybe I can guess the password."

"A fanabla!" Papi yelped. "Just call your dad."

Little Ricky sighed and took out his phone. An excited voice answered on the first ring. "Son! Where are you? Are you okay?" his dad said.

"I'm fine," replied Ricky flatly.

"Are you still living underground? Are those people treating you okay?" he asked.

"I'm fine! Okay? I'm not calling to talk," Little Ricky replied.

There was a long silence on the other end, his dad's heart deflating.

"What's the new password for the Joey Paul experience?" Ricky asked.

"Are you in trouble?" his dad whispered.

"No!" Ricky yelled. "But I will be if you don't give me the fucking password!"

Barry bristled. He wanted to step in and tell Little Ricky to be nicer to his father. But the boy was fuming mad. Now wasn't the time to get involved.

"Okay," his father said, resigned, "The password is *ILoveMySonAndIMissHim*."

Little Ricky rolled his eyes. "Are you serious?"

"Serious as soup," his father replied.

Little Ricky typed in the password and sighed. "It worked."

"Okay, now, son, if you're in trouble—"

Ricky disconnected before he could finish. He scrolled through his account page. He was a "silver" member, and another tier was above him, a costly one called "ultra platinum." Its main perk—a monthly in-person meetup, where fans could get direct access to Joey Paul for five minutes.

"That's a lot of money to upgrade," Lauren said, eyeing the page.

"It's fine," Ricky said, auto-filling his dad's credit card info. "Hopefully, he didn't cancel his card."

A spinning hourglass appeared on the screen, and the Brotherhood held their breath. If Little Ricky couldn't gain access to Joey Paul through this ultra-platinum tier, their goose was cooked. Joey no longer ran his social media accounts. They were managed by AI bots, which helped form a wall between him and crazy fans. This costly ultra-platinum subscription was the only way to reach the influencer.

A ding sound emitted from the phone, and Little Ricky smiled. "We're in."

Everyone high-fived, elated by their good luck for once. Papi tried to locate some Italian snacks to celebrate while Little Ricky stared at the screen.

"Holy shit," he said. "The meet-and-greet is happening right now. I have the invite."

"It's tonight?" Barry exclaimed.

"What are the odds?" Papi said, beaming. "I mean, this is fate right here! We can talk to this kid *tonight*?!"

Little Ricky looked closer at the invite. "The only hiccup is it's just for one person, and it's in my dad's name."

"Hmmm," Papi said, snacking on some roasted peppers, "I'll go and pretend to be your dad. Then I'll corner this kid and get him to broadcast our news. Piece of cake."

Little Ricky smiled weakly.

"What's wrong?" Lauren asked.

"Oh, I dunno," he replied. "I really wanted to meet Joey Paul. I wanted to be there. I guess I'm a really big fan."

"I'm sure you can meet him another time," Barry offered. "This is important. If Papi can go there and get this done, our lives might change."

Little Ricky didn't reply. He was busy poking around the website. There was another ding sound.

"I just added a plus one. I'm going," Little Ricky said, resolute.

Barry peered at Ricky's phone. "Jesus, that's a lot of money for a plus one," he said. "Your dad's going to be in the poor house with this."

"Nah," Ricky replied, "My dad's rich as fuck."

There was a loud rumble outside, and everyone stood up, alert. Papi peered out the front window and saw an ominous white van chugging down the street. They all tensed up and remained quiet as it slowly passed the window and down the road.

Forty

Security Guards lined the front entrance of Joey Paul's luxury apartment complex while a gaggle of desperate fans waited outside. The Brotherhood emerged from a sewer grate across the street. Papi was the last to appear and winced in pain.

"You okay?" asked Barry.

"Fine," Papi said, gritting his teeth, "I'm starting to regret hiding that vial up my you-know-what."

Barry wasn't sure why Papi needed to shove the top-secret ingredient up his ass. "Go on," Barry said, "Lauren and I will hang back as lookouts."

Papi and Ricky beelined toward the entrance. A disheveled young man with patches of facial hair lept in front of them. "Are you an ultra-platinum subscriber?" he asked.

Papi didn't answer, and the Scruffy Man took it as a "yes." His friends grabbed Papi and Ricky and pulled them into their drum circle. They were all dead-eyed, wearing baggy hemp clothing in various shades of beige.

"Can I be your plus one?" asked the Scruffy Man. "Please?!"

"I'm sorry," replied Papi, inching away. "My *son* is my plus one tonight."

Little Ricky smiled at the thought of Papi being his father. The scruffy men looked upset, and Papi clenched his fists, ready to defend the tickets on Ricky's phone. But the scruffy men weren't interested in a fight. Instead, they linked arms and kneeled in prayer around them.

"May you gain infinite wisdom in Joey Paul's presence," the Scruffy Man said. "May he shine the light of lights upon you."

"Madone, these people are weird," Papi grumbled, grabbing Ricky and gliding toward the entrance.

A large human security guard stopped them. Several synthetic guards flanked the man, each stuck in a "waiting" pose as if lifted from a video game.

"It's late," the Guard said. "I'm not sure we can let anyone else in."

Papi's butt cheeks tightened.

"I'm sorry," Papi replied, his mind cycling through plans. "But, uh...my boy...he's very sick. And it took him a while to get ready. He has...a brain...disorder."

"A brain disorder?" asked the guard.

"Yes, it's terrible," replied Papi.

Ricky closed his eyes and groaned like a zombie. He was a terrible actor.

"Uh...Fine," the Guard said reluctantly.

Ricky fumbled with his phone, then displayed a barcode for entry. The Guard scanned it, and Papi tensed, his butt swelling. If the guard asked for ID, he would know they were X-ed, and the game was over. There was a strange screeching sound, and the Guard looked up from his investigation. The scruffy men droned away on their makeshift drums, howling at the moon.

"I saw those people talking to you," the Guard said sternly. "Do you know them?"

Papi wasn't sure what the correct answer was. "No," he shakily replied, "I don't know those people."

The guard studied Papi's eyes and broke into a smile. "Glad to hear it," he said. "They're a little fucking weird, right? IDs, please."

Papi's eyes widened. *Not their IDs.* Little Ricky began babbling nervously, trying to stall. Papi put his arm around the boy to prevent him from short-circuiting.

"I'm sorry," Papi said, an idea forming, "But those words…they trigger me."

"What?" asked the guard.

"Those people over there are not 'fucking weird,'" said Papi. "They are fans of Joey Paul and should not be denigrated. You could get in trouble for that sort of speech."

Little Ricky looked at Papi, a mix of confusion and appreciation. This was either very dumb or genius.

The guard went pale and shrunk inside his mammoth frame. "Please lower your voice," he said. "I didn't mean to offend you."

"Words matter," Little Ricky said, relishing the moment.

"I know," said the guard, and quickly escorted them inside without checking IDs. "There's only fifteen minutes left until the party's over. So make it count."

Papi and Little Ricky entered Joey Paul's penthouse apartment and found a dozen ultra-platinum fans conversing over cocktails. They all hovered around the famous influencer, who was seated, cross-legged on the floor, and wearing a VR helmet. Assistants dressed in black swarmed around him, offering sips of water.

"Alright, we don't have much time," whispered Papi. "You make contact with that kid, and I'll find a bathroom so I can get this vial of Formula Two out of my ass."

Ricky nodded, relieved to no longer hear about Papi's undercarriage. He walked toward the buzzing crowd, and they all glanced up to see if Ricky was famous. They returned to their conversations, momentarily bummed that he wasn't. Ricky inched closer to Joey Paul, observing him like a wild animal. Sweat beaded across the top of the young influencer's VR headset, and his lips were dry.

"Water," his lips said. "Water."

An assistant swung in and replenished him.

"So, that's our savior?" whispered Papi, returning from the bathroom. "That helmet looks pretty lame, right?"

"No," Ricky said. "It's cool."

Papi noticed several pixelated LCD screens mounted on the wall as if it were an art museum. He couldn't help inching closer to study them. Black, red, and blue swirled into a digital mess, pixelated and smeared.

"I thought this kid was loaded," he whispered to Little Ricky. "He can't afford a real painting?"

"That's a non-fungible token," Ricky replied. "Joey may not own the original painting since it's at a museum, but he owns its digital spirit."

"I don't get it," Papi said, squinting at the swirly mess. "Can't anyone just take a bad digital photo of a painting?"

"Sure," said Ricky. "But you wouldn't own the true representation of the painting."

"This is beyond my pay grade," Papi muttered. "Let's go talk to this kid."

"Sirs," interrupted a server, "Would you like a cocktail?"

Papi studied the drinks on his serving tray. "Are these real cocktails?" he asked. "Or a digital representation of one?"

The server gave a loathsome smile.

Papi and Ricky grabbed a cocktail and moved closer to Joey Paul.

"It's go time," Ricky whispered.

An assistant instantly grabbed them. "Please," she said. "Six feet away from Mr. Paul at all times."

"Sorry," Papi replied. "Could we get a word with him? I know there's not much time left."

The assistant stared through Papi and explained that Mr. Paul was in the middle of a live video stream.

"Madone!" said Papi, annoyed. "Is he almost done?"

Ricky pulled the Italian leader aside. "You need to relax," he whispered.

"Why?" asked Papi, "I didn't stick a tube up my ass and walk ten city blocks for this douchebag to play video games!"

"He's not playing video games," Ricky explained. "He's watching others and talking about *them* playing video games."

"I don't get this world!" Papi yelped.

A frazzled middle-aged couple bumped into them, looked down, and muttered an apology. They scattered down a hallway like hermit crabs, miserable, hunched over, and scared.

"Who are those people?" asked Papi.

Ricky tried to get eyes on them but only caught a glimpse of their haggard frames. He looked up something on his phone and whispered. "I think that's Joey Paul's parents."

"They look like hostages," replied Papi.

"Well, if the stories are true. They sort of are," Little Ricky said. "Apparently, they didn't buy him a Playstation thirty-seven for Christmas one year. So, when he got rich, he made them work for him as revenge."

"Jesus," said Papi. "I dunno if I like this kid."

Three assistants lifted Joey to his feet, and a hushed chatter filled the air. His VR helmet slid off, slick with sweat, revealing a seventeen-year-old boy with blue eyes and brown hair. A crowd formed around him, and his assistants barked at everyone to keep their distance. Joey smiled wearily and asked his crew if anyone had his "break shake." They were all dumbfounded.

"No one has my break shake?" Joey asked. "I need my protein blast after a video game walkthrough THAT intense! I was talking about people playing video games for a very long time!"

The assistants didn't know what to do. Panic lit up their weary bodies.

"I have a break shake for you," said Papi.

The assistants turned toward him, eyes filled with daggers.

Joey had a confused smirk scribbled across his face. "How's that?" he replied.

Papi smiled and jostled a cocktail. "There's only one break shake I know of."

Joey seemed weirded out by Papi, and Little Ricky shrank with embarrassment. "I'm sorry, Mr. Paul," Ricky said. "That's my dad... He's a real cornball, but he means well."

Papi was offended.

"It's cool, bro," replied Joey. "Actually, I wouldn't mind a cocktail. As long as no one narcs on me!"

"No one will narc," said Papi, handing him a drink. "I know the party's about to end, but could we talk to you for a minute?"

Joey took a sip and sighed. "Dudes, I'm pooped," he said, "honestly, I hoped we could end this party a little early."

Little Ricky's eyes widened in fear. There was no way they would leave without talking to him, without getting him to broadcast what was inside Formula Two.

"But we have a guaranteed five-minute meet and greet," Ricky said. "I know we got here late, but still."

Joey rolled his eyes. "Fine, let's do this," he said, sucking down his cocktail. "What do you want me to sign?"

Little Ricky was annoyed. "We're not here for an autograph," he said. "We have a...personal story to share with you."

Papi could feel the assistants' eyeballs all over them. "Could we go somewhere private to talk?" he asked.

Joey noticed his fans staring and pulled Papi and Ricky aside. "I need to change outfits for my after-hours bonus stream," he whispered. "Why don't we talk in my room? Five minutes, though, okay?"

They nodded, trying to play it cool, but they wanted to burst with excitement. The assistants told the rest of the crowd that the party was over, and the well-heeled subscribers reluctantly slunk away.

Papi and Little Ricky glided along, Joey Paul leading them down a long hallway to his darkened room. Papi clutched the vial of the mystery ingredient, and a new feeling emerged, one he hadn't felt in years. It was hope.

Forty-One

Joey Paul may have lived in one of America's most luxurious apartment complexes, but his bedroom was a pigsty. Half-eaten take-out bits, crumpled-up clothes, and video equipment were strewn on the floor. The influencer entered his lair to find his parents lying in bed, typing furiously on their laptops.

"Why are you guys in my room?" he asked.

"You said you didn't want us around the party," his mother replied. "That we embarrass you."

"That doesn't mean you can hang out in my room!" shouted Joey, pointing to the door as if they were dogs that shat the carpet.

His father parted his lips, about to speak, when Joey's eyes glowed with rage. He left quietly with his wife.

Papi raised an eyebrow at Little Ricky.

"Don't feel sorry for them," Joey said. "They know what they did and are now paying for it. Anyways, tell me your story while I change. You got five minutes, like I said."

"We want to talk to you about Energoo Formula Two," Papi said anxiously.

Joey sighed. "You guys aren't marketing dudes, are you?" he asked. "Cause I'm not interested in being a brand ambassador. I'm doing too many of those already." He pointed to a cereal box on his dresser, which depicted him floating in a giant bowl of cinnamon squares.

"We're not marketing guys," Ricky assured him. "We're..." he searched for the words, "*truth-tellers* like yourself. We have some important information to disclose."

"Do I need my lawyer?" Joey asked. "You're talking goofy."

"No...no need for a lawyer," Papi interjected. "We want to talk about the explosions. We know why people are exploding."

"Ugh," Joey replied. "Explosions have gotten so political these days. I rather not talk about it. Besides..." he said, inching closer, "I don't really drink Energoo."

"Really?" Ricky asked, surprised. "I thought everyone drinks it?"

Joey seemed concerned. "Eh, I shouldn't talk about it," he said, putting on a navy polo. "I shouldn't talk about *anything* without wearing this." He picked up a shiny metallic helmet and flicked its switch.

"Oh wow," said Ricky, gobsmacked, "You got the Nexus upgrade?"

Joey smiled. "Of course I did."

They chatted for a while, and Papi couldn't understand a word of their tech jargon. It was like two aliens speaking. He smiled and nodded, as one does in a foreign land. But, eventually, he wanted to be looped in.

"Oh, the Nexus upgrade," Ricky explained, "is a chip you can install onto your headset that filters your thoughts. It uses machine learning to do it."

"Hey! It doesn't filter my thoughts!" replied Joey, offended. "I'm still one hundred percent Joey Paul: The truth sayer!"

"Sorry," Ricky apologized. "The new chip prevents you from saying certain thoughts aloud."

"Madone," said Papi. "That would have helped my marriage."

"I don't use it all the time," Joey said, wanting to clear the air. "I only use corporate mode when I'm on camera. It prevents me from saying anything controversial. Stuff that might get me in trouble with a sponsor or X-ed."

The mere mention of getting X-ed caused the room to quiet, and Joey seemed to drift away, focusing on his livestream ahead.

"So, how does that mode work?" Papi asked, growing desperate. He needed to keep the boy talking, soften him up for their big request.

"It's essentially a loopback machine," Joey replied. "Instead of my brain signaling to my mouth to say something aloud, it reroutes those thoughts back into my brain."

"Does your brain ever get tired of all that looping?" asked Papi.

"Sometimes I'll get a headache," Joey admitted. "But it's better than getting X-ed! Speaking of," he slid on his helmet, "I have to be on cam again in two minutes."

Time was running out. They had to quit bullshitting and get to the point. Papi held out his clenched hand. Inside was the vial. He was ready to flick his fingers open and reveal it. But Ricky shushed him.

"What?" asked Papi.

Ricky turned to Joey. "What we're about to tell you needs your unfiltered thoughts. You can't wear the helmet. You can't be in corporate mode."

Joey drained his cocktail, annoyed. "I'm not a corporate drone, you know," he muttered.

"Prove it," Ricky replied.

Joey took a breath and slid off his helmet. Papi instantly unclenched his fist, and the tiny green vial glistened in the darkened room.

"We've found out what's making people who drink Formula Two explode," Papi said. "It's an unlisted mystery ingredient we've isolated in this vial. When enough of this stuff is mixed into someone's bloodstream, they explode."

"What the fuck?" said Joey. "How is that legal?"

"I know!" Ricky said, excited. He and Papi spoke over each other, trying to explain their predicament, when an assistant popped her head in, "Livestream is about to start," she said.

Joey seemed ready to leave and join the livestream, and Papi was pissed. How could he talk about fucking video games at a time like this?

"If people keep drinking this stuff, deaths will be worse than the plague," Little Ricky pleaded. "We need your help. We need your platform to tell everyone."

Joey's helmet rumbled on, and his eyes rolled up into his head.

"Only addicts and degenerates are exploding," said Joey. His speech was measured and smooth. He was in corporate mode. "Honest, hard-working Americans have no reason to worry. I trust that most folks will read the label and won't drink enough to explode."

Ricky was heartbroken. How could his secret idol wimp out like this? Wasn't he the truth-sayer? Joey excused himself from the room, but Ricky rushed him.

"Your whole brand is about 'telling it like it is'!" Ricky shouted, "And you're giving us this corporate nonspeak! You're full of shit, man!"

Joey remained calm. "I will always be the truth-sayer. But your exclusive members-only meet and greet time is over."

Little Ricky's eyes filled with tears. Papi was livid. He hated to see Ricky upset, especially at the hands of this spoiled rich kid with questionable art-collecting habits. Without thinking, Papi grabbed Joey Paul's helmet and ripped it off. The boy shouted in horror as if someone had torn off his skin.

"You need to go on cam without that helmet and tell people what's happening!" Papi demanded.

Joey was on the floor, wrenching in pain. The sudden psychic break from the helmet was alarming. More assistants flooded into the room, ready to call security.

Little Ricky locked eyes with Joey Paul, and he went for broke. "You used to be my idol, man."

His assistants picked him up and asked if they should call security. Joey steadied himself, looking woozy. "No," he said. "Everything is fine. Just let my fans know the feed will start a few minutes late. I still need to talk with these two."

The assistants weren't sure what to do.

"You can go," Joey said.

They dispersed, and Joey turned to Ricky. "Listen," he whispered. "My uncle exploded the other day. But my cousins didn't believe it. They think it was all done with computers. They tried to get me to go on camera and say it was all a hoax. But I didn't want to get into politics."

"This isn't politics," argued Little Ricky. "This is a public health issue."

A dark cloud fell over Joey's face. "They still think my uncle is alive somewhere," he said. "They were shipped his body, and it was just a pile of green goop."

"That's why you need to do something," Ricky said. "Get on your feed and tell the world the truth. Atlas Wake is poisoning us."

Joey stared at his messy bed, hoping the lumpy pillows would advise him. He took a deep breath. "Okay," he said. "I'll do it."

Ricky smiled and handed him a folded piece of paper - a written statement to read to his fans. Joey read it over and swelled with pride.

"Thank you for this opportunity," he said to Little Ricky.

Ricky beamed. Across the room, Papi couldn't help taking a better look at the helmet on the floor. He picked it up and fiddled with its buttons, wanting to know how it worked. Suddenly, the helmet latched onto his skull.

"Improper user," the helmet croaked.

Ricky's eyes widened. What the hell was Papi doing? They were inches from mission accomplished! Ricky tried to rip the helmet off him, but it was stuck. The helmet squealed, causing everyone to cover their ears.

"Helmet compromised," it said, latching on tighter. "Improper user has been X-ed!"

"You're X-ed?" Joey shuddered, "how the fuck did you get in here?"

"I can explain!" Papi said, his eyes rolling back. He tried moving his lips, but no words came out.

Joey hyperventilated and stumbled toward his desk, which was covered with bags of chips. Papi's eyes rolled higher, and he stumbled around like a zombie. Joey located a red button on his desk, and Ricky blocked him from pressing it.

"I'm X-ed, too," Ricky said.

"Are you fucking serious?" said Joey.

He struggled and tried to press the button, but Ricky held him back.

"It was for something I posted on social media!" Ricky squeaked out. "It was something negative about Energoo Formula One. Atlas Wake X-ed me for not liking their product! We need *the truth-sayer* to expose them before it's too late! Before more people die!"

"Agh," Joey shouted, pushing Ricky to the floor. "You guys are going to fuck up my brand!" he yelped and pressed the red button. "Security!"

A large human guard and two synthetics entered.

"Get these two out of here!" Joey shrieked. "They've been X-ed! They're going to fuck up my brand!"

"No one fucks up our sman's brand," said the human guard. "Not no one."

He pointed, and the synthetic guards skittered forward, ready to pin the intruders down. Ricky noticed an open window and grabbed Papi, who was still dazed by the helmet.

"Stop!" yelled the guard.

Ricky pulled Papi onto the window sill and peered below. It would be a long fall to their gruesome demise. He took a deep breath and flung themselves out.

The synthetics were confused by the maneuver and looked back to the human guard, who tried to lift Joey Paul to his feet. The boy was inconsolable, balled up on the floor, and crying.

"My brand!" he wailed, rocking back and forth. "My brand!"

Forty-Two

It was cold outside Joey Paul's apartment complex, and Barry rubbed his hands for warmth. Lauren paced, nervous for their comrades inside. The scruffy men cult noticed them loitering, and Barry ignored their gaze, hoping Papi and Ricky would show up soon.

A large van skidded to a stop across the street. Government officials with hazmat suits climbed out. Their movements were slow and stilted, their shadows creeping along the misty sidewalks. There was a small explosion, and Barry and Lauren reeled to find a homeless man slumped over in a nearby alleyway. His body half-exploded from Energoo. More explosions, humans combusting like bottle rockets. The Hazmat figures plodded over to each puddle of human remains and pulled out a handheld device to scan them.

"What is going on?" Barry whispered.

A massive silver truck pulled up next to the van, and officials quickly unspooled a long hose from the truck. They vacuumed up the green goo, and the truck gurgled as human remains passed through its metallic belly. More people exploded, and the scruffy men cult finally fled. The thick black sky, steaming goo, and strange vacuums proved too apocalyptic for even the biggest Joey Paul fan. Another man exploded, and hot green goo flung onto Barry's forearm.

"Agh!" he cried, leaping back, arm singed.

There was a loud clang in the distance. Two figures brushed themselves off from a fire escape, and ran toward them. Lauren tried to puff herself up for a confrontation.

"We gotta get outta here!" yelled one of the figures.

It was Papi John and Little Ricky, Papi still wearing Joey Paul's helmet. They had landed on a fire escape and were now running toward them.

"What's on your head?" asked Barry.

Papi just looked at him dumbfounded, his eyes spinning like a top.

"He's still in corporate mode," Little Ricky yelped. "Let's move!"

The crew hurried toward the closest sewer grate, and Papi's helmet beeped out of control. Barry and Lauren lifted the grate and peered into the darkness. Barry wondered what had transpired in Joey's apartment. Whatever it was didn't seem promising, and he became depressed. Would they be heading back underground forever?

"Are you Rocco J. Papa? AKA 'Papi John'?" asked a man, his words sailing through the crisp night air.

Little Ricky motioned for everyone to get underground, not to answer the man's question. But Papi's helmet urged him to swing around.

"I am Rocco J. Papa, AKA Papi John," he said, slow and zombie-like.

The man asking the question wore a hazmat suit and held a large industrial vacuum. He was very tall, his face shrouded by a dark shield.

Barry grabbed Papi and pushed him toward the grate. But, several other officers surrounded them. The streets were quiet. Everyone had fled or exploded. All they could hear was the officer's respirator taking in clean breaths. One man slowly pointed to Papi's head. Barry took it as a sign they were mad about the helmet. Perhaps Papi had stolen it?

"If you want this helmet, it's all yours," said Barry.

"We don't care about the helmet," said the tall officer. He flashed a handheld device across Papi's face and swept it across the others like a magic wand. The device let out an ear-piercing shriek.

"They've all been X-ed," he said.

"That's right," Papi replied, his lips betraying him. "We have all been X-ed and should be properly dealt with."

"Agh!" Little Ricky screamed, banging the side of Papi's helmet to reveal a stripe of small buttons on its inside. He pressed several key combinations, and the helmet suddenly detached and hit the pavement with a thud. But it was too late. Handcuffs clicked on all their wrists. Barry, Ricky, and Lauren struggled against them, but it was hopeless. Papi looked around as if just waking up from a coma.

"What happened?" he said, peering at the shackles on his wrists.

Before anyone could answer, they were pushed into the back of a large white van. The vehicle rumbled alive and sputtered off.

The crew were chained together in the back, a privacy glass separating them from their government captors. Explosions rattled around the van. A warzone. They were lucky not to be killed on sight, but who knew what awaited them at the federal X facility? They held each other tight, exploding humans echoing in the distance.

Papi's memory was dizzy from the helmet, but they could see him slowly putting the pieces together. There were no more places left to hide, no more plans, no more hope. Their ultimate nightmare was made real. These were end times.

Forty-Three

The shareholder meeting had disturbed Geena, and she was up all night, pacing and drinking, wrestling with her new role at the company. At four in the morning, she finally fell asleep. But, two minutes after her eyes closed, her nightstand rattled. She sighed and picked up her buzzing phone. It was Meryl.

He apologized for the late-night call and told her she needed to wake up. Make a pot of Energoo, and get dressed. Many things would be coming at her in the next twenty-four hours, and she needed to be in the office early and ready.

"You are my most trusted colleague," he said. "And I care about you. You know that, right?"

Geena wasn't sure why Meryl was acting so serious and sentimental. She wanted to know what was going on. What was "coming at her in the next twenty-four hours," but Meryl dodged her questioning and acted cryptic and weird. He began speaking about his father, the first time he'd ever mentioned the man to her. He mumbled for several minutes. All she could make out was "company man" and "Bell Atlantic." The rest seemed like incoherent mutterings of an elderly person.

"Please remember as we move into the next phase," Meryl said, his voice slowly coming into focus. "That I'll always have a seat for you at the table."

There was a pause, and Geena filled the silence with "Okay."

Meryl sputtered. He seemed like he wanted more from Geena. But she had no idea what he was saying. Just kept replying, "Okay," and hung up.

She brewed a pot of Energoo as instructed and let the energy boost flood her synapses. Meryl's words rattled around her brain. Even if incoherent, everything he said felt imminent and ominous, a dark storm cloud on the horizon. She wondered if it was all a bad dream. She pinched herself but didn't wake up.

Forty-Four

Papi sat in the back of the van, nursing a headache. The Brotherhood was frightened, and he wanted to console them, but the helmet had rattled his brain. The van slowed, and Papi noticed the sunrise peeking through the back window. A sliver of light fell upon his head, and his eyes became misty. Faint words poured out of his mouth, desperate and searching. The others weren't sure what to make of it.

"What are you saying?" Little Ricky asked.

"I'm praying," Papi replied, closing his eyes. "I need to get right with God...But, mostly, I want to apologize to the Mexicans."

Lauren looked at Papi, confused. His eyes were closed, so he didn't notice. The Mexican comment lingered in the air.

"You don't need to apologize to the Mexicans," Little Ricky said.

"What are you guys talking about?" Barry asked.

Papi continued praying to himself, eyes shut.

"We don't need to get into it," said Little Ricky.

Barry looked out the back window. There was a traffic jam. "I think we're going to be here awhile," said Barry. "I'd like to hear why Papi believes he needs to apologize to 'the Mexicans.'"

Little Ricky let out a sigh, and Papi opened his eyes. He told them it wasn't important to rehash the story. What was important now was asking for forgiveness. He wasn't religious but hoped his prayers would be answered or at least heard. The van lurched to a stop, and Lauren fell, smacking into Papi. She was nervous about what awaited them. She needed a distraction, needed their leader to tell them a damn story.

"Please tell us," she insisted.

"Okay," Papi nodded and took a breath. Ricky rolled his eyes.

"I had a pizzeria, as you know," he started. "It was very successful, and I dreamt of expanding it. So, one night, my staff, who were all Mexican, were drinking and having a good time with me. I asked what the name of my next pizza chain should be. Since my last name is Papa, they joked I should name it 'the other Papa Johns'."

"I love Papa John's pizza," interrupted Barry. "Even if it is a big chain!"

Lauren gave him the evil eye.

"Anyways," Papi John continued, "I had a lot of bourbon that night. I was really feeling no pain. And I suggested we call my new franchise 'Papi John' to salute my staff, my Mexican brothers."

"Ugh," Little Ricky interrupted.

"Let me finish," Papi said. "Anyways, everyone laughed at how stupid I was, and no one took offense. And that was that. The next day, the authorities showed up. I was informed that someone on my staff *was* offended. To them, saying Papi was a bridge too far. I was culturally appropriating."

"That's bullshit, and you know it," exploded Little Ricky. "You want to believe that, but we know why you were X-ed."

"It was because I was insensitive to the Mexican people," Papi replied flatly.

"No, it's not," said Ricky. "It was because you refused to sell Energoo in your pizza parlor. You hated the taste! You always preferred soda!"

The van went quiet. People exploded faintly in the distance.

"I do prefer soda," Papi said, deflating.

"Here's what really happened," Little Ricky said, turning to Barry and Lauren. "Atlas Wake knew about his soda preference and tried to find a disgruntled employee to pay off, to create a problem. But, you know what happened?"

Barry and Lauren shook their heads.

"They couldn't *find* any disgruntled employees because everyone loved working for Papi!" he continued. "Days before the authorities raided, Papi hired a new dishwasher. Atlas Wake *planted* the dishwasher. The guy only took the job to set up this fraudulent complaint. No one was actually offended by his comments."

Barry and Lauren looked over to the Italian leader. Despite their bodies casting a long shadow on the man, they could tell he had tears in his eyes. If Papi knew Barry and Lauren any better, he probably would have told them how much that pizza business meant to him. How he craved a family, having none of his own. How those Mexican men truly were brothers to him.

Angry protesters crowded the van. Little Ricky noticed they were waving anti-Energoo signs. "Whoa," he said. "Are people *actually* standing up to Atlas Wake?"

The news encouraged Barry and Lauren, but Papi remained in the shadows, sniffling his tears away. "I'm glad people are protesting," he said, "but there will be just as many people, if not more, counter-protesting. Atlas Wake is too strong."

"You've been in the Brotherhood of the Resigned too long," said Ricky. "Maybe it's time we change our name. Take 'resigned' out of the title, at least."

"No," Papi blurted. The headache that consumed his brain was slipping away. He studied the lines on his hands. "Resignation can be a good thing."

"How's that?" replied Little Ricky. "How can resignation be a good thing anymore? It hasn't worked for us."

Papi sat back and stared at the ceiling, a dreamy look in his eyes. "I didn't get a chance to visit Italy till late in life," he said. "And when I got there, I was shocked. Everyone acted like an asshole. The car rental guy, the ladies at the hotel front desk, the waiters. 'Customer service' is not a word that exists in Italian."

"What does this have to do with anything?" Little Ricky asked.

"Well, on day three of the trip, I realized these people weren't assholes," continued Papi. "They just had nothing to prove anymore. They were already part of a great empire. It fell, and they were over it. They were free."

The angry protesters peered into the stopped van, trying to eye who was inside.

"Here in America," Papi said. "Everyone is in denial. No one realizes our empire is sinking. Instead of resigning like the Italians, we double down and get out our knives."

Barry couldn't believe what Papi was saying. He looked to Lauren, who nodded in agreement.

"You believe this too?" Barry asked.

"I'm starting to see it that way," Lauren replied.

"American corporations have driven most of us into poverty." Papi continued. "Artificial intelligence and automation may have been attractive to folks like you, Barry. Detached from reality CEO-types. But those were real jobs for the rest of us. If you haven't noticed, the streets are filled with homeless people and robots."

Barry wanted to argue with him, argue for *his* American Dream. But staring at his two X-ed brothers (and sister), he couldn't. His heart had slipped into the sea.

"I don't relate to Americans anymore," Papi said, his voice barely registering, "I relate to the Italians. *The resigned.*"

The van's engine kicked on, and there was a loud crunch. A man screamed in agony.

"They ran over someone," Lauren said, paralyzed with fear.

The Brotherhood banged the walls and yelled at their captors for an explanation. The driver shouted back, but it was muffled and unintelligible due to his hazmat suit. The van picked up speed as the Brotherhood peered out the back window, noticing several crumbled dead bodies on the street, protestors swarming.

Several cars behind the Brotherhood sat a large stretch limo, Geena Jackson alone in the backseat. She had seen the van run over the protestors and wanted to scream in horror. She put her hands in her pockets, only to discover the plastic trophy boobs were still inside. She fingered them nervously, wanting to vomit, panic swirling around. She watched the van pull up to the Atlas Wake offices and wondered who was inside.

Several hundred protestors surrounded the Atlas Wake building. And surrounding them were counter-protestors. It was easy to differentiate the two. One expressed anger against Atlas Wake and its corporate disregard for consumers, while the others drank cans of Energoo and shouted about personal liberties. Every few minutes, one of the counter-protestors would explode. The proceedings would pause as everyone ran for cover. After a moment, the two groups would fill the streets again, shouting at each other like crazed animals.

Papi sat in the van, watching an angry middle-aged couple clutching their two young kids. The children held protest signs and drank cans of Formula Two, the enraged father encouraging every sip. The two kids exploded, and before the parents could react, they exploded, too. Their green, gooey remains were so acidic that they began eroding a nearby metal trash can. No one seemed to notice, or at most, viewed it as a minor inconvenience.

"Where did we go wrong?" Papi asked quietly. "Why are people still drinking this stuff?"

The van doors opened, and the Brotherhood was pushed out. Papi squinted at the new dawn, the sunlight cutting like a knife. How could the morning mist feel so ominous, so heartbreaking? He watched protestors and counter-protestors swinging fists. Green goo on their tattered clothes, scarring their skin. The bitter, acidic fight, the endless culture war.

Forty-Five

Geena entered the vast lobby of Atlas Wake at five in the morning. A synthetic security guard scanned her ID, and she wandered the entrance, which was now a ghost town. A lone janitor worked in the corner, clutching a mop, eyes fixated on the floor. His mop was covered in green goo, and he scrubbed hard, sweat dotting his forehead. He noticed Geena staring and wiped his brow.

"Yeah," he said, "People are exploding all the time now."

He lowered his head and got back to work. Geena was unnerved. Watching exploding people on the news or from the comfort of her limo was one thing. But, now, human goo violated her place of work.

"Geena!" a voice cried. "I thought it was you!"

Mitch barreled out of a janitor's closet. His glued-together face appeared normal, but his eyes were wild.

"What are you still doing here?" Geena asked, shocked.

"If I go home, I'll lose my job!" Mitch yelped. "As long as I'm in this building, I'm employed!"

Geena sighed. It was terrible to see the boy so lost and out of it. But what could she do?

The Janitor stopped scrubbing and narrowed his eyes. "This kid's starting to annoy me," he said. "And he's taking up too much room in my closet!"

Geena's phone vibrated. Meryl was calling. She excused herself, and Mitch watched, stunned.

"Geena!" he cried. "Don't leave me here all alone!"

She was gone.

Protesters screamed from outside. Mitch peered through the large lobby windows. The Brotherhood of the Resigned slowly walked up the Atlas Wake stairs, bound and gagged. Lauren led the way, dead-eyed, life drained from her body. Mitch cried out for her, but she never heard him.

Geena tried to compose herself in the hallway leading to Meryl's office. Mitch's descent into madness rattled her, but Meryl's cryptic phone call spooked her more. Closer to his office, the scent of pastries wafted by. It reminded her of a bakery her father took her to as a child. He always let her pick out what sugar cookies she wanted. He was good that way.

Meryl sat in his darkened office, surrounded by baguettes stacked on top of each other as if they were books in a library. Bread loaves not only lined the bookshelves but stuck out of every orifice in the room. Geena had never seen this many carbs in her life.

"Did I overdo it?" asked Meryl, wheeling his way out of the shadows. "With the bread and all?"

"It's quite a bit," she replied, noticing a hearty roll affixed to a lampshade.

"Things are changing, Geena," he whispered. "And we need to be prepared."

"With bread?" she asked.

"Well..." he trailed off, staring at the ceiling. "The Brotherhood of the Resigned has been apprehended," he said. "We plan to get as much information out of them as possible. Find out where the other chapters reside and get them too."

Geena was confused by his use of "we." There was a knock at the door, and the Janitor from downstairs peered inside. Meryl waved him in, and the man wheeled over a large titanium metal tank. It had a transparent lid atop it that exposed its contents—human green goo. Geena shrieked, and Meryl said nothing, didn't move. He waited for the Janitor to leave.

"Now, Geena," he said, "there's nothing to freak out about."

"Why did he bring *that* in here?" she asked, shaking.

Meryl stared into his most trusted colleague's eyes. "I told him to, Geena."

"Why?"

"It would be easier if I showed you," he replied. "But I need you to take a deep breath and remember you have a seat at the table."

"Seat at what table?" she asked.

Meryl's eyes glowed in the shadows. "We're entering a new stage," he said, wheeling over to a coat rack filled with whole wheat bagels. He grabbed a bagel and unscrewed the lid of the tank. He peered into the green goo, a mix of someone's son or daughter, employees who consumed too many cans of Energoo. The smell assaulted Geena's nose. She doubled over, trying not to vomit. Meryl gave her a nose plug.

"This helps," he said.

Tears welled in Geena's eyes. "What's going on?" she pleaded, wobbling to the door.

"Don't go!" Meryl said. "Please. This will make sense soon. I promise."

Sunlight filtered into the office, and Meryl's eyes no longer glowed. They were kind and soft, the way they'd always been. But she felt uneasy, and the room began to swirl. She gripped the doorknob, ready to escape.

"Please," Meryl said. "I just need you to grab some bread loaves and follow me."

The room stopped swirling, and Geena's plugged nostrils adjusted to the scent. She eventually grabbed some bread loaves from Meryl's desk. He smiled, pleased to see she would take a leap of faith with him. He wheeled over to the tank filled with green goo and used a thick metallic container to scoop some up. The container was heavy. "Solid titanium," he said.

They boarded the elevator in silence, Meryl's wheelchair loaded up with a baker's dozen of baguettes and several titanium containers of green human goo. They ascended to the top floor, and Geena was overwhelmed by an old memory—her first job interview with Meryl. The joy on his face. His determination to make Atlas Wake a success. "We have a chance to do *something*," he kept repeating. "We have a chance to get out from under before the whole thing turns to shit."

She wheeled the old man down the hallway and toward the conference room. A stench overwhelmed her, and she plunged the plug deeper into her nostrils. They entered the room, and Geena's body locked up, frozen, eyes unable to process. She stumbled, and Meryl tried to steady her, bread loaves tumbling off his wheelchair and onto the floor.

Sitting around the conference table were twelve human-sized insects—gooey, spindly creatures who smelled like rotting flesh. Tears streamed out of Geena's eyes. This was a waking nightmare, and her limbs went numb. She no longer felt in control of her body. Meryl rubbed her back, trying to keep her from fainting.

"I need you," he whispered.

She staggered around the room.

"I need you," he repeated.

"What?" she mumbled, clutching his wheelchair, trying to stay upright.

"I need you," Meryl said and pointed to the floor. "I need you to pick up those bread loaves."

Geena's brain had melted. An internal monologue no longer steered her. All she could do was listen and follow orders. She picked up the baguettes and handed them to Meryl like a robot, ensuring her eyes never made contact with the strange beings. Meryl smiled wearily and wheeled over to the creatures.

Geena gasped for air in the corner, trying to pull herself together, be a person again. She couldn't help glancing at the shareholders. They possessed long, awkward legs like a praying mantis, with the slick underbelly of a moray eel. Their arms were skinny and deformed, hands gnarled with disease. Their heads were a disfigured mass with rows of eyes like a spider. Instead of mouths, they had long, spindly flesh tubes that dripped saliva and goo. The creatures remained silent, staring, unblinking, at Meryl. Geena had to look away.

The old man placed a few sourdough loaves on the table and offered the shareholders some human goo from the heavy titanium containers. They replied with a low-pitched gurgle, each grabbing a piece of bread. They tried to tear the bread into smaller pieces, but their awkward limbs struggled. They were frustrated and barked at the bread, a bizarre mix of gurgle sounds and low bassy grunts. Meryl, the 123-year-old man, smiled, happy to rip their bread apart and aid someone else for a change.

The tallest creature studied the piece of sourdough in its disfigured paws. It slowly dragged the piece across the top of the titanium container, catching a thin layer of green human goo. Its fleshy tube mouth drooled out of control as it sucked up the gooey bread. It entered the creature's stomach and gurgled with delight, eyes blinking in ecstasy. The others saw their colleague's satisfaction and joined in, slurping and gurgling through the snacks Meryl provided.

Geena noticed human skin draped over their chairs as if they were jackets. These human hides must have been the shareholders' usual costume, a way to blend in. But now they felt comfortable showing their true selves. Why was that? Why was Geena now privy to the truth? Nausea overwhelmed her, and she covered her mouth.

"I'm sorry," she said, bile rising up her throat. "Excuse me."

Geena vanished from the room, but Meryl never noticed. He was too taken by the shareholders. Their appreciation for the meal he curated filled him with pleasure. It was a meal he had honed and prepared for years.

The long conference room table began to splinter. Green goo had splattered onto it, and its acidity dissolved the wood. Meryl smiled, noticing the metallic containers remained intact, fortified by titanium. It was one of the few metals strong enough to resist the acidic goo. The shareholders finished their meal and immediately started barking. Their bodies ached for more. *More. More. More.*

Meryl searched for Geena and finally realized he was alone in the room.

Forty-Six

Geena retched into a porcelain toilet bowl. She felt like she had died, and her life was flashing before her eyes. It was just a collection of career milestones. How sad. There was a knock at the door, and Meryl asked if he could come in. Geena obliged, and Meryl entered, sheepish, like a child whose hand had been caught in a cookie jar. They stared at each other, speechless for a while.

"Are you going to tear off your skin next?" she asked. "Are you one of them too?"

Meryl laughed. "No, I'm not like them. I'm one hundred percent human."

Geena stood up from the toilet and grabbed tissue paper to wipe her chin.

"The shareholders are our friends," Meryl continued. "We have a deal with them. Me and you, we're set for life. We never have to worry."

Meryl's voice seemed miles away. Geena's head throbbed, and the restroom lights burned her eyes. She dry-gulped a pain reliever and turned off the lights. She closed her eyes and curled into a ball on the floor.

"Are you okay?" asked Meryl, squinting in the darkness.

"I think I'm having a migraine," she whispered in pain, "Tell me what the *deal* is."

"The *deal?*" Meryl said, confused.

"You just said we have a *deal!*" she yelped. "So, what is it? For them to turn us into bread dip?"

Meryl sighed and wheeled away from her. "You could look at it like that," he said. "But, they don't need the bread. They prefer it, though, especially a nice crusty sourdough."

"I don't care about the bread part," she said between gritted teeth. "You lied to me. We put those bullshit labels on Formula Two, and you knew this stuff was dangerous."

Meryl could barely make her out in the dark, but he could see the outline of her body shaking, pissed. "I...did...know," he admitted.

"What exactly did the shareholders offer you in exchange?" she asked.

Meryl sunk into his wheelchair with disappointment. "We've worked so hard for this moment," he said desperately. "And the shareholders are going to give us the world in exchange. Don't you get it?"

Geena moaned on the tiled floor.

"How could you be mad?" Meryl asked.

"You...sold...out...the world," she said weakly.

"Well, if I didn't do it, some other asshole would!" Meryl exploded. "I worked for every Tom, Dick, and Harry in the book! And I never moved up! Never got a shot! I was broke for years. Lived in shithole after shithole. And when I finally started my own business, no one gave a shit! I was a fucking failure!"

Geena crawled over to the man, trying to get in a word, but he was too worked up.

"And then one night," he continued, "I was sitting in my God-awful little studio apartment. The pipes were leaking because it had just rained, and I saw this light. It was outside my window. These beings...they offered me a way out of this hell. Offered a way to get out from under. Offered a partnership! A seat at the table! It was their brilliance that got people hooked on Energoo! Their ingredients! Their craftsmanship! Not me! I'm just the human figurehead. Don't you see! *I'm so grateful for the opportunity!*"

Meryl's face was beet red, and his body trembled. This diatribe seemed to awaken a deep pain buried in his bones. Geena slowly sat up and walked over to the sink, where she found a bottle of pain reliever. She gulped several pills and let his words linger in her swollen brain. This man she had trusted for years was trying to justify selling out the human race because his career didn't work out. She knew things were dire, unemployment at astronomical levels. But, still. Meryl didn't have to do *that*. Right?

She caught his reflection in the mirror, and his eyes were moist and hopeful, desperate for her loyalty. But Geena couldn't give him the satisfaction.

Meryl wheeled over and massaged her back. "Geena," he said tenderly.

She removed his hand and moved to the other side of the restroom. She needed a moment to think.

Meryl was surprised she didn't delight in his rags-to-riches origin story. "I always thought it was a strong enough story to be in a Narvel movie," he laughed half-heartedly, trying to lighten the mood.

"Does the government know about this?" she asked, ignoring his attempt at levity. "Or the military? I mean, can't we fight these things?"

"Why fight the inevitable?" replied Meryl. "If I hadn't accepted their partnership, someone else would have. Maybe my next-door neighbor. Maybe one of yours. We could both be piles of goo on the street right now. But we're not. We're alive. We have a seat at the table."

Geena's forehead felt like it could split open. Meryl's words rattled around in her skull, only worsening the pain.

"I just," she stuttered, "What about the others?"

"*The others?*" Meryl replied. "You don't have a partner in this life, do you? Kids? Parents? Anything?"

He knew she didn't, and it made her feel small.

"Don't feel bad," he whispered. "I don't have anyone either." He wheeled closer. "We're just two lone wolves in this world, aren't we?"

She wanted to agree with him.

"Nothing will change for you," he said, touching her hand. "You didn't have anyone in the old world, and you won't have anyone in the new. Except me."

She wondered if he was right. She barely interacted with anyone else outside the company. She had no friends, no outside interests. Her parents were dead, and her food was delivered to her by gig econo-bots. It was just the job, always the job, a footsoldier to the corporation. Would it be *that* different for her once the shareholders took over? Was there any real downside for her in this new world order?

"The only thing that will change," Meryl said, "is your wealth. You will have access to only the best things on earth. And when I say earth, I mean *earth*. There will be no borders, no countries. We can travel freely, live like king and queen."

Geena had never traveled, never had the time with work. The pain reliever finally kicked in, and Meryl's vision for the future took shape in her mind. Without the job and responsibilities, she could become a human being with interests, hobbies, and places to travel.

"We're going to be just fine," Meryl said, nuzzling his head into her.

"Yeah," she replied, rubbing his back. "We're gonna be okay."

Meryl smiled, tears in his eyes. He looked up at Geena, who dwarfed him and found liquid in her eyes too.

"You don't have to worry anymore," he said weakly.

"Okay," she whispered, shoring up her nerves. "But what about everyone else?"

"Well," the old man said, holding her close. "Everyone else needs to worry."

Forty-Seven

The Brotherhood was confined to a small metallic room deep in the bowels of Atlas Wake. They were chained together and gagged, synthetic guards at the ready. Vats of Energoo gurgled just outside the door, and the room rumbled with a low vibration.

Barry frantically rubbed their chains together, hoping the friction would free them. The others shook their heads, embarrassed by his attempt. Barry knew their dismissive look well. It was the same look his ex-wife gave him, the same used by his business partners. He was *tired* of that look.

Dan stepped in the doorway, popping a Xanax from a prescription bottle. Barry struggled to take a swipe at him, but his chains yanked him back to the floor.

"What the hell are you doing, Barry?" Dan asked, annoyed.

Barry mumbled through his mouth gag, and Dan reluctantly removed it.

"Why are we at Atlas Wake?" Barry yelped. "I thought we were going to an X facility?"

Dan sighed. "I wish they threw you in an X facility. You think I want to be doing this?"

The others mumbled through their gags, and Dan scratched angrily at his neck. Their muttering reached a fever pitch, and Dan grunted in pain. He undid their gags.

"We happy now?" Dan said. "Everyone can talk."

They did, and all at once.

"Shut up," said Dan, annoyed. "Let me just cut to the chase. We need to know where all the other chapters of the Brotherhood are located."

Barry looked to Papi and Ricky, the only members who could answer this question. They remained tight-lipped and steely-eyed.

"Don't make me escalate this," Dan said. "You don't want this to escalate." The synthetic guard lifted its gun. Dan moved closer. "Tell me where they are."

"I'll tell you," Barry blurted out. "In exchange for our freedom."

The others gasped, and Papi stared daggers at him. But Barry didn't care. It was time to be a badass boss bitch once and for all.

"You will get no assurances," Dan slithered, his forehead dripping with sweat. The Xanax no longer had any effect on him. Even his strange trademark slang drifted away. He was a raw nerve.

"Fine. I don't know anything," Barry said. "I was lying anyways."

"What the fuck, Barry?" Papi whispered.

Dan flew into a blinding rage. He grabbed Papi by the throat and pinned him up against the wall. The others tried to push him off, but the synthetic guards were activated, and they quickly walled the Brotherhood off. Dan pushed his forearm into Papi's neck until his face turned blue. Papi thrashed against the wall, trying to breathe.

"We don't know where the rest of the Brotherhood lives!" Papi gulped. "No one talks to us. All the other factions think we're a joke."

Dan was shocked and accidentally loosened his grip. Papi slid to the floor, grasping at his throat. He sucked air desperately, panicked gasps turning into sobs.

Dan watched, stunned by the man's vulnerability. People never cried at Atlas Wake. Barely showed emotion. But here was Papi, crying his heart out. The synthetic guards crowded the Italian leader, ready to inflict more harm, but Dan had them stand down. He walked to the only chair in the room and slowly deflated into his seat.

"I don't know why *I* have to do this shit," he mumbled, scratching his face.

The Brotherhood was speechless. What the hell was he talking about? Dan continued scratching, growing agitated. "Why didn't Meryl get Geena to do this?" he asked his prisoners. "Why me? Is it because of what I am?"

"Are you upset because you're not CEO?" choked out Barry.

Dan sneered. "I know why I'm not," he said. "It's for the same reason. It's because of what I am."

Barry bit his lip. "And what are you?" he asked.

Dan scratched at his cheek, then attacked his forehead with fingernails. His skin loosened and swayed back and forth in time with his fingers. He kept scratching an itch that could never be relieved. His glasses fell off, and his skin began to tear.

"Oh my God," said Barry.

"Oh fuck off," croaked Dan. He scratched his forehead harder, eventually sending his skin to the floor. A gooey spider-like face peered beneath his human neck, gnarled in fake fleshy skin flaps. Barry shrieked. The others too, their cries echoing through the basement of Atlas Wake.

Dan's tiny, mucous-laced ear nubs flattened at the sound. Their screams irritated his sensitive system. "Shut up," he rasped. "Shut up, stop it with the noise." He hyperventilated, flailing his awkward fleshy limbs as he slinked out, grunting and gurgling, a slimy trail behind him.

Forty-Eight

Dan stood in the elevator, fully exposed for the first time in years. He tried pressing the button for the top floor, but the mucus dripping from his spindly finger nubs caused the elevator to malfunction. The doors opened to the ground level, and three security guards entered. Dan stared at them, a row of insect eyes. The one guard, a human, screamed and ran away, while the other two stepped on. They were synthetics and eager to please.

"Get me to the top floor," he told them.

The shareholders were excited to see Dan, but the sentiment quickly faded when they discovered he had no intel on the Brotherhood.

Dan swung his insect limbs in frustration. "I told you I didn't want to do this!" he said in a high-pitched shriek.

Geena recoiled in horror. She couldn't believe Dan wasn't human this whole time. She thought he was just another guy who failed upward. Turns out he wasn't even a guy.

The shareholders bellowed, upset.

"Dan," Meryl said. "You tried *everything*, and they still wouldn't talk?"

Dan was annoyed by the insinuation and clicked his slender tongue. "If you think I'm so bad at it, maybe you should send Geena down there." He sneered. "Maybe *she* should torture them."

Everyone looked at Geena, and her mouth went dry. She didn't want to torture anyone. She didn't want to be in this room anymore. Fuck. Fuck. Fuck.

"See!" Dan exclaimed. "Why don't you do it, Meryl? Show us what you're made of!"

The largest shareholder gurgled, mucus flying to the floor. Dan translated. "The shareholders agree with me."

Meryl looked at Geena. She was barely hanging on, ready to faint. "Fine," he said. "Bring them up."

Guards were dispatched, and Meryl punched a code into a metal safe under his desk. He pulled out a tray of large hypodermic needles, each filled with a neon green substance.

"Oh God," Geena said. "What is that?"

Meryl placed the tray of needles on his lap. "If you want a seat at the table," he whispered to her, an edge to his voice. "I suggest you shut up."

Dan's unblinking eyes were trained on the pair. "We're hungry," he said. "Get us more dip."

Meryl obliged, and the shareholders ate. Green goo sloshing and splattering everywhere. The conference room stunk like human excrement. Mouth flaps shuddered with pleasure. The shareholders no longer hid their lust for human goo. They ate like animals, limbs struggling to keep up. Geena had to excuse herself from the room.

The Brotherhood exited the elevator, chained and gagged, two synthetic guards pressed against them. They noticed Geena outside the conference room, hyperventilating. They tried to ask her questions, but their mouth gags muffled their voices. She just stared at them, hollowed out inside.

She opened the door to let them in, and the death stench wafted out. The Brotherhood felt the urge to vomit, but nothing materialized.

Dan and the shareholders were covered in goo. Their bodies appeared immune to the acidity, and none of them flinched when it dribbled down their slick, frog-like skin. Papi watched the horrific creatures slurp their final bits off the table. He gripped Little Ricky's shoulders, trying not to faint.

"We need to know where the rest of the Brotherhood chapters are," Meryl said, placing the tray of green hypodermic needles on his desk. "I don't want to kill you for these answers, but I am prepared to do so."

Barry sized up the needles. His heart beat a mile a minute.

Meryl signaled to the synthetic guards to remove their gags.

"I swear," Barry said. "We don't know anything."

"No more bullshit!" Meryl shouted, wheeling closer. "Where are the other chapters?"

Papi looked at the shackles on his wrists. "I told you before. We don't know."

"Bullshit!" Meryl screamed.

The conference room went quiet.

"I don't know what these things offered you," Lauren said, gesturing to the shareholders. "But there's an ocean of people outside who want answers. You can torture us, but you're still fucked."

The shareholders roared.

Meryl tried to reassure his colleagues. "It's not true," he muttered, "Simply not true."

Geena locked eyes with Lauren. "Maybe we should let them go," she said to Meryl. "They don't know anything. Besides, their days are numbered."

The shareholders erupted in anger. Meryl grabbed Geena's hand and squeezed it tight. His eyes willing her to shut up.

"You're not one of them, Geena. Are you?" asked Lauren. "You're human, right?"

Geena shuddered at the thought.

"Enough of this," said Dan, skittering forward. "It's time to make an example out of one of them. Let's do Barry first."

Meryl looked at the needles on his desk and grimaced.

"What's in them?" asked Geena.

Meryl didn't have the heart to answer, but Dan took pleasure in replying. "Each of those needles is filled with a highly concentrated form of Formula Two," he said. "Once it enters the bloodstream, the person will have ten seconds before they cease to exist."

Barry instantly fainted, collapsing onto Lauren, who clumsily held him up. Little Ricky pissed himself, scared, and Papi hugged him to his chest.

"Do it!" Dan shouted. "Now!"

Meryl struggled for an excuse. He didn't want to kill Barry. He always liked the guy. He wanted to tell him he was only fired because the shareholders pushed him. They were always watching his office remotely. Saw everything. Sure. Meryl was angry when Barry asked too many questions, but he also believed Barry was dumb. That he had no intentions of being a whistleblower. The shareholders didn't see it that way.

"What's the point of giving him a needle now that he's fainted?" Meryl asked.

Dan just pointed at the needles.

"Would you be open to...*other* forms of torture?" Meryl asked. "They can't tell us anything if they're dead."

The shareholders gurgled, and Dan argued with them. He turned to Meryl and reluctantly said, "They're open to it."

Meryl wheeled to a closet and returned with a long leather whip. His best one. Kangaroo hide. The most cherished in his collection. He patted the weapon in his palm.

"Don't make me whip you," he said. "I'll whip you good. Now tell me where the rest of the chapters are."

No one made a sound.

"I'll whip you good!" shouted Meryl.

"How could you do this?" Lauren burst. "How could you both sell out the human race?"

Geena looked upset. Meryl snapped his whip in anger.

"Enough!" he screamed.

He lashed Lauren's shoulder, and she cried out in pain. Barry regained consciousness just in time to take a blow across his face. The shareholders gurgled approvingly, their gooey mouth flaps dripping in anticipation of every impact.

Meryl slowed quickly. He was sputtering out, exhausted. Paused to catch his breath but never caught it. He needed a time-out. The shareholders turned their row of eyes toward Geena. It was her turn. This was her moment to prove loyalty to the corporation. If not, the shareholders might make her their next meal. Meryl placed the whip into her palm.

She struck Barry in the face, and his blood sprayed onto the beige conference room carpet. She came down hard on Lauren, and the shareholders vibrated with pleasure. She thrashed Papi. But froze at Little Ricky, his innocent eyes piercing her soul. She shrugged it off and whipped him. Blood poured from his cheek, and he wailed in agony. Geena gasped and dropped the whip.

Her hands drifted to her pockets, and she felt the plastic breasts inside. She thought about the hours she spent alone in a tiny office, trying to climb the ladder of Atlas Wake. The stupid, meaningless trophies that lined her wall.

"Again!" screamed Dan, saliva splashing from his tongue. "Again!"

Geena remembered what Meryl told her in the restroom—that nothing would change for her. Maybe he was right, and this made her profoundly sad. She clenched the plastic breasts in her pocket so hard they cracked.

"Pick up the whip!" shouted Dan.

Meryl stared into Geena's eyes and realized she had lost the plot. He tried desperately to pick up the whip and continue the torture himself, but his ancient fingers struggled. He was so close to the final act. For years, he doubted he would witness the shareholder's plan come to fruition, and he was determined to see it through, to be seated at the table of the new world order.

Geena calmly approached Meryl's desk and studied the green hypodermic needles. She grabbed one and turned to the Brotherhood.

"Yes," Dan slithered, excited. "Do it!"

Geena walked toward Barry.

"Oh God, no!" he cried.

She suddenly pivoted to Meryl, who lifted his hands and closed his eyes.

"Please," the old man pleaded.

Geena's eyes filled with tears. She stabbed herself in the shoulder and exploded. Green goo went everywhere, dissolving the Brotherhood's chains. Lauren stood up, shocked, and grabbed the others. They hightailed out of there.

Dan commanded Meryl to wheel after them, but the 123-year-old had lost the will. The old man was elsewhere. He stared out the windows and saw a city filled with the homeless, a city destroyed by automation and reckless capitalism. He was part of this great destruction and could no longer feel sorry for himself.

"Fifty years," he stuttered to no one. "My father worked for the Bell Atlantic company for fifty years. Got a pension and everything."

Dan stabbed Meryl in the neck with a needle, and the old man's eyes watered. The shareholders slowly closed in on him. In a few seconds, he would be their snack. The whole idea felt so absurd that Meryl couldn't help but laugh. It was a joyous laugh. A detached laugh. The laughter of a small boy, his father's son, the son of a company man. The last American dreamer.

A BRIEF INTERLUDE ON THE SHAREHOLDERS

The shareholder is a disgusting creature with sweaty mouth flaps, gnarled digits, and rows of multifaceted eyes. They are a wealthy race, perhaps the richest in the galaxy, but before they met Meryl, they were utterly bored.

They had conquered every inferior species in the galaxy, from Slapnoid to Argnot, and they did it by brute force thanks to an army of AI-powered insectoid robots. Yes. It was good to be shareholders, the kings and queens of the galaxy. However, their reliance on AI caused two problems.

A.) Art was dead. Or rather, handmade art was dead. Everything the shareholders consumed was AI-generated. A copy of a copy of a copy. At a certain point, the ruling class questioned this move to AI "art." They were no longer surprised by the content they consumed. And if the ruling class can't be adequately entertained, what's the point?

B.) The food sucked and was in short supply. Before their reign of terror, the shareholders enjoyed peasant labor. They produced fruits, vegetables, and meat. Items they could blend into smoothies, for they had no teeth. But, peasants needed to earn a living, even meager, and replacing them with AI-powered farm bots was much cheaper. Unfortunately, these robots had no spiritual connection to the land and overharvested, devastating the planet's ecosystem. That, coupled with several natural disasters, found the shareholders starving.

And so, they boarded their luxury spaceships and cruised the galaxy. Looking for sustenance, looking for entertainment, looking for *anything*. They passed planet after planet until they found one beautiful orb, gleaming blue and green: Earth. They were awestruck by the planet and might have teared up if capable of emotion. But, something got in the way of their ascent to Earth—a giant rocket ship.

To be precise, it was a rocket ship from the United States of America. One of many rockets sent into space by billionaire freedom-of-speech advocate Arliss Munk, another wealthy creature bored of his depleted home planet. Unlike the shareholders, Munk's rockets mostly exploded upon entry into space. And this particular launch was no different. But this time, it sent seven dead astronauts hurtling through the cosmos.

The shareholders viewed these spacemen with disdain from their luxury ships. These human bags of trash were in the way and needed to be disposed of quickly. Luckily, the shareholders' ship was equipped with a liquidator, a powerful ray gun capable of turning space debris into compact goop. But a curious thing happened after vacuuming and liquidating the human astronauts. And it's all thanks to a particularly bored shareholder whose name has no reasonable translation in English.

This bored shareholder was so desperate for food that he did the unimaginable. He consumed some of the liquidated astronauts. His eyes instantly lit up, his senses tingled and buzzed—humans tasted terrific. The others joined in and found that they, too, loved the taste of human goop. They wondered if all humans were this delicious.

Despite the strength of the shareholders' AI army, they were no match for Earth's massive size, which dwarfed every planet under their grip. They stared at the giant gleaming orb and sank with despair. If only they could figure out how to turn Earthlings into goo on a massive scale. They could sustain their appetites for generations. But how?

They arrived on Earth, disguised in AI-manufactured human skin suits, and their solution became clear in less than an hour. Sure, they couldn't take the planet by force, but there was a smarter strategy that played into human frailty. The shareholders needed to create FOMO, a fear of missing out. They could take over the entire world by creating something that harnessed this notion. All they needed was a lusty, addictive product...and a great marketing department.

The shareholders (still dressed in human skinsuits) traveled to Silicon Valley and raised vast sums of venture capitalist cash. They found the fundraising process easy. All they needed to do was prove that their new corporation wouldn't rely on costly human labor. Simple. Their entire production line would be manufactured with robots and their human staff would be small and mighty. Atlas Wake was born.

Atlas would go on to develop Energoo Formula One while sister companies sprung up in support. The shareholders knew that with enough corporate synergy, they could infiltrate American society on multiple levels and, eventually, the world. These shareholder-backed conglomerates ran the gamut from entertainment to government lobbying and community building. They ensured every Hollywood celebrity enjoyed Energoo on the red carpet and that famous athletes mixed the beverage into their heavily photographed water bottles.

But the shareholder's true genius stroke was their human staffing process. Yes, the Atlas Wake building was massive, but the number of humans occupying the building was small: just a handful of CEOS and assistants managing AI. All of the human workers had one common trait—they were aggrieved. They believed they were passed over and deserved more, and the shareholders exploited that fact. Meryl was their first target. The elderly man was bitter in the twilight of his years, hanging onto past failures. Not only did the shareholders offer life extension therapy, but they also made him head of the company. The rest of the small staff fell like dominoes. Geena, constantly passed over by less talented men, jumped at the opportunity. And, Barry, well, Barry ran out of places to fail upward. He was desperate for anything.

And so, this unholy alliance of aggrieved CEOS and extraterrestrial shareholders created one of the best-selling beverages ever: Energoo Formula One. The team was delighted by its success and bided their time to roll out Formula Two. The lethal dose. Shareholders believed humans would consume it without batting an eye. They were too hooked.

No human working at the company knew the contents of the new formula or the master plan; only Meryl shouldered that weight. He was distraught when Desean exploded prematurely, believing the incident might unravel their decades-long plan. But Meryl didn't need to worry. Planet Earth was way dumber than anyone anticipated.

Forty-Nine

The Brotherhood stumbled out of the elevator to find the Atlas Wake lobby empty. Security had fled, frightened by rumors of insectoid creatures on the top floor. Panic washed over the Brotherhood. What should they do now?

They argued over plans, but Barry lingered by the elevator. A dark cloud hovered over his head.

"I'm sorry," he interrupted.

"About what?" asked Lauren.

"That I didn't save the day back there." Barry's eyes welled with tears. "Every time I think I'm going to be a badass boss bitch...I..."

"Hey!" a voice yelled in the distance.

Doors swung open from a janitor's closet, and Mitch sprung out. "Is that really you?" he asked. Hand tools spilled out of the closet, and he tripped over them. Lauren helped him up.

She noticed his cheek had slid off his face, still attached by a lone thread of crazy glue. "Dude, are you okay?" she asked.

His eyes looped around like a Ferris wheel. "Everything's fine," he muttered.

There were a few booms outside. They peered out the windows to find protesters imploding at random. A guy filming with a selfie stick also exploded.

"We need to get out of here," Barry said.

Papi clapped his hands. "Ceto Isles. We should go to Ceto Isles."

"The place with all the rats?" asked Mitch.

"They've cleaned it up," explained Papi. "Not only is it remote enough to hide. But, it's also home to the largest chapter of the Brotherhood."

"So you *did* know where they were?" Barry smiled.

"Well, yeah. Barry. I told you this before."

"Right," Barry replied.

"How can I help?" Mitch asked desperately. "I've been cooped up in that closet for a long time, you guys."

Papi was hesitant to engage with Mitch, whose cheek finally detached and plopped to the floor.

"Oh God!" yelped Barry.

"I can explain," said Mitch.

"No need," replied Papi. "Time is of the essence. Do you have a car? If you can get us to the docks, I might have friends who can charter us a boat."

"I don't have a car," Mitch replied sadly. "But, wait, if you agree to bring me to this rat island, I can use my ID to hail us a taxi bot."

The Brotherhood smiled at each other. This was it. Their last great plan. Mitch took out his phone to hail a ride. The lobby doors burst open. A mob of angry protesters flooded in. The Brotherhood stood still, slowly taking in their wave of hostility. Could this uprising be capable of toppling the beings that resided on the top floor? Would humanity have a shot? Despite being encouraged by this unrest, the Brotherhood realized it was best to hide in the janitor's closet until their ride appeared.

They huddled inside the claustrophobic space, listening to the wave of protesters storming in. Panicked cries echoed. The shareholders had made their presence known. No longer burdened by human hides, they flailed through the lobby, snarling through long mouth flaps. Dan led the way, snacking on a bagel topped with human green goo. Mitch poked his head out to see what was going on and nearly fainted.

"Don't pass out on me," Lauren urged. "How close is the car?"

Mitch then did, in fact, faint, the phone toppling out of his hand and onto the floor. Lauren attended to him while Barry scooped up the phone.

"The car's already here," he said. "It's outside."

Little Ricky got to the car first and waited for the others, struggling with Mitch in their arms. The car beeped for identification, and they quickly rotated Mitch's comatose body so the vehicle could scan his eyeballs. The car dinged, and the doors opened to a taxi bot with a "Make Mine Narvel" bucket hat.

"Hell of a lot of congestion around this building," the taxi bot smiled. "Am I right?"

Barry disguised his voice and pitched it higher. "You're right," Barry squeaked. "And when you're right, you're right."

Lauren suppressed a laugh. His disguised voice sounded like a cartoon character. A fleshy limb flopped onto the windshield, and everyone screamed. It was Dan, flicking his tongue angrily.

"Well, I'm not one to overstay my welcome!" said the taxi bot cheerfully. "Buckle up!"

The car sped off, and Papi stared out the back window. He wondered why the shareholders had let them flee the conference room so easily. Was it really their lack of physical prowess? Or was there some other goal? A loud booming noise erupted through the sky, and he noticed a giant spaceship landing on the roof of Atlas Wake. At that moment, he realized the shareholders had bigger things on their minds.

Fifty

The rideshare vehicle was packed to the brim. Little Ricky sat in the passenger seat while the rest of the Brotherhood sat in the back, a passed-out Mitch laid across their laps. The town was in upheaval. Cars were on fire. Stores looted, windows smashed. Mobs of people flooded the streets, some protesting, some counter-protesting, and others just wanting *content* to post on social media. People exploded so often that it punctuated the silent car ride like a disco beat. They approached the docks anticipating anarchy, but everything seemed quiet and normal.

"Beautiful time for a swim, isn't it?" the taxi bot asked.

Papi agreed and used Mitch's phone to tip the robot.

"Ah, you're very generous," it said. "God bless you and your family. And see you at the cinemas this October for Metal Man 243!"

Papi shook Mitch awake.

"My face," the young man said, distraught. "What happened to my face?"

"We'll find you a new one," Lauren quipped. "Let's go."

They searched the ports for a while, the crisp, salty air invigorating them.

"Who are we looking for?" asked Barry.

"The Mexicans," Papi replied.

Lauren looked at him cross.

"They would be okay with me calling them that," explained Papi. "Because they are, in fact, Mexican."

Everyone nodded, not wanting to argue about semantics during the possible end of civilization. They spotted a large, pristine white yacht at the end of the dock. It could easily fit forty people and was the most beautiful boat Papi had ever seen.

"That's them!" Papi shouted joyfully.

"Wow, they're rich," said Lauren.

"Yeah. I guess they did well for themselves," Papi replied, rushing over. "Hola, mis amigos!"

On the ship's deck sat three Mexican men and their wives. They stared at Papi as if he were a mirage.

"My friends, can you help us?" asked Papi.

The men looked at each other and told their wives to retreat to the cabin. They inched closer to Papi and rubbed their eyes.

"Papi?" the eldest man asked, peering down from the bow. "Is that really you?"

Papi smiled and explained they needed a boat to get to Ceto Isles and that everyone should join. A national emergency was on the horizon, and they should flee the city immediately. The men asked for details, but Papi figured they wouldn't take him seriously if he mentioned the giant spaceship he had seen.

"I'm sorry," the eldest man said, "But we can't let an X-ed person on board."

Papi pleaded, but they wouldn't budge, and he began to cry. He apologized for his past transgressions. He never meant to offend anyone who worked for him. "I thought of you as my family," he sobbed. "My brothers from another mother."

The men were embarrassed for Papi and shushed his tears away. They explained that the three opened their own restaurant after he got X-ed. It became a massive success with multiple spin-off establishments. The truth was, he had nothing to apologize for. The collapse of his pizza business only inspired them to work for themselves.

"My friend," the eldest said, "We can't let you board our ship, but our neighbor has a boat. They haven't used it in years and likely wouldn't miss it."

He pointed to a rickety four-passenger fishing boat, and Papi couldn't hide his disappointment. The boat looked like it would sink under the weight of a single large dog.

"It's tiny," said the youngest man, "But like you once told us, 'you get what you get, and you don't get upset.'"

Papi was happy the young man remembered one of his cheesy sayings. He thought they had erased him from memory.

"We would never forget you," the man said.

There was a high-pitched whine, and everyone faced the city. Tiny spaceships headed toward them.

"Aye, Papi," said the eldest Mexican man. "Is this the danger you spoke of?"

"Si," replied Papi sadly.

The Mexican men quickly drew their anchor and pushed off to sea, waving goodbye and wishing them well. Papi looked at the tiny fishing boat and urged his crew to board. But, before they could reach the vessel, winds pushed them backward.

Above them was a tiny spaceship, its orbit kicking up winds so violent it threatened to rip off the rest of Mitch's face. The spacecraft settled onto the dock, and the breeze dissipated, instantly causing them to fall over.

The Brotherhood gripped the docks, frozen in fear. They eyed the spaceship door, waiting for the shareholders to flood out. But the ship just sat there. Ominous steel. The Brotherhood hurried off, trying to find weapons, but they could only procure wooden oars.

The spaceship door opened, and a hideous creature emerged. It was a thicker, squatter version of the conference room creatures. A working-class variant. It looked like someone had grabbed a share-holder by the head and pushed down. It still sported rows of eyes and a mucous-covered mouth flap, but its arms were more muscular. In its hands was a glowing laser sword, a weapon that resembled something from Star Force 185.

"Oh God," said Barry, afraid.

The creature slowly walked toward them, laser sword pulsating.

"What are we going to do?" cried Lauren.

Papi watched in horror as another muscular creature exited the ship, laser sword in hand.

"We gotta get to that boat," Papi said, inching backward.

They coalesced around Papi, ready to dart away, except Mitch, who stood resolute before the creatures.

"What are you doing, Mitch?" asked Lauren.

"Go on. Get out of here," he said, his face a goopy mess.

"What?"

Mitch slammed his wooden oar against a metal pole and shat-tered it, turning the boating instrument into a jagged bayonet. He faced the Brotherhood. His eyes were stone, lips askew. He seemed broken. Maybe it was an undisclosed gas leak in the janitor's closet that scrambled his brain. Or maybe he was just a young man without a purpose.

Lauren motioned toward him, but Papi held her back. They finally ran for it. The squatty creatures roared angrily and plodded toward them, swinging their laser swords. Mitch quickly countered, thrusting the broken oar into the first creature's belly. Its stomach filleted open, green goo oozing out.

Papi reached the boat and grappled with the small outboard motor while the others boarded. It chugged to life, then quickly took off. The waves were violent, and the tiny fishing boat bobbed up and down. The Brotherhood watched Mitch battle the squatty creatures like a coked-out war hero.

Relief washed over them. But it was short-lived. A squatty creature appeared out of Mitch's periphery, swinging a laser sword. Mitch pivoted with his oar, but he was too late. The creature lopped off the young man's head. The spaceship's door zipped open again, and the shareholders, the awkward-limbed variety, quickly filtered out to blend him into paste and feast.

The Brotherhood watched from afar, stunned into silence. Lauren wanted to jump into the ocean and let the sea consume her. Why run away to an island if this was ultimately their fate? Lauren cried, and Papi took her hand and whispered, "No time for tears."

The motor putted away as they watched people run for their lives on the dock. Some threw themselves into the ocean and tried to swim away. Their terrifying cries echoed across the water and became fainter as the Brotherhood moved away. Eventually, their screams were muted by the ocean's unending waves.

Fifty-One

The Brotherhood's tiny boat moved through a thick blanket of fog. There was nothing, no land in the distance, no reference point. They wondered if Ceto Isles still existed —if the Brotherhood had even made it there. After all they'd been through. Now this? Lost at sea. Destined to die by starvation or heat stroke.

Lauren's mind drifted to Geena. Did she know her acid goo would melt their chains? Is that why she exploded on them? And if so, why would she make such a sacrifice? Lauren wondered if she, too, could ever be so selfless. Probably not.

Waves licked the side of the boat, and hours slipped away. Hunger gripped them. They tried to fish but were ill-equipped.

"If I could only have a piece of meat," Little Ricky whined.

He thought about his wealthy father. If he were here, they'd probably eat lobster on a yacht. When Ricky was X-ed, his dad tried to shield him from the world. He offered to build the boy an elaborate underground bunker, a powerful gesture on its face, but Ricky found it hollow. He believed his dad spent money to make up for being unavailable. His mom was no different. When Ricky met Papi and the Brotherhood, he found a real family.

Papi noticed Little Ricky looking uncomfortable and patted him on the back. The gesture displaced Ricky's memories across the rolling waves, and he smiled, relieved to be free of them.

It was pitch dark, and the sky and the ocean blended into one large inky mass. Stars popped from this sheet of black and illuminated the small boat as if it were a movie.

"It's so beautiful," Lauren whispered.

Barry smiled. Despite the situation, he felt happy here, dazed before the ocean's majesty. Glad to have friends to share it with. They stared silently at the stars, soaking it up like a sponge. For a brief moment they forgot their hunger.

The sun peeked through the clouds, and a morning mist formed around the boat. The Brotherhood looked to the sky and hoped there was a God that could save them. Instead, a wayward seagull took a shit on Barry's face.

"Agh," Barry said, recoiling and almost falling off the boat. The others couldn't help but laugh. It was a welcome respite from their dire situation.

Papi's eyes grew large. "We can't be far from land, right?" he asked. "If a seagull is hanging around here?"

The others looked up, squinting through the fog, hoping for more gulls. But there was none—no sign of life.

"Getting crapped on by a bird is good luck, right?" asked Barry, cupping his hands over the ocean and washing his face.

"I've never heard that before," said Little Ricky.

A whine filled the air, and an object whizzed above. The Brotherhood looked at each other with dread.

"That's them," Papi gulped.

They panicked, heads on swivels, trying to find a way out. But they were weaponless against the invaders. Sitting ducks. In the distance, the fog began to lift, and the shores of an island emerged about a mile away.

"Holy shit!" yelped Papi. "Is that Ceto Isles?"

He grabbed the small outboard motor and shifted gears. The boat lurched forward, only to sputter and die.

"Oh no, no, no, no," cried Lauren.

Papi hit the side of the motor, but it stayed silent. He desperately flicked its choke button off and on. Nothing.

There was a small plop. Something had landed in the boat. Before they could examine the object, they looked to the sky. Their eyes widened in terror. Hundreds of tiny parachutes dotted the cloudy sky, Energoo cans dangling from each one.

"This isn't happening, is it?" said Lauren in disbelief.

A loud boom thundered across the water. They turned and squinted through the fog. A large, menacing figure emerged—an ocean liner.

"They're coming," said Lauren weakly.

The mammoth ocean liner ripped through the waves. Papi was frightened and turned back to the island. Energoo parachutes plopped on its shores.

"They're bombing the island with Energoo," Papi said. "Then once everyone drinks up and explodes, they'll swoop in and eat them."

"Jesus," Lauren whispered sadly. "Energoo is everywhere."

Spaceships materialized above the distant island. The shareholders were now poised to overwhelm them by air and by sea.

Papi looked at his crew's frightened eyes, the eyes of people contemplating their own death.

"I don't believe any of us has truly sinned," he said, turning to the rolling waves. "But if we have, I believe we've done our penance. If we die here, we die as human beings again."

The others nodded, glad for the sentiment to be vocalized. Barry was visibly moved. He cleared his throat to speak, but no words came out. Papi began reciting the serenity prayer as the others held onto each other, trying not to weep. There was no fight left. They were resigned to their fates.

"God, grant me the serenity to accept the things I cannot change, the courage to change the things I can, and the wisdom to know the difference," Papi said.

The ocean liner boomed again. A death toll. There was muffled shouting in the distance. Incomprehensible. The Brotherhood perked up and looked over to the massive ocean liner approaching.

"That sounds like humans," said Barry. "Maybe it's the military?"

A figure gestured wildly from the ship.

"Come aboard!" the figure shouted.

There was writing scrawled across the boat. But they couldn't decipher it in the fog. The boat slowly moved through the mist, revealing words that shocked Papi.

"The Brotherhood of the Resigned" was etched on the ship's side. Papi almost fainted, and Barry caught him. They squealed like happy schoolchildren.

"It's really them!" Papi said, near tears.

"Hey!" said Lauren, eyes moist. "There's no time for *that!*"

A rope fell into their boat, and a man in a black spandex suit ushered them aboard their giant ship. Several other men were on deck, all wearing the same black uniform. They had machine guns trained at the sky.

Papi was so shell-shocked he wanted to faint. But, a man, presumably the captain, held him up and shook his hand. He scanned Papi's eyes with a mobile device, which dinged.

"Rocco J. Papa, aka 'Papi John,'" the Captain said. "I'm honored to meet you."

Papi was emotional. "That's the first time anyone's ever said that to me."

"Well, it's an honor to meet any of our other chapters," the Captain replied.

He gestured to his crew, who handed out machine guns to Barry, Lauren, and Little Ricky. A weapon landed in Papi's hands, and the Italian leader's smile faded. He studied the instrument of death, unsure how it worked.

Another loud boom caused the ship to vibrate. A spaceship was in striking distance.

"Get down!" the Captain commanded.

BLAM! The spaceship's missile hit the mast of the Brotherhood's boat, causing it to splinter. The Captain and his crew swung around the deck in unison. A choreographed dance. The crew sprayed bullets across the spaceship, causing the vessel to implode.

The crew yelped with joy.

Barry was so impressed that he began clapping.

The Captain searched the sky for another spaceship, saw none, and relaxed on his knee. Papi and Lauren were dumbstruck.

"That was awesome!" Little Ricky shouted, clumsily holding his weapon. "How do I use this gun? I wanna fuck these things up too!"

The Captain nodded to his men and calmly pulled Ricky aside.

"We'd appreciate you not using that sort of language on the ship," the Captain said.

"Oh," Ricky replied, confused. "Sorry about that?"

"It's okay," the Captain said. "We just have to mind our Ps and Qs now that we have corporate sponsorship."

Papi was shocked. "The Brotherhood of the Resigned is corporate-sponsored now?"

The Captain nodded proudly. "Yeah, we just signed the paperwork!"

"I guess that explains how well-equipped you are," Barry said.

"It sure does," replied the Captain. "We used to be held together by duct tape. You guys know. But, now look at us! This beautiful boat, these weapons, it's all thanks to a little corporate help!"

A trio of spaceships hovered in the distance.

"Look alive, everyone!" The Captain shouted. "They should be in our airspace in five!"

Papi was speechless.

"So, who's the corporate sponsor?" asked Lauren.

"Oh," replied the Captain, reloading his weapon. "Narvel!"

"What?" said Papi in disbelief.

"Yeah," said the Captain. "Narvel bought the rights to the Brotherhood!" He spun around, revealing a cape pinned to the back of his black spandex shirt. "Our new uniforms are pretty cool, right?" he asked. "Much better than the old gray sweatpants and hoodies!"

"I suppose so," said Papi, baffled. "I guess they look cool."

"Hell yeah, they do," replied the Captain. "Besides, the old uniforms didn't test well anyways."

"Didn't test well?" asked Lauren.

"Nope," replied the Captain. "Focus groups thought the sweatsuits were lame and depressing. Narvel wants the Resigned brand to be more uplifting and aspirational."

Papi felt like he was going crazy. Narvel, the family-friendly studio, wanted ownership of the Resigned, the most "toxic" group on earth?

A crew member noticed Papi's bewildered face. "Permission to speak freely," he said.

"Granted," the Captain replied.

The man turned to Papi. "I know you might be sentimental about the gray sweatsuits," he said. "But I like the new branding. And I like wearing these capes. It makes me feel like a badass boss bitch."

"Where can I get one of those uniforms?" Barry asked.

The crew members were happy to find everyone a uniform. But Papi wasn't ready.

"C'mon, Papi," Little Ricky said, thrusting his new black cape into the wind. "The Brotherhood of the Resigned joining the expanded Narvel universe is pretty F-ing cool!"

The Captain smiled, pleased the boy self-censored himself.

The three spaceships were a hundred yards out. The Captain nodded at the approaching threat and yanked a wooden lever. The deck slowly pulled apart, revealing a massive pulsating cannon underneath. The crew climbed aboard it like ants, pulling switches and punching in codes.

"They're really close!" shrieked Little Ricky.

The Captain smirked and clapped his hands. The cannon let loose a supercharged laser blast. BLAAAAM! It annihilated the first spaceship, causing it to spiral and crash into the second.

"Reload! We got one more!" The Captain yelled.

Papi watched the crew work, his mind reeling. "Where's the military?" he asked. "Are we the last line of defense? None of us are trained for this!"

"Don't worry!" the Captain said, spinning his gun like a cowboy. "Narvel put us all through intensive training! You'll learn, too!"

Lauren picked up her gun and felt the weight in her hand.

The last spaceship screamed toward them.

"Hey! The cannon isn't ready!" yelped a crew member.

The Captain was unphased. "Everyone! Lift up your weapons!"

The crew snapped into action. Barry and Ricky joined them. Even Lauren lifted her gun reluctantly.

But Papi refused to pick up his weapon, grabbing the Captain's shoulder instead. "What happens if we all die?" he whispered.

The Captain was annoyed and shoved another gun into his hands.

"I don't know," he replied. "But, it'll make great *content!*"

The Captain reloaded his gun and got the spaceship in his crosshairs.

"*Content?*" Papi asked. "For who?"

The Captain fired, and the rest of the crew followed. The spaceship lit up in flames and careened into the ocean. Everyone whooped and hollered.

"*Who* are we making content for?" shouted Papi over the cheers.

The Captain pointed to a parrot sitting atop a deck ladder. Its eyes were strange and metallic. "Say cheese," the Captain said.

The parrot got closer, and Papi recoiled. It was robotic. Its eyes were camera lenses.

"We're being recorded right now?" asked Papi.

Barry took a sudden interest. "We are?"

"Yep!" replied the Captain. "And the audience loves you!"

"They do?" replied Barry, flattered.

"*Who* is the audience?!" shouted Papi.

"Everyone," the Captain replied. "The shareholders thought it would be a great intergalactic reality TV show. I guess their planet is bored of their local AI-generated content."

"We're being broadcast on another planet?" asked Barry, turning toward the parrot. "Hi, Mom!"

The Captain smiled. "They've been watching you closely over the last few days, Barry. I'm telling you. Your numbers are through the roof. Their planet thinks you're one loveable goofball! A real badass boss bitch!"

Barry gasped. "Wow," he said, near tears.

"What about me?" said Little Ricky, putting down his gun. "What do they say about me? Do they like me?"

The Captain paused. "Well, uh, they're warming up to you, kid."

Lauren studied the parrot's artificial plumage. It reminded her of the fake pile of important documents in her fake executive office. She put her weapon down and distanced herself from the others.

"Do you think I could get a spin-off series?" asked Barry, wiping away happy tears. "I mean, if my numbers stay good?"

"I'm sure that's in the realm of possibility," the Captain replied. "This is all new ground, a brand new world of intergalactic entertainment. Anything is possible."

Another spaceship appeared in the sky, and Barry quickly grabbed two guns. He was puffed up, boosted by his newly discovered popularity. He fired at the sky, and every shot missed his target. He winced, hoping the cameras didn't see. The Captain and his crew picked up the slack. The spaceship erupted into flames.

"I could do this all damn day!" Barry yelped.

But Lauren and Papi were no longer with them. They had drifted to the boat's stern to contemplate their future. The shareholders' spaceship slowly sank into the sea.

"I don't understand," Papi said softly.

"Me either," Lauren replied. "We're all just reality TV stars now? That's worse than living underground."

Several insect shareholders struggled out of the sinking ship. But, once in the water, they quickly drowned. Their skinny limbs were ill-equipped to swim.

"They want to turn us into goop and eat us," said Papi, trying to process the madness. "But they also want to do battle? Turn this into a giant TV show they can watch back home?"

Lauren searched for words. "I guess so?" she said. "Dinner and a movie."

"Christ," Papi replied.

The rest of the crew continued celebrating on the bow, popping open cans of beer and drinking merrily. But Papi and Lauren could no longer hear them.

"What should we do?" Lauren asked. "Everyone seems checked out, completely fine with all of this."

Papi stared into the water. A school of seabass swam free. The waves were calm, and the sun poked through the clouds. It was quiet and serene, not a shareholder in sight. They had all drowned.

Papi jumped from the ship, and Lauren reached out, trying to stop him, but it was too late. He cannonballed into the perfect blue ocean.

His body refused to surface, and Lauren panicked. Suddenly, he bounced up in the water, breathing rapidly, the sunlight beating on his face.

"What are you doing?" yelled Lauren.

Papi spit out some water. "This is a real situation nowhere," he replied.

"What?" Lauren asked.

"Situation nowhere," he said, as if repeating it would make more sense.

She looked past him, the ocean calling her. Still pure, uncorrupted by human hands.

"Come on down here," he said. "The water feels great."

His breathing began to slow, the shock of the jump wearing off. He smiled and swam toward the horizon. Lauren jumped in too. The water was cold and alive.

Barry finished a beer on the boat's bow and noticed Papi swimming toward the island. Lauren, a few strokes behind. He tried yelling to get their attention, but they never responded. Kept swimming. Little Ricky noticed them too and screamed. But, no luck.

"What are they doing?" asked Little Ricky.

The Captain squinted at the ocean. "Might be heading to Ceto Isles?"

"That seems like quite a swim," Barry said.

The Captain took a sip from his beer. "I'm not sure *why* they'd want to go to Ceto Isles. The shareholders are turning that place into an Energoo offshore production facility."

"Really?" asked Barry.

"Yep," the Captain replied, swirling the last of his beer. "They've been raining Energoo on that island all week. Pretty much all the indigenous people have drunk it already and exploded. Think some rats even exploded by accident."

"Wow," replied Barry. "Rats too."

Barry watched Lauren catch up with Papi. The two smiled at each other, relieved. They swam together confidently, with big, forceful strokes.

"Well," Barry said wistfully. "You have to admit one thing."

"What's that?" asked Little Ricky.

"They sure look like badass boss bitches."

ACKNOWLEDGEMENTS

To my wife Daron for her unwavering support and countless reads.
To my mom and family, who always supported my writing even when I started getting weird.
To Sam Pink, whose early edits made me a better writer.
To my beta readers, especially Arthur Douglas, Amber Lilyquist, Brittany Nefcy, and Kyle Wilamowski.
To Garth Miró, for his generous and honest advice.
To Mallory Smart, who published my first short story and gave me the confidence to attempt a novel.
To Griff. I'll explain the book when you're older.

ABOUT THE AUTHOR

Bobby Miller is a writer and filmmaker from New Jersey who lives in Los Angeles. His films have premiered at Sundance, SXSW, and Fantasia. His short stories have appeared in Maudlin House, Expat Press, and Bending Genres. SITUATION NOWHERE is his first novel.

If you enjoyed this book, please consider leaving a review on Amazon, Goodreads, or social media.

Subscribe to Bobby's free newsletter, www.BobbyMillerTime.com, for more writing.